I0610345

Copyright © 2020, K.G. Kilpatrick

Published by Crying Cougar Press

Cover art by Benito Gallego
Typesetting by Julie Melton, The Right Type
Critiqued by the Penny Dreadfuls
Proofread by Zeus

All rights reserved. No part of this book may be reproduced, stored, or transmitted by any means—whether auditory, graphic, mechanical, or electronic—without written permission of both publisher and author, except in the case of brief excerpts used in critical articles and reviews. Unauthorized reproduction of any part of this work is illegal and is punishable by law.

ISBN 978-1-7339646-2-3

K.G. KILPATRICK
A Pound of Fur

Crying Cougar Press ™

··· **Prologue** ···

Lieutenant Kitch held the handkerchief tightly against his nostrils. Stepping over stinking splotches of brain and blood, he motioned for his men to carefully collect samples of everything they encountered. As he cautiously entered the main room of the warehouse, he nearly puked his coffee down the crease of his pants.

Two decapitated bodies lay crumpled against the near wall. Someone had brutally murdered the men and kicked the remains to the side as they moved farther into the room. The scene suggested fierce hatred for the victims, something Kitch noted in his mental folder.

The heads weren't cleanly severed. *These men never saw death coming,* thought Kitch. *Someone had come up silently from behind them.* He looked at the stringy remains on the necks and shoulders. *Shotgun blasts at close range. Effective and immediate, but hardly professional.*

One of Kitch's men stepped into the room. A second later he ran toward the door, dribbling vomit from cupped fingers beneath his chin. Another officer stoically inserted samples into plastic baggies, labeling them casually, as if he was helping design a float for a parade. Kitch looked over at his man, giving silent approval. The sergeant who left urgently would have to be reprimanded, of course, even though

Kitch sympathized with his reaction. What they were seeing wouldn't make it out of the cut room in a horror movie.

He glanced back at his sickened officer. The man seemed healthier, but Kitch motioned for him to stay by the door. The scene in the central warehouse would no doubt have ushered him into the nearest hospital.

Lieutenant Samuel Kitch had placed his life in the hands of the Los Angeles Police Department nearly three decades ago. He steadily worked his way through the ranks until reaching his desired goal. He loved his work, the meticulous detail involved in solving complex crimes, the sordid personalities he came upon, and the horrid scenes he encountered. What he witnessed in the warehouse had nearly sent him to the door with his fellow investigator. It was a scene that made Kitch question human sanity.

The place obviously housed one of the many dogfighting rings in the county. Men with a lust for blood and gambling would gather at a location and bet on the outcome of a battle between two animals that ripped each other apart until one of them lay dead. Kitch despised such practices, but in the order of importance for detective work, the hobby ranked quite low on the scale.

A man lay prone in the well, the hideous battleground where dogs fought their atrocious battles. His ears, nose, and lips had been torn away from his skull, his throat slashed open in a gruesome display of ferocity. Hideous wounds riddled his broken body, leaving his motionless remains awash in blood.

A massive pit bull lay close by him. For some reason Kitch couldn't fathom, the dog had mercilessly attacked the man in the well. Barely alive and whimpering, it licked its broken hind leg repeatedly. It looked up at Kitch, growling and yet wagging its tail as well as it could. Kitch felt the urge to drop down into the well and comfort the injured animal.

Two conflicting thoughts fought for primacy in his mind. The first admonished the men who became involved in such barbaric activities. He'd never experienced a connective bond with animals, but he felt a kinship with those who protested against such sickening entertainment.

The second thought finally won out. He would assign an investigation into dogfighting raids to one of his junior detectives. A vigilante had taken up arms in his city, perhaps more than one. Whoever they were, their tactics were brutal and callous. Tracking them down would be his first priority. He couldn't imagine the bloodbaths that would emerge once word of these attacks hit the street.

••• 1 •••

Hunter

The man pointed both barrels of a shotgun directly at the base of his target's skull, then squeezed the trigger gently. If it weren't for the splattered pieces of brain, skin, and bone flying in every direction, the sound of the blast would no doubt have frozen everyone in their shoes.

The headless body slumped to the floor in front of the attacker. The man wearing the aviator sunglasses scanned the room quickly, looking for anyone foolish enough to challenge him. No one came forward. Instead, many in the audience bolted for the back door. What they saw there caused them to abruptly change their minds.

Three men stood inside the dank, dimly lit room, each holding an AK-47 rifle. The man on the left fired off a short burst, halting the running men in their tracks. The audience members, their faces wide with fear, backed up toward the bloody pit in the center of the warehouse.

Oddly, even with the gunfire and the apparent panic surging through the room, the two fighting dogs in the well continued their onslaught. One of the dogs had taken the worst of it. It limped horribly while snapping its head back, trying to inflict any damage it could to its opponent. The other dog, a huge Rottweiler, seemed to sense that the battle had turned in its favor. It carefully measured its attacks to cause maximum damage. The first dog would be dead in a matter of minutes.

"Turner, Michaels," the man holding the shotgun said, "the dogs."

Two of the men guarding the back door moved swiftly toward the fighting pit. The third man held his ground. None of the audience members moved at all. They realized their night of gambling and drinking had gone terribly awry. Most of them silently prayed they would live to see daylight.

"Who's in charge here?" asked the man with the shotgun.

No one said a word. Even so, every man in the stinking fighting arena stared at the man wearing the sunglasses.

"I'll ask one more time. Who runs this operation?"

He waited three seconds before turning toward the man closest to him. Slowly, without ever losing eye contact, he freed two shotgun shells from his belt clip. Opening the chamber with a flick of his wrist, he removed the spent casings and replaced them with the fresh shells. Snapping the shotgun back into firing position, he aimed the gun at his next target.

"M-me," came a voice from the back of the room. "This is my building, and you're trespassing."

"So, you're in charge of this slaughterhouse?" asked the stranger, turning his weapon toward him.

"That's right," said the other man, showing more confidence. "Who are you to barge in like this and kill a man in cold blood?"

A Pound of Fur

Kevin Collins spat at the floor in the man's direction. "Nobody special." He glanced over at Turner and Michaels, making certain they had the fighting dogs under control. Michaels knelt in front of the injured dog, tending to its wounds and cooing to it quietly. "Good job, men. Let's get ready for the next fight."

The comment didn't register with the warehouse owner at first. He stood firm as Turner and Michaels walked over to him. When four strong hands grabbed hold of him, however, he suddenly realized their intent. In a panic he struggled, calling out for the others to come to his aid.

The men went about their business, removing his clothing an article at a time. When all that remained was a pair of briefs, the man squirmed ferociously, trying one last time to free himself. Michaels flashed a large, imposing switchblade. He stilled the man by holding it to his throat before cutting the briefs from his quivering body. Now naked as the day he was born, he felt the smooth steel of handcuffs around his ankles. He began screaming, suddenly terrified of the strange men and their intentions.

Turner slugged the man in the solar plexus, silencing him. He and Michaels lifted him off the ground and threw him down into the pit. The man landed hard on the coarse dirt, face down, wheezing with pain and terror.

While his men readied the warehouse owner, Collins walked through a side door into a small alcove. The room swam in the rancid stink of piss, excrement, and forced aggression. Breathing through his mouth, Collins scanned the cages until he found the right dog. The animal stared through the bars, eyes burning with a feral rage born from a life of brutal combat.

"Don't worry, fella," said Collins in a calm, low voice, "only one more fight, I promise." He went to the wall of the small room and selected the strongest choke lead he could find. Rolling the handle in his right hand, he walked back to the dog's cage. The animal saw the lead and growled menacingly. When he moved it through the bars, the dog reacted violently, snapping at the loop and at Collins' hand.

"Turner," called Collins in a loud voice. "I'm going to need help with this one."

Turner's head moved through the doorway. He glanced quickly in the direction of the cage. "Jeezus."

After a riotous struggle, the two men emerged from the "locker room" with a massive Presa Canario fighting dog. It wasn't the largest of the breed at ninety pounds, but the animal had a countenance that would make a bear turn and run the other way. Countless scars and cuts dotted the muscular body. The eyes spoke of a lifetime of hatred, hatred for those who had forced it into battle time and again, with no reward for victory and swift punishment for defeat. Fortunately for this animal, losing occurred rarely. They had turned it into a savage killer and it served its masters well.

"Let's bring him to the edge of the pit," instructed Collins.

The dog's sanity unraveled upon seeing the fighting pit. It fought its handlers mightily, almost breaking free at one point. After a titanic effort, the two men positioned the animal at the rim of the blood stained well. Collins handed his lead off to Michaels and walked around to the other side.

When the warehouse owner saw which dog they had brought out, he pissed himself with fear. Whimpering like a child, he pleaded with the men to take anything they wanted and go. He would give them money, his home, even his daughters if they would stop this madness. He squirmed around in the pit, trying to face his enemies, but the handcuffs on his ankles left him severely crippled. No matter how much he begged, or how hard he tried, he would not be allowed to escape.

The huge dog registered fear in the man. As it had been trained to do, it growled viciously, barking like the psychotic assassin it was. After four savage years of brutally killing whatever it found in the pit, it reacted as it always had. What it fought made no difference. Another dog, a man, a smaller animal, it didn't matter; it would follow its orders without pause.

The warehouse owner looked into the bloodshot eyes and saw imminent death. He swore he could see the animal smiling at him. It knew who lay across from him, and it wanted more than anything to charge into the pit and rip him to pieces. The man scrambled over to the side of the blood soaked well. With a mighty heave he wrenched himself up and over the edge. Collins walked over and kicked him back into the pit. The man rolled over to the side of the wall, balling himself up to protect his face and throat.

One of Collins' men still held the rest of the audience under guard. Collins waved his shotgun around, and when he got their attention, he spoke to them.

"Whether you believe me or not, this is your last night of dogfighting. All of your pictures have been taken. By tomorrow morning, we'll know your names, where you live, and where you work. If we see you at any other raid, we'll kill you without hesitation."

Collins pointed his shotgun toward the headless body on the floor. A few flies and gnats had already laid claim to the foul-smelling gore oozing from the neck and shoulders.

"This man ignored our warnings. We knew him from another fighting ring located not far from here. He chose to die because he didn't listen."

The big Presa Canario interrupted Collins' speech, nearly pulling Turner and Michaels into the pit. They had to use every ounce of strength to hold it on the lip of the well.

"Boss," said Michaels. "He's ready. We can barely hold him."

Collins shouted over the din of the snarling animal. "Tell everyone you know. These fighting rings are finished. This kind of cruelty will no longer be tolerated."

Collins turned and looked into the pit. The warehouse owner was shrieking like an infant. The terrifying reality of what was about to happen had shattered his nerves. The dog sensed every ounce of panic in the sweat dripping from the man's face. It became ravenous in its desire to charge and kill its opponent.

"Let him go," said Collins.

Turner and Michaels loosed the straps simultaneously. The dog skidded one paw on the hard dirt, losing traction for a brief second. Frustrated, it dug all four paws into the ground and launched itself at the warehouse owner. It landed less than thirty inches from its target, vaulting into the man's midsection with a frightening thrust.

Everyone in the blood caked room looked down at their feet. They couldn't bear to witness the horror they heard coming from the pit. Only Collins stared straight ahead, watching the Presa Canario rip huge swaths of flesh from the man's body. The warehouse owner bawled horribly as the giant dog tore into him again and again. He could do nothing to thwart the attacks. If he raised his arms to protect his face, the dog lunged at his midsection, or his armpits, or his groin. He couldn't lower both of his arms at any time; if the dog took one swipe at his throat, he would die a horrible, gagging death.

In a rage born out of fear and adrenaline, the man grabbed the dog and threw it away from him. It immediately charged, but the warehouse owner kicked his legs out. He connected twice, once to the chest and once on the nose, causing the dog to back off for a moment. The bleeding man actually smiled, thinking he had won himself a reprieve.

Slowly, however, the horror returned as he watched the Presa Canario pacing slowly back and forth in front of him. The dog was performing a ritual well known to the man lying in the pit. When a wounded animal lashed out at a superior opponent, the winning dog usually waited a moment for the surge to pass. This gave it two advantages, a time of rest and a better angle of attack. The fighting dog in the pit took stock of both. Seconds later, seeing the edge it had hoped for, the dog charged. The warehouse owner tried to fend off the attack, but this time the Presa Canario would not be turned away. Smelling fresh blood everywhere on his prey, it bit both of the man's hands simultaneously, causing him to rip them away from his head. An instant later, the giant dog slashed the man's throat with its paws and then with its huge fangs. The man squealed one last time and then lay still.

The dog, sensing death in the pit, began staggering around the ring. It ignored the dead man lying prone on the ground. It was waiting for its handlers to cage it again and feed it the meager winner's rations.

"You men," ordered Collins. "Help us load those dog cages into our van. We're taking them with us."

The audience members hurried to do the strange man's bidding. One of them owned three of the animals in the side room, but he wouldn't think of asking the man with the shotgun for any favors. He hustled along with the others, picking up cages and ferrying them to the van outside the warehouse. When all the dogs had been stored, including the Presa Canario, Collins dismissed his captives with a stern look. The men stared at their newfound benefactor, someone they hadn't any knowledge of sixty minutes earlier. They waited to be excused. They didn't want to anger a man so comfortable with firearms.

"Remember what I said tonight. If we find you at any other dogfighting events, we'll kill you." He looked each man in the eye, making sure all of them understood. "Now go home."

The men turned and ran. They wanted one thing only, to put as much space as possible between them and the man with the mirrored sunglasses.

"Well," said Collins, "that's one more fighting ring out of commission."

"That makes two dozen we've hit," said the man who had guarded the back entrance. "They don't seem to be any harder to find, boss. There must be hundreds of dogfights in this county every weekend."

"There'll be fewer once the word starts spreading," replied Collins, not entirely sure of his comment. "At least I hope so."

"What if we can't end it, I mean stop all the fighting for good?" asked O'Neal.

"Then we'll always have something to do on Friday and Saturday nights. I get frustrated sometimes, thinking about what we're fighting against, but then I remember why I'm out here."

"We're *all* here because we care about animals, boss."

"Yes," sighed Collins. "But I'm here for another reason."

"What's that?" asked Turner and Michaels at the same time.

Collins looked toward the van and the rescued dogs. "I love animals a lot more than I like people."

... 2 ...

The vast and mostly drunk crowd cheered wildly, issuing a raucous welcome to the Bertram 700 sport fishing boat as it negotiated the shallow waters around the dock. The impossible had been done at the Bi-Coastal Marlin Championship. Brett Jeffries, a newcomer and a Montana rancher no less, had smashed the record for marlin fishing with eighty-pound test. The previous record had been set at just under twelve hundred pounds. Jeffries had hauled in a billfish that weighed over thirteen hundred and fifty pounds.

Jeffries launched himself over the gunwale onto dry land as the boat pressed against the pontoons on the dock. Hands reached in from every direction, hoping to touch the hero of the day. No one had landed a marlin this size using eighty-pound test line in the history of organized competition, and now Jeffries had quite possibly set a record that might never be broken. Shouted offers rattled his ears as he walked toward the scorer's table. Everyone wanted a piece of Jeffries. He heard people proposing free hotel rooms, free dinners, even nights of lusty romance coming from a few of the more inebriated female attendees. Jeffries brushed everything aside except an offer from a very attractive brunette. He winked at her, smiling coyly. She returned his attentions by sliding her tongue along the bottom of her upper lip.

As Jeffries reached the scorer's table, the captain of the gleaming vessel winched up the tail of the record setting fish. Swinging the mechanism out over the dock, he punched the controls and watched the massive marlin float above the crowd. The tournament attendees roared anew as the dripping carcass rose into the air like some freakish caricature representing man's dominion over the creatures of the earth. Several partiers close enough to do so put their thumbs over the mouths of their beer bottles and shook them vigorously. They sprayed the huge fish, christening it with their version of holy water.

The winch finally reached its maximum height. The immense marlin stared at the swaying crowd through dead, dark eyes. Seawater, combined with blood and intestinal fluids, dribbled lazily from its bill. At various intervals, empty beer cans and used food wrappers bounced mutely off of the streamlined body. Looking at the gigantic, record setting catch, the crowd worked itself into a delirious frenzy.

"How about that for the first day of competition!" boomed the tournament director, Matt Mayfield. The crowd went ballistic with its response. "If we have three more days like that, we'll all have something to tell our grandchildren!" More raucous applause and cheering accompanied each of Mayfield's comments.

■ ■ ■

A man sat in a coffee shop at the far end of the pier. He watched the scene unfold. He saw everything, the boat, Jeffries, the fish, the onlookers, and that blowhard Mayfield pumping up the crowd. All because of an innocent creature whose only crime had been swimming in its natural environment.

"More coffee, sir?" asked the thirty-something waitress, hovering to the man's left carrying two steaming pots.

"Yes, please," replied the man, removing his sunglasses and massaging the bridge of his nose. "I wonder if you'd know of a hotel in town where I might find a room."

"I'm afraid you're out of luck," said the waitress, beaming with her prettiest smile. "This is the biggest thing in Greenwich Falls all year long. You won't find a vacancy for fifty miles."

The man smiled back at her, brushing his dirty blond hair with his thumb and index finger. "I bet if I were competing in the fishing tournament, I could get a room."

"Oh, yes, sir! We put all the anglers up at our best hotel, the Rocky Bluff Inn, on the west side of the pier."

"Well, I guess I better start learning how to fish."

The waitress giggled, trying to flirt with the stranger. She looked longingly at the man, thinking he could certainly keep his shoes next to her bed if he felt so inclined.

"I'll take a check, Miss," said the attractive, middle aged man. After re-tying his right shoelace, he stood, donned his sunglasses. He reached down to the table and grabbed his mug. After swallowing the last of the coffee, he set the mug down and grabbed a fresh glass of ice water. He drained that just as the waitress returned with his bill. She hustled away to grab a pitcher of ice water and had his glass refilled by the time he'd opened his wallet. The check came to twelve dollars and change. He gave her a twenty, telling her to keep it. She smiled a mile wide, gushing her appreciation a bit too generously. The man drank another glass of ice water, watched her grab the pitcher again, and held up his hand signaling to her that he'd had enough.

"Is there somewhere I can make a call privately?" he asked the waitress.

"Sure thing," she said, stretching her smile again. "Out toward the front door. Turn left just before you leave the restaurant. You'll find two employee tables just past the bathrooms."

"Thanks."

"My pleasure and come again."

The man smiled, jamming his right hand into the front pocket of his jeans. Pulling his cell phone out, he punched numbers as he made his way along the deck.

■ ■ ■

Matt Mayfield sat at the scorer's table interviewing Brett Jeffries. The crowd had other ideas, they wanted to party now that the first day of competition was over. Most of the attendees were there just for the booze and the parties anyway, the fishing being mostly an afterthought.

"Did you ever think you'd be able to fight a marlin that big with eighty-pound test?" asked Mayfield.

Jeffries took a long pull from a pint glass of locally brewed porter. "Hell," he said, "all I was thinking about was hanging on. I knew it was a big bastard, but world record big, who can think about that when your arms feel like they're going to break off." He took another pull.

Mayfield grinned. The crowd roared again. "So, are you going to stay here for the rest of the weekend, or are you leaving now that you have the trophy and the world's record?"

Jeffries looked out over the crowd. It took a few seconds, but he found her eventually. It was the gorgeous woman who'd caught his eye earlier. He smiled, she smiled back. He winked at her; she gave him a look that melted his loins.

"I think I might stay for the weekend, Matt. It's always a good idea to cheer on the other competitors, right?"

"Right on, Brett," said Mayfield. "We'll be glad to fix you up with anything you want, including another beer. That one's looking a little short."

Jeffries signaled to his crew for another beer. He was on top of the world. He had just landed the biggest fish ever in his weight class. He would eat and drink on the house for the whole weekend, and some supermodel with a medically enhanced rack wanted to fuck him silly.

■ ■ ■

After dialing his number and listening to the mechanized voice, the man tapped five more digits on his cell. After hitting the last number, he paused to take in the breathtaking scene. He watched the water glisten, the boats lazily floating out to sea, and the birds jousting for scraps. For a moment he forgot about his mission. The ringing of the telephone on the other end of the line brought him back, prompting his memory.

A Pound of Fur

"McCarthy Stevens," said the delightful secretary answering the call.

"Kevin Collins, please."

"May I ask who's calling?"

"If you feel you must," said Turner, giving the proper coded response.

"One moment, please."

Turner listened as the phone line offered a series of clipped tones. The secretary was locating Collins and informing him of the situation. When Collins received the information, he would locate his burner phone and return the secretary's call. What Turner now heard was the final connection between the two phones.

"You've arrived in North Carolina?" asked Collins.

"This morning," answered Turner. "I've already located our next target. I've had breakfast, assessed the situation, and placed the enticement. I've even discovered where the tournament directors and competitors are staying."

"Excellent work," said Collins. "When do you expect to make contact?"

"I'll wait until the evening of the last day. The enticement should keep Jeffries here over the weekend, and Mayfield will have to remain until everything's taken care of. I think by that time both men will be quite exhausted. There won't be any problem."

"What about the facility?"

"There's an industrial site less than 30 miles from here. Looks like it's abandoned. They have a guard shack with one minimum wage hack. I'm sure he'll do exactly what we ask of him once he sees we have the right incentive."

"And the equipment?"

"Already here, sitting in the back of a semi. It's parked up the road with about a hundred other semis. Nobody will make it for anything but another show vehicle."

"Well done, Turner," said Collins. "The team should start arriving tomorrow night. Keep an eye on our targets until then."

"Will do, boss."

Turner gently hung up the phone. He walked toward the front door of the restaurant and nearly collided with Brett Jeffries and his new paramour.

"Excuse me," he said, glancing once at the prostitute.

"I'll let it go this time, mate," slurred Jeffries, already teetering from one too many beers. He shouldered his way to the bar, dragging the enticement in his wake. "Any other day and I might hang a hook on you." He smirked and hugged the woman a little closer.

Turner let one corner of his mouth inch up the slightest bit. *Amazing how a few beers turns the biggest dullard into a prophet.*

··· 3 ···

"Lieutenant Kitch here to see you, sir."

Kevin Collins put his feet up on the corner of the scraped and discolored veneer stripping covering his desk. Moving his rump down a bit, he pulled his shoulders forward in order to adjust his clothing. Then he sat back and eyed his secretary.

"Send him in."

Sam Kitch moved quietly through the door and into Collins' office. He was a slight man, not someone you would expect to hold the rank of lieutenant in a major metropolitan police department. He wore three quarters of a suit; his coat lay slumped over his chair back at headquarters. His slacks looked neatly pressed, but his shirt and tie reflected the untidy condition of Collins' office.

"Have a seat," said Collins, gesturing to one of the well-worn reception chairs sitting opposite his desk.

Lieutenant Kitch passed by the stiff, uncomfortable chairs. He slumped down on a tired, sagging couch positioned against the wall farthest from Collins.

"I think," said Kitch after placing his interlaced fingers behind his head, "you should spend some of your profits on new office furniture." The diminutive lieutenant placed his feet on the coffee table. He used one foot to nudge a pile of papers and reports a little to the left. As the top of the stack spilled off the table, he made his feet comfortable.

"Sorry," he intoned dispassionately.

"Forget it," replied Collins. "Those are fake reports. I leave them there on the table to impress and intimidate potential clients."

Kitch stared but didn't answer.

"Kind of like the rest of this office," continued Collins. "Not very impressive at first glance."

The lieutenant rolled his eyes around the room before nodding his head once.

"That's the way I like it," said Collins. "Makes people think I don't care very much about details. Or that I'm sloppy, or I spend all my money on booze and hookers."

"You don't?" asked Kitch.

Collins smiled. "So, who should I thank for this visit?"

Lieutenant Kitch's body didn't even twitch. His arms, his head, even his cockeyed feet sitting on the table didn't move at all. The voice seemed to emanate from a dead shell.

"Another dogfighting ring got hit a few nights ago. Two men dead, one of them ripped to pieces by a huge animal. The other one's going to keep the M.E. busy for the next month. Seems whoever doesn't like dogfighting hates the people involved even more."

"Good," said Collins, assuming the same relaxed posture. "Fuck 'em. I hope every one of them gets the same treatment."

"So do I," answered Kitch, "but that's not my call. Unfortunately, when these assholes are finished raiding one of these rings, I have to go in and try and figure out how to stop them from having their little parties."

"Why don't you focus on stopping the people organizing the dogfights?" asked Collins in a less than friendly manner.

Kitch's feet wobbled slightly. "Where were you last Saturday night, Mr. Collins?"

"Kevin, please."

Kitch didn't say a word. His gray eyes remained locked onto Collins' face.

"Spending the night in a hotel about five hundred miles from here," said Collins. "We had a booth at a security convention in Stockton."

"Yes, but can you prove you were actually there?" asked Kitch.

Collins smiled broadly. "If you mean, can I provide you with photographs taken of me with the mayor of Stockton or the governor of California, then no, I can't prove I attended the conference. However, if charge receipts for rooms, flights, restaurants and rental cars will suffice, then I guess I'm covered."

"Anyone could have made those arrangements," replied Kitch. "Someone on your management team could have signed those receipts or given your name as theirs to conference attendees."

"What are you driving at, Sam?" asked Collins. "Do you think I had something to do with those jerks getting what they deserved last weekend?"

"As a matter of fact, I do. Unfortunately, I can't prove it."

"Then stop trying. As much as I despise them, I wouldn't jeopardize what I have just for a shot at revenge."

Kitch stared at Collins, dissecting the man with his eyes.

"What?" asked Collins, perturbed.

"Did you know that the man who managed the fighting ring was killed by a Presa Canario?"

"I flipped through the story, but I don't know the particulars."

Kitch continued staring.

"Big ass dogs, those," said Collins. "Wasn't that the kind of dog that killed that lawyer in San Francisco?"

"The man's head was nearly torn away from his body," Kitch said. "The throat had been shredded, the tip of the spinal cord crushed in three places."

Now it was Collins' turn to stare.

"We never even found his genitals. Apparently, fighting dogs are trained to go for the vital areas as quickly as possible. That must be why the man lowered his defensive guard from his head and neck. Can't very well leave your privates exposed when a vicious dog is snapping his jaws at them."

"Sounds like a hell of a party," said Collins. "Listen, Sam, I have a meeting if you…"

"We're still trying to find a full set of teeth from the other man," interrupted Kitch. "The only way the medical examiner can make a positive identification is with both jaws. Too bad they exploded from his mouth when he took a shotgun blast to the back of his neck."

"Well, I guess I don't to have to read the paper this morning. You've given me quite an account."

"Always happy to oblige," Kitch said. "By the way, will you be attending any conventions in the near future?"

"Nothing on the schedule right now." answered Collins, "Although, sometimes I'm needed at the last second. You just never know in the security business."

"You will tell me if you leave town?"

"Sam," asked Collins, "am I a suspect in these murders?"

"Nothing of the sort," replied Kitch. "I've suddenly become very interested in your line of work, that's all."

"It certainly pays better than a lieutenant's salary. Hours are better, too."

"My point exactly. Perhaps if I learn enough by hanging around your organization, you might one day offer me a position."

"Anything's possible," said Collins. "We're always looking for good ex-military or law enforcement folks. I really have to go, though, my meeting, as I said earlier."

"Of course," Kitch said. "Thank you for your time."

Kitch moved forward and tried to stand. The couch was so low and deep he fell back after trying to grasp the edge of the coffee table for support. He made it up the second time, glancing at Collins shamefully. He saw the man smiling and holding out his hand in a mock gesture of assistance.

"That's another great thing about this office," said Collins. "It affords me quick getaways."

... 4 ...

Andrew Michaels opened the front door of the modest, three-bedroom home he shared with his wife. The ranch style house wasn't large; at slightly over sixteen hundred square feet it looked downright stunted next to most of the other homes on his block. However, the back yard of the Michaels residence matched or surpassed anything within twenty miles.

Michaels had bought the home specifically for that reason. He and his wife had worked, scrimped and dreamed for fifteen years while living in a cramped town home located next to one of the busiest municipal airports in California. The noise had been unbearable – planes, helicopters from every civil and private company in the city, car alarms, sirens, dogs, babies, assholes; Michaels and his wife had withstood the onslaught every day. In the cool dawn of early mornings, they would tell each other that someday their plans for a better home would come to pass.

For more years than he cared to remember, Michaels had harbored doubts about whether he and his beloved wife would ever see that home. The figures just never added up;

there was always one more issue keeping them from making their move. Michaels might have ignored the facts and bought a home if the decision had been his alone. Thankfully, Darla, his wife, had a cool head and a brilliant mind for numbers. She would stroke his cheek during those peaceful discussions and tell him for the umpteenth time that someday their dream would come true.

Kevin Collins made their hopes materialize. Michaels had first met Collins at a pizza and micro beer joint located a short walk from the ocean. After shaking hands and toasting to a good day in the waves, Collins had begun questioning Michaels about his livelihood. He sensed Michaels' military background, and he wanted to know whether his career path had served him well.

Michaels had told him without embarrassment that since leaving the service, his jobs had been interesting but not lucrative. Collins queried him further; he wanted to know what his specialty had been in the army, if he'd ever been deployed with or commanded a group of soldiers. He asked at length about Michaels' employment history since leaving the armed forces. He dug deeply, inquiring about companies, jobs, pay, and any acquaintances or friends he kept in touch with, either military or civilian.

Michaels told him everything. He answered all of his questions openly. He trusted the man from the moment he shook his hand. There was something about this Collins fellow, he remembered thinking, and so he laid himself bare over two beers.

After the two men hammered down a large bar-b-qué chicken pizza, Collins offered him a job. Principal investigator and advanced detail director, a title that confused Michaels so much he almost refused the offer. After Collins had reassured him, telling him the expected salary and that he would personally walk him through his first three months, Michaels had acquiesced.

When he returned home that night, accompanied by the sounds of sirens, planes and a very loud hedge trimmer, he scooped his wife up into his arms and told her to start looking for another home. Cautious as always, Darla questioned him about the strange man he'd met at the restaurant. After checking out the man's company on the internet, however, her excitement grew. She hugged him, kissing his neck and whispering her love for him. They bought their dream home two months later. Since then, Michaels had worked for Collins nearly six years.

"I'm home," shouted Michaels as he dropped the mail onto the kitchen table. "I'm home!"

He heard his wife call out from the master bedroom. "My Baby's home," began a ritual they'd enjoyed for years. She raced down the hallway toward the kitchen, proclaiming her husband's arrival again and again. They embraced, did a peculiar little dance, and kissed repeatedly.

"And who have we here?" asked Michaels as he felt a heavy body pressing against his legs. Disentangling himself from his wife, he looked down and saw a huge, golden tortoise shell cat.

"Kitty!" he exclaimed as he reached down with both hands. He grunted mightily as he picked up the heavy feline. "Someday you'll have to pick me up, Kitty," he said while throwing the beautiful cat's forepaws over his shoulder. He scratched her back while talking to her, smiling broadly as he looked upon her contented grin.

"You'd better go into the back yard and say hello to your sons before they tear the deck to pieces," said Darla.

As if on cue, a huge, woofing bark exploded from beyond the den. The Michaels household, as all their neighbors repeatedly said, was safer than a police station. Anyone crazy enough to try and break into their home would find a few nasty surprises waiting for them.

"Okay, Kitty," Michaels said, "I'll leave you here with your mother. I'm sure she can find a snack for you."

Michaels walked down the hall, through the living room and into the den. On the way he intercepted two more cats. One was a glistening, midnight black Siamese mix, the other a stunning flame point Siamese.

"Hey, boys," he said as he gingerly picked his way past the cats. "Back in a minute, alright?" The two male cats, put off by their father's quick passage, stared after him like spurned lovers.

Michaels flicked the blinds back, exposing the sliding glass door that led to the deck and back yard. He saw only a glimpse of the expansive redwood deck, however, because three large, furry dogs blocked his view completely. He scrunched down, placing his hands on his knees. In this way he stood eye level with the joys of his life. He pursed his lips and kissed at the dogs, making their tails wag quickly. He pressed his lips together and forced a stream of air through them. This created a high-pitched sound, not unlike the squealing cry of a puppy. This caused the dogs to whimper excitedly.

Michaels slid the door wide open. As much as the dogs wanted to cross the threshold into the house, none of them even placed a paw on the runner. As a group, they backed up, giving Michaels enough room so he could walk out onto the deck and join them. After he did so, the three dogs took up positions in front and to either side of him. They sat down, their tales wagging vigorously.

"Hello, Hoss," Michaels said, addressing a stunning brown and black German shepherd. The dog barked once, staring directly into Michaels' eyes. "You still the smartest dog in the world?" Another quick retort followed.

He moved to stand in front of a massive Alaskan malamute. "Did you find another way to break out of the yard, Tank?" The giant sled dog squirmed, his body rocking back and forth with his desire to be petted. Michaels smiled, looking at the one hundred sixty-pound brute. *If he only knew how strong he really was, he could probably run right through the fence.*

He stepped over to the third dog. He'd never show it to the other two, but he loved Pip more than any other animal he'd ever owned. The slight Australian shepherd, a female, weighed only forty-five pounds. She made up for her smaller size with lightning fast quickness and an incredibly keen mind. Pip was the first female animal Michaels and his wife had ever brought home. They loved males, and every other time they had visited a shelter, they'd always adopted another son.

When they met Pip and heard her story, however, they took one look at each other and signed the papers. Pip had been abused and then abandoned at four weeks old. A migrant worker had found her limping through a strawberry field. The young man had immediately fallen for the fluffy, smiling puppy, but knowing the tenuous nature of his living arrangements, he decided to bring the young Aussie to a shelter. Pip undoubtedly would have been spoken for in a matter of hours, but fate had been on the Michaels' side. Darla had been running errands that day, on a whim she decided to stop by the shelter for a walk through. Both she and Andrew visited pounds and shelters regularly, if only to visit with the animals and bring a moment's joy into their lives. On this day it would be Pip who filled Darla's world with delight.

Upon seeing her and asking the shelter about her, the attendant on duty declared that the small Aussie had only arrived that day. They were required to keep all animals for seven days in case the owners came in to claim them. Darla asked when she would be able to adopt her.

"One week from today," said the shelter employee, "at nine o'clock in the morning."

At eight fifty-five on the morning in question, Darla and Andrew Michaels pulled into the parking lot. They waited by the door until the same attendant opened the shelter for business. She recognized Darla immediately, greeting Michaels and her warmly.

"Is the Aussie puppy still here?" asked Darla, holding her breath.

"She is, and I think she's been waiting for you. Would you like me to bring her to a petting alcove?"

Darla and Andrew had smiled, nodding their heads. The attendant led them down the hall to the first alcove. She unlocked the door, holding it wide for them. When they were both seated, she closed the door, addressing them one last time.

"I have to warn you: the puppy seems to be quite fearful of men. Our guess is that a male abused her, so she naturally shies away from people who resemble him." She noted the pained expression on Michaels' face. "The good news is she loves women." The attendant smiled again before disappearing.

Darla had cautioned her husband about any potential shyness or fear on the part of the puppy. Both she and Michaels understood animal psychology very well, from a practical point anyway. He would do what the situation demanded, no matter how painful.

The shelter employee returned with a squirming puppy. She was a puffy ball of fur with two eyes and a stubby tail. The coloring in one of her eyes was luminescent white, a telltale mark of a purebred Aussie. The attendant leaned over the gate and placed the young shepherd on the floor of the alcove.

Michaels neither moved nor made a sound. He sat still, allowing the small dog the time she needed to explore the two newcomers. His wife, however, couldn't resist the urge to call the puppy over to her. Pip smiled while running across the alcove and into Darla's arms. When she lifted her up to her face, Pip smothered her with puppy breath and kisses with her tiny tongue.

Pip looked over at Michaels a few times without showing any sign of fear or uncertainty. Even so, Michaels had stayed perfectly still. He tried not to make eye contact; he wanted Pip to feel completely comfortable with him. She turned toward Darla again, who had just announced their decision to adopt the young Aussie pup. Michaels smiled in agreement. Even without direct interaction, he knew Pip would be going home with them that day.

Then the most remarkable thing had happened. Pip squirmed out of Darla's loving hands. Darla hastily lowered her to the ground. Pip rolled awkwardly, trying to get to her feet. When she finally did stand, she walked over to Michaels. She looked up at the unmoving man, offering a very light, squeaky bark. Michaels lowered his chin, looking down at the small dog that would one day be his closest companion. Pip met his eyes evenly, yipping again.

"I think she wants you to pick her up," said Darla.

"I'm almost afraid to," replied Michaels. "I don't want to ruin the progress we've made."

At the sound of a male voice, Pip cringed to the ground, backing away from Michaels. Both he and his wife could see the fresh memories of the pain someone had inflicted upon her. Michaels had a passing thought of finding the man and introducing him to Collins. He let it float from his mind quickly; he didn't want anything negative to radiate toward Pip.

Michaels decided to gamble and see if he could calm the little puppy. He kissed and squeaked softly, without moving. Pip responded, though still cowering behind Darla's legs. Michaels lowered one of his large hands to the alcove floor, cupped and inverted, as if he held a treat. Pip looked around Darla's shin timidly. Then she looked up at Michaels. Then she barked again, twice. Michaels squeaked quietly, drawing her over to him with the tantalizing call of a puppy or a kitten. Pip slowly crawled across the alcove, finally placing her nose a hair from Michaels' thumb.

Andrew Michaels had known better than to initiate contact. He held his hand still, waiting for Pip to judge him as non-threatening. The courageous little puppy sensed something likable about him. She jumped up and barked three times, startling Michaels. The man couldn't resist the cute dog's invitation, but still he held back. Flicking his eyes up to look at his wife, he saw her make the tiniest gesture, telling him to welcome young Pip into his arms.

Michaels opened his sturdy hand, allowing the small puppy time to sniff each finger and then his thumb. He rolled his palm over, placing it next to Pip's flank. Alarmed, Pip jumped to the side, but only for a moment. Soon she stood next to his hand again, sniffing his wrist. She stopped suddenly, looking up at Michaels as if to say, *what next?*

With the first knuckle of his right index finger, Michaels very lightly rubbed Pip's left shoulder. When she didn't move away, he rubbed her rib cage and her hind quarters.

Pip turned toward Michaels' hand and began licking his finger. Michaels wouldn't have moved a muscle at that moment if his life depended on it.

The shelter attendant returned to the alcove in time to see Pip showering her father's hand with kisses. "I don't believe it," she'd gasped, explaining that none of the male shelter employees had been able to stay in the same room with Pip. Her reaction to men had frightened all of them, to the point where they almost decided to restrict the adoption to females only. Looking upon the scene in the alcove, however, the attendant nearly broke down in tears.

A Pound of Fur

"You *have* to adopt her," she had said. Darla and Michaels had exploded with laughter, frightening Pip momentarily. The small puppy yipped and barked excitedly, causing everyone to laugh anew.

Michaels smiled, reliving the memory of his first encounter with the little puppy. "Pip," he said while holding her head in his hands, "if there's another one like you out there, I'll never find her in a million years."

Pip shot her tongue through her lips, licking Michaels' fingers as best she could. Hoss and Tank sat patiently next to their sister, knowing what would soon be coming.

"Okay," he said to his three canine children. "You've all been very well behaved, but now I think it's time for…"

Michaels vaulted over Pip, running away from his dogs at a remarkable clip. The three animals bolted away from the sliding glass door, hot on his trail and barking as if they had treed a skunk. They caught up to him in seconds, but Michaels had mapped out his trail long ago. He knew every square foot of his massive back yard. He shot through the trees on his left before dancing over a series of rocks springing up from a rather deep pond. As he reached the other side, he heard the three dogs splash through the water. It slowed them just long enough for Michaels to reach a large grassy area surrounded by solar powered lamps; accent lighting for his and Darla's frequent parties.

Hoss, Tank and Pip had given him enough grace. As a team, they tackled him roughly on the soft grass. Pip raced around to his front while Hoss nipped at his heels. When these two slowed him to a crawl, Tank slammed into Michaels like a runaway truck. The four of them went down in a heap, legs, paws, slacks, shirt, tails and all.

The dogs tried to outdo each other in showing their affection. Tank stood over Michaels, unmoving, his great, slobbery tongue pushing against his master's face. Hoss and Pip worked from the sides, nuzzling into Michaels ears with exceptionally eager kisses.

"Okay, okay, I love you, too," said Michaels amidst his rousing laughter. He hugged each dog individually, and then as a group. He loved to bury his nose into the thick fur of a good-sized dog. He felt unusually secure in their presence, and not because of Tank's size or Hoss's protective nature. It was more than that to him. For Michaels, the bond between man and canine completed him in a way unlike any other relationship, familial or marital.

"Dinner's ready, if anyone wants to stop playing long enough to eat."

At the sound of Darla's call, six furry ears stood straight up. The licking continued, but the three dogs recognized the inflection in their mother's voice. Food would be coming soon. They had a tough choice to make – stay here with Pop or go see about having some dinner.

"All right, you kids," said Michaels, "time for me to go clean up." He grabbed the thick coat around Tank's neck and gave the big malamute a verbal command. Tank dragged him clear of the other two dogs while giving him the support he needed to climb to his knees and stand. Michaels faked like he was going to run to the back door. He laughed as Pip bolted ahead of the other two before stopping. She looked around, giving him a look of wounded misunderstanding. He called her back to him, waiting to reassure her with his heavy fingers.

"I love you, Pip," said Michaels while drawing her near to him. Tank and Hoss nuzzled up against his legs as they reached the deck. He shot a quick hand out to them, rubbing the crowns of their heads.

With the animals fed and dinner served, Michaels sat down with his wife. Jingles, the beautiful flame point Siamese, stood quietly at the end of the table, waiting for a few scraps of chicken to be passed his way.

"I have to go away tomorrow, for the weekend," said Michaels.

"So soon, again?"

"I'm afraid so. Collins has lined up another conference. He says some important contacts will be attending. It might mean a lot of new business for the firm."

"Where is the conference being held?"

"North Carolina."

"I'm not aware of any convention facilities there," said Darla.

"I think it's in Greenville if I'm not mistaken."

"How long will you be gone?"

"Just the weekend, maybe Monday as well," replied Michaels. "Definitely not one minute longer than I have to be away from that delicious banana bread." He reached across the table, hoping to filch a few slices.

She slapped his hand away. "It's nice to know there's something here you'll be eager to get back to." She gave him a sassy little smile.

■ ■ ■

Darla Michaels had her suspicions about her husband's weekend assignments. At first, she wondered if he'd found a girlfriend and the weekend duties served as a cover. After she came to her senses and ruled that out, she still suffered from a terrible intuition. She knew that Collins, her husband, and a few other well chosen "executives" from the security firm were engaging in some form of illicit activity. While there might actually have been conventions in the towns they visited, some grisly crimes seem to occur every time they took an out of town assignment.

She recalled that on some occasions Michaels would leave the house in the middle of the night and not return for hours at a time. Darla had no idea what occurred during those late-night forays, but she didn't care for her husband's attitude whenever he returned home. It reminded her of the close calls they'd had after he'd come home from the war. If his leave lasted only a few weeks, it seemed as if he never left the battlefield behind. Some nights he would wake, terrified, in a shivering panic. It would be days before she could touch him or talk to him again.

He exhibited similar behavior after returning from an assignment with Collins, and it gave her cause for concern. Everyone who worked for Collins was ex-military, even the sales force. She imagined some might even be mercenaries. No one who visited the office would suspect anything; however, Collins' men were extremely polished and professional. During normal office hours, the employees of Collins' security firm looked like any other group of nine to five working stiffs.

A Pound of Fur

Even so, Darla worried a great deal. They had built a wonderful life together. She wasn't sure she wanted Michaels to risk their happiness for a man they'd barely known five years. The situation was complex, however, because if not for Collins they wouldn't have the life they enjoyed.

■ ■ ■

Tank nosed open the sliding glass door, worming his way into the kitchen. He walked in, set his ample chin on the glass table. His eyebrows twitched back and forth as he searched his parents' faces. Jingles' tail flashed back and forth vigorously, smacking Tank in the nose a few times. The cats ruled the house, that was certain, but the sight of Tank never ceased to worry them.

Michaels flipped a potato skin in Tank's direction. The huge Malamute caught the treat in midair, swallowing the hefty snack without chewing. With the signal understood, both Pip and Hoss wedged their way into the kitchen. Three other cats hopped up onto the table; Kitty, Jamie and Schmoozer, an older Abyssinian. The dogs squirmed on the floor while the cats weaved back and forth on the table.

"Well, now you've done it," said Darla, moving down to the end of the counter. "If one gets a treat, they all get a treat."

Michaels walked over to the pantry. Seven pairs of eyes followed his every move.

"Treats?" he asked.

All four of the cats, including Schmoozer, stood at the extreme edge of the kitchen table, chins out and eyes wide open. Tank, Hoss and Pip took up their positions directly beneath their feline family members. Jingles and Kitty swiped their right paws in Michaels' direction a few times, catching Pip's ear more than she cared to tolerate. She nipped lightly at them, chasing their limbs away.

After the critter desserts had been handed out, Michaels washed his hands and walked over to his wife. She let him place his strong arms around her but did not return the gesture. She felt him pull her close, felt his strong chest squeezing against her breasts.

"Andy, what exactly do you do on your weekend jaunts with Collins?"

"We fight the good fight," he answered. He loved his wife, but this was something he couldn't possibly share with her.

Darla slid her arms inside of his shirt, embracing his strong back. "Would it make any difference if I told you how worried I get whenever you leave in the middle of the night, or for a long weekend conference?"

Michaels let his arms slacken a bit. He didn't relish the idea of keeping things from her. This was the third time she'd broached the subject, and each time she persisted a bit more. He'd given a little more with each discussion, but he knew it had to stop here. If she kept this up, she would eventually learn the truth.

"Darla, I can only promise you this. When it's all over, and my association with Collins is ended, then I'll tell you about our boring conference trips. Until then I'd rather you not question me about it again. The men involved in these projects are all decent, loving family men who believe strongly in what they're trying to accomplish. I promise you, we take every precaution to assure our safety every minute we're on assignment."

"Great. Now what the hell am I supposed to think? What do you have to keep yourself safe from?"

She slid her hands out from underneath his shirt. Wriggling away from his grasp, she walked over to the sink and began cleaning. Some of the dishes were dirty; others were fresh from the dishwasher. She didn't care either way; she just wanted something to occupy her mind.

Michaels let her go. He knew she needed time to sort herself out. If he tried to soothe her feelings right now it would only backfire and make things worse. He looked over at Pip. The sweet Aussie shepherd was staring at Darla like a nurse looking at a new patient. The dog understood completely. It never ceased to amaze Michaels how animals could sense things humans couldn't, and all Pip wanted to do was make things right for her Mommy. Michaels loved her all the more for it. It reinforced his belief in what their little organization was trying to achieve.

He called the three dogs over to him. "Darla," he said, "If you knew the truth, you'd call me a hero, then you might just leave me. Sometimes people have to use evil to defeat evil, and that's what we're doing. We're trying to make the world a better place."

The tears came, plopping into the sink along with water from the faucet. "And just how are you doing that?" she asked.

"By giving people something to think about," replied Michaels.

··· 5 ···

At precisely eight forty-five on Friday morning the sleek Lincoln Town Car swerved into its predestined parking space at the Los Angeles International Airport. The driver exited, immediately hustling around to the rear passenger door. He opened it, allowing the businessman with a handsome, lined face to heave himself out of the car.

A steady wind blew across the parking lot, bringing with it the smells and small pieces of garbage that normally inhabit a large airport. The roar of jet engines cooked the sky every few minutes; another flight had received clearance for takeoff.

The driver retrieved three items from the trunk of the Lincoln; a large traveler's suitcase, a smaller carry on, and a laptop computer. He arranged these in such a way so that the businessman would be able to comfortably maneuver them through the terminal. After passing off the main handle to his employer, he looked him in the eye.

"Anything else, Mr. Collins?"

The businessman shook his head no.

"Four-thirty Monday afternoon, then?"

A Pound of Fur

"Meet me outside the baggage claim. I might have a dinner engagement, so be prepared to work late."

"Yes, sir. Have a good trip, sir."

Kevin Collins navigated his way through the endless stream of travelers at LAX. Sprinkled in here and there were spiritual appeals from dozens of ecumenical devotees. Ignoring these petitioners, he checked the Delta counter as he swerved through a nervous pack of vacationers, all buzzing around a man wearing a coat and holding a poorly made sign. The regular line at the Delta counter snaked all the way back to the end of the rope barrier. Luckily, there were only two people standing in the Delta Preferred Travelers queue. Collins moved purposefully toward the shorter line.

Once situated, Collins removed his cell phone from his coat pocket. Feigning interest in his dialing list, he secretively scanned the airport for those he knew must be present. He didn't expect to see Kitch here; the man was too clever to give himself away that easily. He did, however, observe two of his men standing innocently about the terminal. One fondled a magazine at the concourse gift shop. The other had placed himself at the standing bar at Starbucks. He sipped a large coffee that no doubt had grown cold an hour ago. They both stuck out like mannequins at a ballet performance. Collins registered their presence and dismissed them.

No doubt Kitch wanted to keep an eye on him, especially if he planned on leaving the state. That was fine with Collins; he wanted more than anything to be seen here at the airport. He wanted as much of his itinerary as possible to be catalogued by law enforcement. They would provide his alibi, both here and in North Carolina.

Collins pressed a button on his cell phone. The number of the boarding house where his two pets would stay for the weekend popped up on his screen. He punched dial, listening to the tiny device as it ran through its commands. After a short, high pitched ring, he heard the connection being made.

"Coast Pet Hotel," sang a cheery receptionist.

Collins identified himself, gave a description of his animals, and followed up with a confirmation number for their prepaid stay.

"Yes, sir, Mr. Collins, paid in full through Monday. You'll be picking them up that afternoon?"

"Someone in my employment will be by to collect them," said Collins. "If by chance I need them to stay an extra day or two, I'll telephone and make arrangements."

"That shouldn't be a problem," said the receptionist. "Monday through Wednesday is usually the slowest part of our week."

"Thank you for being so helpful. Those two mean a great deal to me."

"I can see why. Those have got to be the biggest cats I've ever seen. That Maine Coon must weigh thirty pounds, at least, and the Bengal isn't too far behind."

"Yes," said Collins. "Well, I'm afraid I have to go; I'm at the airport now."

"Have a good trip, Mr. Collins."

Silencing his cell phone, he looked ahead to the security checkpoint. He scoffed at the procedures the airport used to scan for illegal materials. A nine-year-old could walk a pistol around the barrier and no one would ever know.

As he approached the metal detector, he laid his carryon

bag on the conveyor belt next to his laptop. He unpacked nearly everything, putting the individual articles into separate bins. With that task completed, he walked over to the detection tunnel. He eyed the person holding the scanning wand. He hadn't emptied his pockets at all, since the Glock nine-millimeter in his shoulder holster would set off the mechanism anyway. He approached the determined looking woman standing on the other side of the threshold. He held up his identification, flicking it open with his middle finger.

"Come through, please," said the woman.

He walked through the slim, plastic tunnel. The detection monitor bleated.

"Your weapon, sir."

Collins deftly removed the Glock. With a swift, practiced motion, he released the clip, letting it fall into his hands. He drew back the chamber lock, ejecting the one remaining round. Then he handed the gun, clip, and the single bullet to the airport security officer.

"Step this way please, sir."

Collins followed the uniformed woman into a small MTA office. She turned his weapon over to another official, one of higher rank. She nodded to Collins and left to return to her duties.

"Identification, please," said the second guard.

Collins went through a routine he'd followed a thousand times previously. His papers were examined, his weapon assembled and disassembled, his life gone over with a microscope.

"You have a career in military intelligence?" asked the officer in charge of the MTA team.

"Yes," answered Collins. "I left the service fifteen years ago. I retain my rank as an inactive member in case of national emergency."

"Why do you continue to carry a weapon if you are not on the active roster?"

"I own a private security firm. We offer many of the same services that intelligence provides for the armed forces. Sometimes my business requires that I carry a firearm."

"Does this trip demand that you do so?" asked the security officer, digging in a little too deeply.

"No."

"Then may I ask why you are armed today?"

Collins raised his eyes until they met the MTA officer. "Habit," he said. "I am licensed to carry a concealed weapon. You must have learned that by scanning my papers."

"I am aware of your certification, Mr. Collins. I'll ask you again. Why did you feel it was necessary to carry a firearm today?"

Collins shifted his eyes, looked at the man directly. He saw a cool confidence combined with extreme competence. Definitely a military background. He made a mental note to come back and offer him a job.

"Sometimes you just have a feeling," he said, still staring at the officer. "Know what I mean?"

The MTA commander nodded his head once before placing Collins' Glock into three separate plastic baggies. "Sometimes I get that very same feeling." He placed the disassembled, packaged gun in a bin behind the counter. "You may collect your weapon after you deplane in North Carolina."

"What's your name, soldier?" asked Collins.

"As you can see, my name is Delgado."

What is your given name, Mr. Delgado?"

"Guillermo Roberto."

"Perhaps we can enjoy a cup of coffee someday soon."

"Perhaps," said Delgado. "Enjoy your flight, sir."

Collins left the MTA office. He gathered his belongings from the hallway and accessed the escalator that would take him to the main gateway. His flight was scheduled to leave from gate forty-one. After checking his watch, he decided to visit the commander's lounge for a quick bite.

··· 6 ···

"Back Monday night, then?" asked Darla.

"Yes," said Michaels. "Maybe even Monday afternoon. We'll see how quickly we can clean up after the convention."

"Be careful," she said. "I love our home and our children, but I love you more than anything. Just make sure you come home."

"I'll call you when we reach North Carolina. Take care of the kids."

Darla nodded her head once and kissed her husband. She stood in the doorway between the kitchen and the garage, watching Michaels store his luggage in the trunk of their wagon. When he backed out of the garage and turned to wave, she smiled her best smile and pressed the button to close the garage door.

··· 7 ···

Brett Jeffries stretched out on the soft, king sized bed, looking out the open window toward the pier. A light breeze, scented by the ocean, wafted over him and into the hotel room he shared with his latest conquest. He felt the soft wind rolling over his naked shoulders, buttocks and feet. He smiled the contented smile of a man completely satisfied. He had won his division with a world record, eaten the freshest seafood, drank the most delicious beer, and fucked a sexy woman for three straight days. He couldn't have been happier.

The dazzling woman he met on the pier the first day of the tournament came out of the bathroom wearing nothing but a sarong. The material was sheer enough so that just the right amount was left to the imagination, and it made Jeffries' loins flare. He turned and looked at her, at her perfection. She had tied her hair into a loose ponytail, so the fine brown strands touched by the sun draped loosely to the sides before gathering up again by the nape of her neck. Every inch of her skin was flawless, light brown, California beach tanned, and accented by small groves of tiny blonde hairs in all of the most enticing places. Her sensational figure seemed to enjoy every movement the woman made, whether writhing on a bed or sofa, walking across the room, or breathing. Her stunning breasts, legs, stomach and behind took his breath away. For Jeffries, she was a rare find, a truly gorgeous woman who loved nothing else but to please her man in myriad ways.

"What are you watching?" she asked, glancing at the television.

"You'll love it," replied Jeffries. "Here, let me start it at the beginning." He flicked a few buttons on the remote.

A tiny calico kitten rolled around on a tile floor. A few feathers danced lightly above it. The little paws flashed as it tried to catch them. Every few seconds a wee meow escaped the kitten's mouth.

The prostitute smiled, watching the animal's antics. She opened her mouth to tell Jeffries she had a calico cat at home named Magic.

A woman's spiked heel slammed down onto the kitten's belly. The startled animal rolled over, frantically trying to escape. Its paws slipped on the freshly cleaned tiles. The heel came down again, splitting the kitten's jaws. Teeth, blood, and fur shot in every direction.

The shoe fell again and again, crushing the helpless kitten in a scene of savagery so shocking the prostitute nearly doubled over and vomited. She watched the kitten screeching for help. She could barely compose herself, but she had a contract to complete. She'd be away from the creep soon enough.

"Interesting," she said dispassionately.

"It's a crush video," said Jeffries. "I watch them all the time. Funny, huh?"

A **Pound** of Fur

Sashaying across the room holding a beer in her delicate hand, she sat on the edge of the hotel room bed. She wanted to break the bottle and slash his face with the jagged neck. Instead, she upended it slightly, sending the dark ale tumbling into a chilled glass. Jeffries never detected the small pill she'd deposited before pouring the beer; he was busy brushing the tiny hairs along her taut, flat stomach. Even with all the fabulous sex he'd had over the last three days, he still became aroused at the sight of her. She was without a doubt the hottest piece of ass he'd ever fucked.

"Beer?" she asked, holding the glass in front of and level with her supple breasts.

Jeffries grabbed the glass from her hand, took a long sip and swallowed most of the liquid. He retained a small amount in his mouth. Moving toward her on the bed, he propped himself up on one elbow and placed his free hand on the small of her back. Pulling her forward, he swallowed one of her delicious nipples between his lips.

The woman arched her back, pressing the meat of her ample breast into his face. This pushed him over the edge, for how many times he couldn't recall. She had a way about her he'd never experienced with anyone else. She could say a word, touch him with a finger, or move her body in such a way that he would be instantly aroused. Today it was the feel of freshly showered breasts in his face.

The woman let him suckle her nipples, trading one for the other every few seconds like all men did. She inhaled deeply while placing her hands on the top of her head. These actions moved her breasts into their most supple position, taut and inviting. She watched Jeffries vigorously boost his attack, grabbing and sucking like a newborn babe.

And then, as if the air simply left Jeffries' body all at once, the champion of the marlin tournament collapsed. Completely paralyzed by the drug, he slipped off of the bed and hit the floor like a pile of dirty laundry.

The woman leaned toward her nightstand. She grabbed the disposable cell phone she'd purchased at the drug store the day before. Flipping it open, she dialed the number Turner had given her. She listened as the call chimed through several forwarding links before settling on the desired location.

"Turner Securities, Inc."

"Your package is ready, sir," she said while fingering her aroused nipple.

"Are there any shipping charges?"

"Four dollars and thirteen cents, sir."

"Understood," said Turner. "Thank you for the call."

Turner took a pen from his shirt pocket and wrote the information on the back of his breakfast tab. *Room 413 – Rocky Bluff Inn.*

··· 8 ···

Matt Mayfield sat at the helm of his brand-new Cabo 38 fishing boat. Drunk out of his mind and feeling on top of the world, he took another swig from his bottle of Blue Label. The people on his and the surrounding boats partied all afternoon and into the evening. The sun set maybe twenty minutes ago, and Mayfield still felt the soothing warmth on his face.

The tournament had been a smashing success. Two world records had been broken, one on the first day and one on the final day. The turnout exceeded his expectations.

The financial return on the event drew the attention of the right people. Three more sponsors had signed on for the remaining tournaments of the season. With the news of the broken records sailing through the internet seconds after their occurrence, the gates for the last five events had nearly sold out.

Mayfield gripped the steering wheel so he wouldn't tumble out of the captain's chair. Staring out to sea, he slowly brought the bottle up to his lips. A brisk onshore wind blew in from the ocean, scattering a few strands of his hair.

Mayfield turned the bottle up and drank. A few drops of the expensive whiskey dribbled from the side of his mouth. He swallowed, tipped the bottle forward and wiped his lips. The motion brought his head around enough for him to see the strange man standing on the dock.

He stood motionless, like a wraith, in jeans, work boots and a worn, khaki shirt. He had the sleeves rolled up to his elbows; Mayfield could see he could handle himself. The man said nothing. He simply stood there staring at the drunken man playing captain in his flashy, new boat.

"Ain't it kind of dark for sunglasses?" asked the tournament director.

"Yea," replied Turner. "I guess I forget I have 'em on sometimes. Sun goes down pretty slow around here."

Mayfield grunted an inaudible response. He turned once in the captain's chair, looking out toward the ocean. His hand slipped, almost separating from the wheel. In his haste to correct his body's imbalance he dropped his bottle. Falling from the high perch of the helm, the bottle shattered on the deck of the boat. Mayfield slouched in the seat, trying to look below him.

"Shit," he said in the drunken slur.

With his head still hanging down, he looked under his armpit at the man in the sunglasses. He now stood on the dock immediately behind the gunwale of Mayfield's boat. Still wearing the shades, he stood with arms folded, silently staring at the sweaty, sunburned tournament director.

"That's a damn waste of some fine whisky."

"What do you want?"

"I'd like you to come with me."

"What the fuck for?" asked Mayfield.

"I want to show you something."

"Go fuck yourself."

"It can be easy or hard," said Turner. "Either way you're coming with me."

Mayfield craned his neck left and right, his drunken field of vision looping like an unbalanced pendulum. What little he could focus on didn't raise his spirits. He and the stranger were the only people on the dock. Most everyone had left the tournament hours ago. The people he had been partying with were all at the restaurant on the pier, and that was more than three hundred yards away. Mayfield listened for any sound of humanity close to his boat.

He fumbled for a flare gun locked in a quick release holster underneath the wheel housing. Once he held it in his hand, he smiled, thinking the encounter with the stranger would soon be over. He ripped the flare gun from its casing, spun around, and promptly fell belly first from the chair. Before hitting the deck, he managed to fire the gun. The blazing flare flew less than six feet before slamming into a life jacket rack on the port side of the boat. It remained there, spreading its burning chemicals among the orange vests.

Swearing under his breath, Turner vaulted over the gunwale and into the boat. He grabbed a utility bucket and reached over the starboard railing. Filling it with seawater, he hauled his hand back over the side. He took three steps and doused the growing fire. Just to be certain, he scooped another bucketful of water and dumped it on the steaming life jackets.

He stood up, breathing as quietly as he could. He heard bells clanging softly around the dock, lanyards slapping against masts, and the cries of people drinking and dancing quite a ways away.

Finally, he turned, scanning the dock area closely. Even with Mayfield's blunder with the flare gun, the two of them were still the only ones occupying the dock. A military man for over twenty years, Turner waited another five minutes before moving Mayfield off the boat.

He sat him on the gunwale, grabbed a baseball cap and pulled it snug over Mayfield's head. Hugging him around the waist, Turner hefted the man up over his right shoulder. Mayfield was surprisingly heavy, even for someone of Turner's build and strength. Shrugging the dead weight a little higher on his shoulder, he turned and walked toward the dock entrance.

··· 9 ···

Lieutenant Kitch sat in the office he shared with two other Los Angeles Police Department investigators. In one hand he held the medical examiner's report on the unfortunate man who lost his teeth along with his head during the raid at the dogfighting ring. Identified as Raul Contreras, he was a day laborer in any of a thousand construction sites around the county. No fixed address, no phone number, no family members living nearby. As a clue to follow, Señor Contreras proved to be a big, fat zero.

In his other hand he held a flat, plastic ruler. Moving it lightly down a list of printed locations, he scanned every known dogfighting contest that had occurred over the last month in L.A. County. There were hundreds within the city limits alone. A good number found their way out toward San Fernando Valley, and another ten or twenty percent occurred in Covina and West Covina.

Kitch could find no regularity in the pattern of the raids. He had hoped to find a linear direction in the group's attacks, say a starting point in Covina and movement west toward the valley. The twenty-six attacks showed no definitive pattern at all. The first happened downtown, the next in West Covina. The bulk of the attacks occurred in South Central, and the last few, including the one Kitch suspected Collins of engineering, were held east of Tarzana.

If it was the work of a small, tight knit team, they took their orders from someone very familiar with investigative police work. The style of the raid changed with each location. Sometimes they shot everyone in attendance. Some received non-lethal injuries, others were less fortunate. In other cases, like the last raid near Tarzana, the organizer of the event became a participant, usually dying a gruesome death. Sometimes the raiding party came early, at other times they hit their target late. At a few of the locations, some of the attendees decided to bring guns and fight back. The military trained vigilante team cut them down easily.

Nothing they did established a pattern except for one constant; they always took the dogs when they left. Those sponsoring and attending the fights paid a terrible price if a raid occurred, and the dogs always disappeared without explanation.

Kitch visited or telephoned every animal shelter in the county, asking if large groups of dogs had been donated over the last six months. Most had laughed, telling him they took in at least fifty dogs a week, many times in groups. He asked about particular breeds, and if they remembered any dogs arriving that were fairly chewed up, possibly refugees from fighting clubs. None answered in the affirmative, but they reassured the lieutenant that if any animals arrived in that condition, they would contact the authorities immediately.

A Pound of Fur

Kitch had even assigned men to work undercover at a few of the fighting rings, hoping to get lucky. They either didn't, the team of vigilantes had inside information, or they could smell a cop from five miles away. It was by far the strangest and most perplexing case he'd worked in a dozen years.

Obviously, the men engaged in the raids didn't become involved because they liked to torture or murder civilians. If they wanted to do that there were a thousand streets in Los Angeles they could get their jollies on. *No*, thought Kitch, *these men are acting as protectors. They are executing these raids out of a serious love of animals.* He shook his head. *The world gets stranger every day.*

The other certainty in the case had to do with the number of illegal dogfights in Los Angeles County. They had dropped by at least half. The message was spreading; no one dared show their face at a fighting ring with vigilantes running loose.

"Lieutenant K," said Detective Brennan, one of Kitch's office mates. The younger man slapped a pile of manila folders down on his desk. The mass of paper swayed to the left, leaning precariously toward the edge of disaster. Brennan set a mug of steaming, black coffee down on the desk mat before catching the sliding mess with his left hand. Instead of centering the pile, he pulled the fulcrum all the way to the right, letting the paperwork fall into his desk lamp.

"How goes the hunt for the puppy lovers?" he asked Kitch.

"Not well, I'm afraid. It is beyond me how a team of heavily armed men can move about a city dense with population, late at night, engage in urban warfare, leave bodies everywhere they go, and disappear without leaving a shred of evidence."

"What about witnesses?"

"Usually gone by the time units arrive on scene," said Kitch. "The handful of men we did interview refused to say anything or give even the most remote descriptions of the attackers."

"Intimidated?" asked Brennan.

"Terrified," replied Kitch. "Whatever they see rips the tongues from their mouths."

"Must be pretty bad if they refuse to cooperate."

Kitch looked over at Brennan. The look in his eyes told the junior detective everything he needed to know. Brennan grabbed his cup and lifted it to his mouth. Taking a delicate sip of the scalding hot coffee, he wondered for a moment what it might be like to manage such a case.

"At least you get to work on something interesting," said Brennan. "Look what I got, two homeless murders on skid row and a domestic violence gone wild."

"There are cases everywhere that need your delicate touch. But while you're having grandiose dreams about solving the crime of the century, perhaps you could help me brainstorm."

Brennan took another sip of coffee. "Sure thing, K. As you can see, my desk is completely clear."

Kitch looked at the mounds of paperwork smothering Brennan's workspace. He smiled, looking back at the young detective. "Let me ask you something, Arthur."

Brennan preferred Art, but he always gave Kitch a wide berth.

"You know the background of this case. What kind of men do you think would be capable of such brutality?"

"Ex-military, without a doubt."

"Why do you say that?"

"They obviously plan their excursions down to the last detail. More than that, they don't deviate, no matter how grisly the assignment. They walk in, take care of business, scare the living daylights out of everyone they don't kill, grab the dogs and split."

Kitch stared across the room, deep in thought.

"You'd have to have seen combat in order to carry out raids like these; normal everyday people wouldn't have the stomach for it."

"Do you believe this is the work of one organization?" asked Kitch.

"Normally, I'd say yes. But the world is so off its rocker these days I wouldn't be surprised to learn that some of these raids had been pulled by copycats."

"Yes. The remaining evidence has the look of different parties. Something bothers me about it, though."

"What's that?" asked Brennan.

"Have you ever worked a case where all the physical evidence pointed one way, but your gut told you that the solution would be found in an entirely different direction?"

"Sure. So what?"

"Nothing. Thank you for your assistance."

"Anytime, K, and if you ever want to trade cases, let me know."

Kitch managed a tight smile. He fanned through the pages of his report until he found the phone number he sought. Holding the page open with his left palm, he lifted the receiver from the handset on his desk and made his call.

"Safeguard Protection Services," said the lively voice.

"Kevin Collins, please."

"I'm sorry, but Mr. Collins left this morning for an out of town convention. May I take a message or transfer you to his voicemail?"

"May I ask where the convention is taking place?"

"Who am I speaking with?"

"This is Lieutenant Samuel Kitch of the Los Angeles Police Department. I visited Mr. Collins a week ago in his office."

"Yes, I remember now. Mr. Collins is attending the private firearms convention in Greenville, North Carolina."

"When do you anticipate his return?" asked Kitch.

"He's planning on returning to Los Angeles the day after tomorrow. He did mention a possible stopover in Washington, D.C., but unless I hear from him, he'll be back on Monday."

"Would you please ask him to telephone me when he gets back?"

"Yes, sir," said the receptionist. "Does he have your number?"

"Just have him call the LAPD and ask for Sam Kitch."

"I'll surely do that. Have a nice day, Lieutenant."

Kitch heard the dull click in the earpiece before he hung up the phone. He sat there, mummified, thinking about what to do next. His right hand remained on the telephone.

"What's up, Kitch," asked Brennan. "You look like you just lost your house at the track."

A Pound of Fur

"If I said Greenville, North Carolina, to you, Arthur, would it stir any thoughts about animals?"

"Huh?"

Kitch removed his hand from the phone and stared at Brennan. "Do you know of any events that happen in that part of the country, anything that has to do with animals?"

"Do fish count?"

"I beg your pardon?"

"Well," said Brennan, "I don't know about animals, but Greenville's one the stops on the Elite Sport Fishing Tour."

"Say again?" asked Kitch.

"Marlin fishing, you know, big billfish tournament. Why?"

··· 10 ···

The men sitting on the slimy, stinking floor heard the dull sound of boots entering the room. One of them sat up slightly, startled at the sound of company after such a lengthy imprisonment. The other, hung over beyond all human capacity, held his body slumped against the grainy wall. The cool cement, although gritty, felt good against his sweat soaked forehead.

"Who's there?" asked Jeffries, suddenly awake and alert. No reply came, but Jeffries and Mayfield could hear a low, whispered conversation occurring in the room.

Mayfield stayed silent. He wasn't hung over enough to forget the man standing on the dock last night. If his current predicament had anything to do with him, he wouldn't give a dime for their chances.

Someone ripped the thick flour sacks away from their heads. The two men blinked repeatedly, trying to focus on the sparsely furnished room they had occupied for the last twelve hours. It looked like the main floor of an industrial plant. Long forgotten in the recession two years prior, the factory owners had grabbed everything they could salvage before running to the protection of bankruptcy court. The windows had all been shot out; a few of the walls had crumbled. The natural flora had invaded the plant, growing through the windows and from beneath the cement slab. Some parts of the ceiling remained, but the coloring highlighted deterioration from years of heavy rains.

Everything had been removed by the last owners of the plant. Today, however, a strange looking machine stood dead center in the middle of the room. It looked downright medieval. Jeffries and Mayfield stared at it incredulously, wondering why in God's name these men would bring it *and* them here under these bizarre circumstances.

"I said, who the fuck *are* you?" Jeffries shouted, "and why are we here, tied up like prisoners?"

The man in the aviator sunglasses glanced over at Jeffries and Mayfield. He held something in his right hand, something made of steel. Neither Jeffries nor Mayfield could make out what it was until the stranger tossed it in their direction.

A giant fishhook, almost two feet long, rang out as it hit the cement floor. It bounced once high in the air, clanging loudly, and then a few more times closer to the ground before it came to rest next to Mayfield's left thigh. The two men looked at the hook with dumbfounded disbelief.

Those following the orders of the man wearing the aviator sunglasses pulled away the tarp lying in front of the peculiar machine. Both Mayfield and Jeffries suddenly realized why the room reeked so badly. Jeffries' world record marlin lay in front of them, lying on the floor with one fin awkwardly splayed out toward the machine. Interestingly, the position of the fish caused it to stare straight at Jeffries with one of its dead, dark eyes. Its mouth hung open; strings of half-dried spittle danced between the upper and lower jaws. A large hole pierced the underside of its lower jaw, the exact location where Jeffries's hook had tugged so brutally during the competition.

"What the fuck are we doing here?" asked a clearly alarmed Jeffries. "What kind of sick fucks are you assholes?"

Mayfield broke away from his hammering hangover long enough to understand Jeffries' assessment of their predicament. "Y-You can't do this to us."

"Shut up," said Collins, "both of you."

The group of men continued to converse. Questions were asked, answers came, and finally, Collins nodded his head once. The men under his command broke away from their impromptu meeting to attend to their duties.

One of them fired up a large, noisy generator. Another hefted buckets of seawater from a five-hundred-gallon drum sitting near the strange looking machine. He doused the marlin with the water, but he also wetted down the cement surrounding the huge fish. Still another man worked off to the side with a small but powerful communications array. His job was to listen in on the Greenville Police Department's radio calls. The location worked out perfectly; it was thirty miles to anywhere or anyone. If a call happened to be put in about their little party, they'd know about it in plenty of time to pack up and split.

Turner and Michaels walked over to the giant machine with its single mechanical arm hanging silently askew. Turner grabbed the thick electrical cable and walked over to the generator. He plugged it in and gave thumbs up to Michaels.

A Pound of Fur

Michaels pushed the thick, rubber startup button on the side of the machine facing him. As Turner walked back over, Michaels worked the machine's controls.

A raspy, grinding, metal on metal noise erupted within the industrial site. The mechanical arm, looking like some apoplectic elephant trunk, began thrashing about wildly. The direction changes were completely unplanned; the arm followed no set pattern, but it was very, very strong. After letting it twist and slam against the metal casing of the machine for a minute, Michaels released the controls and shut the monstrosity off.

Collins walked over to Jeffries and Mayfield. Without saying a word, he picked up the giant hook and tossed it to Turner.

Turner and Michaels fastened the eye of the hook to a thick cable protruding from the end of the mechanical arm. With a great deal of effort, they managed to run the point of the hook through the wound in the marlin's jaw. The thirteen-hundred-pound fish lay on the rough cement, one eye still staring at Jeffries. Turner looked over at Collins, nodding his head once.

"Let her rip," said Collins.

Michaels restarted the hydraulic motor on the bizarre machine. The grinding wheeze began at a low pitch, while the mechanical arm became taught as it tried to pull the giant fish along the cement floor. Michaels cranked up the engine. With the increased power, the noise became deafening, and the arm of the machine started moving more freely. The marlin, dead for three days and stinking to high heaven, slid to the right and then back to the left. The powerful winch built into the arm lifted more than half the fish into the air before dropping it back to the floor again. The fish landed with a sickening, squishy splat and lay there for a moment. Michaels increased the power again; this time the marlin flopped around on the floor chaotically. It looked oddly like the last few minutes of a struggle with a sport fisherman. The noise from the machine and the fish became hideous. To look upon the grotesque scene made one wonder when man's sanity had departed. Blood and intestinal liquids sprayed from the interior of the marlin in every direction. Jeffries and Mayfield sat still, covered in it. Collins had stains on his boots and pants, as did Turner and Michaels. The other men brought along to accomplish the mission sat or stood well away from the action, keeping their clothing clean.

Michaels shut off the machine. The giant fish flopped over on its back, bloated and oozing foul liquids by the pint.

Mayfield's stomach couldn't take the odor any longer. He leaned over as well as a handcuffed man could under the circumstances, vomiting onto the floor, his clothing, and his right arm. After expelling his insides, he strained to right himself again. He breathed heavily, his mouth wide open. Every few seconds he emitted a high-pitched plea. The rotting whisky hammered away at his head, increasing his painful discomfort by the minute. His stomach churned again. He leaned over and dry heaved, feeling as though his head would explode.

After unhooking the marlin, Collins worked with his men to slide the huge bill fish away from the winch. Sweating and breathing heavily, they moved it about five yards.

A **Pound** of Fur

They might have continued pushing it away, but Collins determined there would be enough room.

Jeffries had stopped yelling momentarily while his captors had their fun dragging his prize-winning fish around with the winch. When he saw them shoving the marlin off to the side and then glancing in his direction, and then watching Turner and Michaels walk toward him, he suddenly realized why they'd brought him along. The imagery of what was about to happen made his blood run cold. He felt a rush of numbness soak his testicles before they receded into his crotch. He couldn't fathom what kind of men would do what these maniacs had planned.

Turner grabbed Jeffries handcuffed arms and lifted him to his feet. Jeffries kicked wildly at Michaels as he came forward to help Turner bring him over to the winch. After one particularly vicious kick nearly connected, Turner threw Jeffries to the ground. The men rolled him over, sitting on his legs and shoulders. Jeffries cried out, the wrenching pain in his limbs combined with the nightmarish anticipation terrified him.

"You bastards!" he screamed. "You crazy fucking bastards, what the fuck are you trying to accomplish?"

"A paradigm change," said Collins. "Think of it as a crush video."

Turner and Michaels lifted Jeffries to a standing position. As they did so, Collins casually walked over to where Mayfield was dying a slow death. He squatted down next to the overweight, wheezing tournament director.

"You know what I always wonder?" he asked the pale, sweating hulk. "I wonder if a fish ever suffers when some jackass has it on the end of pole with a hook in its mouth."

Collins glanced over at his men as they prepared the winch. They positioned Jeffries on the ground in front of the machine. The powerful mechanical arm dangled in front of him like some freakish gallows' attendant calling him to his death.

"You ever wonder about that?" Collins asked Mayfield.

Jeffries shrieked like the demons of hell when Turner pierced his right cheek with the massive fishhook. He kept bellowing, half from the sting and half from the pain he knew he would soon endure. Before leaving him, Turner removed the handcuffs from Jeffries' wrists.

At Collins' signal, Michaels pressed the button, cranking the massive winch to life. He dialed the controls lightly, giving a small amount of power to the arm. As it pulled up and away from the ground, Jeffries bore out his pain with a scream that sent tremors through most of Collins' men. His mouth became distorted, stretching and spewing blood. Finally, the skin found the strain too much to bear. The huge metal hook ripped through Jeffries' shredded cheek. The champion of the tournament, who less than twenty-four hours ago had been living like a king, flopped down on the cement like a fish landing on a boat's gunwale.

"Stop it!" Mayfield screamed, suddenly awakened from his stupor. Spittle flew forward from his pale lips as he yelled again and again. He wasn't so much looking out for Jeffries as he was protecting himself. After all, there was only one other man in the room wearing handcuffs. "Stop it right now! You're killing him!"

Collins looked over at Mayfield while lighting a cigarette. Then he looked back at Jeffries.

"Push the hook through his lower jaw," he ordered through an exhalation of thick smoke.

Turner and Michaels didn't hesitate. Turner walked straight over to Jeffries' quivering body. He rolled him over onto his back, holding him there while Michaels pulled the blood-stained cable down toward his jaw. With Turner holding Jeffries' mouth wide open with one hand, both he and Michaels jammed the sharp point of the hook through his tongue and the moist skin just behind his teeth. The work went slowly; Jeffries' body writhed in pain, his uncontrollable bellowing made a clean puncture almost impossible. Together, they finally pushed the huge hook all the way through.

"Assholes!" screamed Mayfield, eyes wide open with unfettered shock and fear. "You fucking assholes!"

Collins took a drag off his cigarette. "I'd shut up if I were you."

Mayfield piped down immediately.

Collins turned and nodded to Michaels, who cranked up the winch again. Jeffries cried desperately when the arm holding the fishhook began to tighten against his jaw. He reached out with his hands, grasping the slick steel cable. He wanted to lessen the strain on his mouth, but the oil and grease made it impossible.

He tried to beg for his life, but no one could make out the words. His jaw and tongue became useless as the powerful winch yanked him forward.

Soft skin wouldn't save him this time. His lower jaw held fast as the winch arm began moving in chaotic directions. Jeffries flopped left and right, up and down, rolling over at times, only to have his body lurch in the opposite direction once again. After a while the screaming stopped. The delirium of excessive pain had vanquished Jeffries' ability to respond. The machine jerked him around like a fishing pole pulling a catch along a slippery dock.

Collins dropped his cigarette, smashed it with his boot. He drew his right hand across his throat, a signal for Michaels to shut off the winch. Michaels complied immediately, watching Jeffries body slump to the floor in a half turn, his limbs splayed out awkwardly.

Jeffries' eyes were closed, but the steady rise and fall of his chest told the men huddling around him he was still alive. The right side of his jaw had broken away from the skull. The swelling around his face reflected the power of the winch; they could barely recognize him anymore. A wide pool of blood spread out underneath his broken skull.

Mayfield looked like a man waking from a horrific nightmare. Never in his life had he witnessed such brutality. He looked at the strange men who'd brought him here, who had done this to Jeffries, who no doubt planned to kill him as well. He saw the leader walking toward him. He involuntarily squirmed away, trying to move his body in the opposite direction.

Collins squatted next to the terrified tournament director. "So, what do you think about my question?" he asked.

"I think you're the sickest fuck I've ever seen."

"Wrong answer," said Collins. He stood, signaled his men. Turner worked the hook from Jeffries' mouth while Michaels walked over to collect Mayfield. The tournament director shit himself while screaming at the top of his lungs.

Michaels grabbed the handcuffs holding Mayfield's wrists together and dragged the overweight, distraught man toward the winch.

As he rolled over, Mayfield caught a glimpse of Turner dragging Jeffries's body away from the machine. His face didn't even look human anymore; the beating the machine gave him had caused that much swelling. A thick trail of blood stained the floor behind Jeffries' path. Mayfield closed his eyes to the horror of it all.

Michaels pulled Mayfield to a spot directly in front of the blood-stained machine. The giant hook, once perfectly pristine before commencing its duties, now looked like exactly what it was, a huge implement of torture straight out of the inquisition. It hung in the air, waiting, five feet above Mayfield's head.

Collins adjusted his sunglasses, squatting before Mayfield. "Do you think hooks hurt fish as much as they hurt humans? I mean, when you have a half ton marlin twisting in the sea spray, do you think it might be in any pain?"

Mayfield stared at his captor, the shock of his predicament stealing his voice. A line of spittle dripped quietly from his mouth as he stared into his reflection in the aviator sunglasses.

"Well," asked Collins, "do you?"

"Let me go," cried Mayfield, begging for kindness. "Just let me go."

Collins shook his head, standing slowly. He locked eyes with Turner and Michaels before walking to a safe distance.

Michaels grabbed the slimy hook, pulled it down toward Mayfield's mouth. Turner sat on the man's back while lifting his jaw. Mayfield screamed like a man being dragged to his doom by all the servants of hell. He tried to bite Turner's fingers and received a few punishing blows for his effort. Collins' men finally wedged the hook into his mouth. They began forcing the tip against the side of his cheek. With one heaving push, they could puncture Mayfield's skin and have him ready for the winch. Mayfield bellowed his confession to any god that might listen. His hangover forgotten; the tournament director turned his head away from the pointy end of the hook. When he opened his eyes, he found himself staring at his own reflection.

"I'm going to say this slowly. You've got one chance and one chance only to escape the pain Mr. Jeffries endured."

Mayfield's body reacted to this statement by becoming repulsively flatulent. He colored his already stained jeans with a series of putrid expulsions. He couldn't speak with the hook in his mouth, but his eyes said everything. He would do whatever they asked to save himself.

"You own the largest sport fishing agency in the world," said Collins. "As of tomorrow it no longer exists. Within a week you will cancel the remaining tour stops for this year, and in one month's time you will have dissolved the company."

Collins issued a hand signal. Michaels removed the hook from Mayfield's mouth.

"Is that clear?" he asked Mayfield.

"Yes, yes, anything," the horrified man replied.

A man monitoring a stack of communications equipment interrupted his boss. "Sir, I'm getting missing person calls for the area around the docks. Seems as though people are starting to worry about our two guests."

A Pound of Fur

"Keep me posted," said Collins. "If they send units we'll need to vacate pretty quickly."

He returned his attention to Mayfield. "I want you to become the world's most vocal advocate for marine life, is that clear?"

"Yes, clear, I mean I will," said Mayfield. "I promise."

"It's not enough that you stop your tournaments and close down your company. You must press the issue with every other agency, especially since when you bow out a couple of dozen companies will swoop in and scoop up your action. I want to believe that you'll be doing everything you can for the good of marine life the world over. The moment I lose faith in you is the moment you'll end up back here, at this very spot, with this machine waiting for you."

Mayfield closed his eyes, trying to force the machine and the strange men to vanish. He opened them when he heard Collins begin speaking again.

"If you talk to the police, we'll bring you back here. If you tell anyone anything about what happened here today, you'll be swinging on the end of that hook. Do you understand me?"

"Yes."

"Do you believe me?"

"Yes."

"Do you think I'm capable enough to stay one step ahead of the police long enough to find you?"

"Yes," said Mayfield. "Yes, for God's sake, just go, leave me. Go away, all of you."

Collins' assistant interrupted Mayfield's pleading.

"Boss, local police just sent two units to the Rocky Bluff Inn. They're on their way right now."

"Take off his cuffs," Collins ordered.

Turner knelt on one knee while deftly working with the keys. In seconds, Mayfield's wrists and ankles were unshackled. The severely unkempt tournament director rolled over and perched himself on his large, stained ass.

Collins lifted a Glock pistol from his rear waistband holster. He crouched in front of Mayfield without looking at him. He fingered the weapon, not lovingly, but as a man who understood firearms.

"Remember, Mayfield, if you do anything except keep your mouth shut and change your life in the manner we discussed, you'll wake up some day in a place very similar to this. Even if you spill your guts to the police, identify every one of us and have us all incarcerated, I have dozens of operatives I can call upon to see that your sentence is carried out."

He raised his eyes and met Mayfield's. "So don't be a fool."

Collins men had been busy wiping down the machinery for prints. Everything small enough to carry went into a brace of duffle bags. The rest, including the giant winch, remained behind, clues with which the Greenville police would begin their investigation.

"Ready, Boss," said Michaels.

Collins tapped the barrel of his Glock against Mayfield's head. "Don't be a fool."

He walked over to the twisted form of Brett Jeffries, whose head looked more like a mangled gourd than anything remotely human. Collins watched the man's belly, waiting for it to rise and fall with Jeffries' breathing. When he saw proof of life, he raised his Glock, targeting the back of Jeffries' head. He squeezed off three rounds. Jeffries stiffened once and then lay dead. Collins sheathed his gun in the holster he wore next to the small of his back. He looked up at his men, nodded once, and then jogged with them out to a waiting helicopter. Mayfield sat in his own feces, staring at the architects of the most horrifying episode he would ever experience.

··· 11 ···

"I'm sorry, Lieutenant," the efficient voice on the telephone said, "Mr. Collins left word that he would be returning tomorrow evening. He was called to Washington for a meeting with another security consulting firm."

"I understand," said Kitch. "May I have his cell phone number? I have an urgent matter to discuss with your superior."

"I'm afraid not, sir. Mr. Collins doesn't give that information to anyone. I don't even know that number."

"Very well then, please ask him to phone me when he returns to Los Angeles."

"I'll post the message right away, sir."

"Thank you," said Kitch.

Sam Kitch sat at his desk with the Los Angeles Times spread out in front of him. He had arranged a front-page story, including the interior supplements, in various positions so he could scan the information at his leisure. A sizable picture graced the front page. It showed the covered body of a mortally wounded man next to a very peculiar piece of machinery. It looked like a thick post of some sort, containing gears

and a small engine, and one solitary moving part. It captivated Kitch's attention. The bloody hook dangling from the
end of the mechanical arm had caught his eye immediately.

On page seventeen the story continued. Apparently when
the Greenville police arrived on scene, they found another
man waiting for them. Although blood spattered and foul
smelling, the man ran to the troopers' cars waving his hands
frantically. He hugged the uniformed men, refusing to leave
their side while they commenced with their inspection.

The first trooper to get a good look at Jeffries lying next
to the hideous winch lost his lunch. Jeffries face looked like a
science fiction freak show, with his left cheek horribly shredded and a hideous, gory hole bored through his lower jaw.
The trooper had glanced at him, then at the machine, with
its blood caked, flesh coated hook, and promptly puked his
Juevos Rancheros everywhere in front of him. It wasn't so
much the putrid sight that caused the reaction. The trooper
had instantly put two and two together and imagined himself
flailing about on the end of the hook. Not quite a rookie with
four years on the force, he explained to his superiors that he
had never seen anything so terrifying in his life.

Kitch shifted his eyes to page eighteen. A head shot of
Matt Mayfield occupied the upper right corner. A very strange
but inviting article accompanied the picture. Apparently, Mr.
Mayfield, after arriving at a hotel for a much-needed shower,
had completely clammed up as soon as the local detectives
started questioning him. Mayfield not only wouldn't answer
questions about the incident, he refused to entertain inquiries
about anything. He telephoned his attorney and asked him to
come to Greenville immediately. The state troopers had used

every possible psychological ploy; coercion, offers of protection, even threats of prosecution as an accessory. Nothing had worked. One of the detectives had been overheard telling his captain that Mr. Mayfield looked like a man scared beyond speech. The only thing he'd given them all morning was his announcement that the remaining tournaments for the year were canceled.

Odd, thought Kitch, turning back to page one. He looked at the machine, a simple, yet effective tool, something a man of similar qualities might use for such a job. He thought of Collins, of what he had learned about the man. Collins possessed the expertise to build something of that nature, but did he have the inner strength to use it, or to command others to do so? The questions baffled Kitch. All of his experiences as a law enforcement officer convinced him that Collins was responsible for these bizarre attacks. First it was dogfighting, and now sport fishing. Kitch pondered where the vigilantes might strike next. Dozens of possible venues shot through his mind. He discarded all of them, there were too many to consider. Better to focus on current activities. After all, Collins wouldn't return to Los Angeles until tomorrow night.

Leaving the newspaper scattered about his desk, Kitch leaned back while opening the top right drawer. A single forest green file folder lay within. Thick with papers and photographs, it contained a thorough synopsis of Kevin Collins' life. Kitch grasped it carefully, pulling it from the drawer and setting it directly in front of him. Gently, he peeled back the left wing of the folder. The first item in the list was an old black and white Polaroid of Collins. Standing in front of a church, the young boy proudly displayed his altar boy vestments. A cast covered is right hand, a trophy from a recent bicycling accident. Even with only one good hand, Collins lovingly held two puppies his family had adopted at a church function that day. One of the puppies crouched in Collins' arm, happily frozen with her tongue fully extended toward her new friend. The other puppy held one of the first dog's front paws in its mouth. In between the two giggling, loving dogs was Collins' beaming face. Anyone could see the boy loved animals.

Kitch lifted a few photographs from underneath the altar boy image. He looked upon Collins with a college sweetheart hugging him tightly while riding behind him on a motorcycle, Collins in high school, obviously stoned and wearing his unkempt hair well below his shoulders, and another photo of Collins bent over at the waist, staring straight into the eyes of a stunning golden retriever. After giving each a cursory glance, Kitch set the pictures aside. He looked at a lengthy report assembled by his staff. He paused, as he always did before inserting himself into another man's life. After a moment of silent consideration, he licked his left thumb and peeled the first page from the report.

··· 12 ···

Kevin Collins began his life as a fortunate child. The son of scholarly parents, an aggressive father and dedicated mother, Collins attended one of the finest parochial schools in the state of California. A brilliant child and very charismatic, Collins prospered in the social and ecumenical atmosphere of the Catholic school. That is, of course, until his sixth year, when his parents divorced.

On a warm Southern California September night, Collins' mother gathered her children in the living room of their custom home, casually announcing that their father had gone on vacation and was never coming home. Collins' oldest brother broke down in tears, understanding his mother's pain. The next brother in line sat stoically, absorbing what he had seen coming for years. The eldest child, Collins' only sister, hadn't even attended the announcement; she'd seen too much and had decided to spare herself the agony of another emotional breakdown.

Collins and his younger brother, sheltered from the unpleasantness over the years, at first sat numbly with their mouths gaping. Seconds later they exploded in a flood of anguished tears, the security of their family suddenly shattered. For Collins it became a defining moment. He would never forget that intimate family meeting, nor would he forget the horrible consequences of his mother and father's decision to divorce.

Kitch suspended his reading for a moment, jotting a quick note on the legal pad he kept balanced on his thigh. *Catastrophic occurrence early in life – feelings of abandonment – fear – anger – revenge?*

The report continued through the remainder of Collins' grade school experiences. Once a star math student at St. John Fisher by the Sea, after the divorce his grades plummeted to the lowest percentile in his class. He became a bother to every teacher he encountered, boasting to anyone who would listen that he "spent my entire eighth grade year in the principal's office."

While still quite popular, Collins began to exhibit behavioral traits the school counselor termed as disturbing and worthy of meriting close observation. He began playing bizarre practical jokes on other students, the type of pranks he never would have pulled prior to the divorce. The pattern became more pronounced during his last year. Once, after smiling cordially and saying hello, he tripped a sixth-grade girl as she reached the top of the stairway next to the school's main entrance. She tumbled down the twelve steps and crashed awkwardly on the cement walkway below. Bloodied and stunned, she turned and gave Collins a look of sheer bewilderment. Even Collins' best friend had condemned the stunt as cruel.

On another day Collins brought a sewing pin to school. Carefully concealing it in his cupped hand, he would wait for students to walk by him in the hallway. After their heads were turned away from him, he would jam the pin through their school uniform and deep into their skin. Sometimes he hit the arm, sometimes the leg, but mostly he slammed the sharp tip into their buttocks. The victims always whipped around, wondering who the strange student was who delighted in their pain. Collins never said a word or changed his expression; he merely cruised the hall looking for his next target.

In another incident, Collins was hanging around the hallway with some friends during the last week of school. On a whim he entered his home room. After a quick inspection to ensure his privacy he began throwing desks and chairs all around the room. They crashed loudly off of each other, the teacher's desk, and the cupboards on the back wall. After five or six minutes of the bizarre behavior, Collins simply left the scene. Kitch's report didn't reveal any psychological follow up by school officials, but it did state that disciplinary action came swiftly.

Kitch clicked his pen again. *Aggressive and cruel behavior – fits of unexplainable violence – remorseless attitude.*

The lieutenant scanned another dozen pages. They dealt with Collins' high school experiences, which seemed to be quite normal, his brief stint at the local university, and his recruitment into the navy at age twenty-two.

One particular segment of Collins' life jumped right off the page. It occurred just prior to his enlistment. It intrigued Kitch to no end. It might be just the wedge he had been hoping for, a tool to bore into Kevin Collins' mind.

A Pound of Fur

Weary of college after only one semester, Collins decided to volunteer twenty hours a week at a county animal shelter. The affiliation impacted him more than any other experience in his life. Collins deeply loved animals of any sort, and he took to his duties at the shelter with a passion he never felt before.

He started by cleaning cages, changing litter boxes and food bowls, and straightening up the canine enclosures. He watered down the patio areas where prospective owners interacted with their hopeful strays and lugged endless bags of food and litter into the facility from rental trucks. The managers of the shelter saw potential in the young man. Soon Collins was checking in strays and other animals discarded by their owners.

It was while performing this duty that Collins experienced an epiphany. Day after day he presided over the shelter's new inhabitants, mostly dogs and cats, but also a few exotic pets. In nearly every case, Collins befriended the new animal, becoming a surrogate parent in the process. He cared for them, cleaned them, loved them, and did anything he could to make certain they felt safe and content. On many days he stayed long after his appointed volunteer hours, especially if an animal arrived that had clearly been abused by their owners.

The more he witnessed this pattern, the less respect he felt for people in general. The experience also formed a deep bond between him and the animals under his care. He realized at the end of that summer that his love for animals nearly matched his disdain for human beings.

His association with the shelter ended the day before Halloween. He had stayed on after the summer at the request of the shelter manager. He volunteered close to thirty hours per week; his boss at his paying job had threatened to fire him if he took on any more hours at the shelter.

One episode rendered everything academic. It happened on a Monday morning, immediately after the facility opened. A rickety, thirty-year-old Chevy pick-up rumbled into the shelter parking lot. A man in his fifties, filthy, wearing a dirty t-shirt, sagging shorts and no shoes, opened his door and slid out of the driver's seat. A small boxer puppy happily followed him toward the door. The filthy man turned on the little dog, viciously hammering it a few times with a closed fist. The tiny, fragile puppy yelped and squealed, rushing back toward the passenger door.

Collins came around the corner a second later. He inquired about the crying puppy and received a curt reply.

"None o' yer fuckin' business," said the foul man.

"Excuse me, sir," replied Collins, "but this is an animal shelter, so that makes it my business."

Ignoring Collins, the man stormed around to the back of his truck. He ripped down the tailgate, slamming it open like someone with little time to spend on a nosy volunteer. He grasped two leashes, yanking hard on the leads and pulling two terrified dogs toward him. The two animals shrieked as they moved closer to the rear of the truck bed. Obviously afraid of their master, they wanted to vault over the side and scamper away.

"Assholes," the man groused as he heaved one last time. Both of the dogs flew out of the truck bed, hitting the hard-packed dirt driveway awkwardly. They both stumbled, whining like the terribly abused dogs they were.

A **Pound** of Fur

"Here," said the man, throwing the leads at Collins. "I don't give a shit what you do with them."

The leashes slapped against Collins legs before falling to the ground. Collins didn't see or feel them. His focus lay exclusively on the bruised and bloodied dogs standing in the driveway of the shelter, shivering like lost refugees. The sight sickened him so completely he lost all sense of self. He looked over at the man climbing into his stinking pickup truck.

He walked to the truck, ripped open the driver's side door, grabbed a fistful of hair and pulled the disgusting man from the bench seat. He slammed his head onto the ground with such force the dog abuser lost consciousness immediately. Collins fell to his knees, hammering the man's face, breaking teeth and bones with every closed fist that found its mark. He stood and spat on the man, then began stomping him repeatedly. By the time the shelter manager arrived to pull Collins away, he had butchered the man's knees with a rusted shovel. The manager and three other volunteers finally subdued the enraged Collins, who hurled insults at the man lying on the ground, only a few breaths from death.

Favors animal rights over human life. Fits of extreme rage and murderous violence. Inability to maintain moral restraint.

After the lawsuits made their way through the court system, Collins had been given a choice; join the service or face serious penalties. He chose the sea, enlisting in the navy the next day. After thirteen weeks of boot camp, Collins left the shores of his home country for the first time.

Fortunately, the regimented existence of shipboard life

agreed with him. After only eighteen months of service, he elevated his rate to Petty Officer First Class. This enabled him to be considered for a position in The Office of Naval Intelligence. He applied twice and gained entrance the second time.

The report in Kitch's hand seemed to weigh less after this revelation. Apparently, many of Collins' records for his service to the ONI were classified. Kitch wouldn't be able to examine that part of his life. The information he did have listed Collins as a student of ciphers, espionage, deep penetration planning and execution, and stalking and pursuit. The report also listed Collins' intelligence quotient as superior, something Kitch had already guessed from his brief conversations with the man.

Exceptional intellect. Extremely disciplined. High intensity intelligence training.

After twelve years of service to his country, Collins received an honorable discharge. He immediately signed a contract to work for a civilian security firm. Aside from protecting corporate, civil, and military dignitaries the world over, the small firm also contracted out teams of ex-military personnel to watch over valuable information. Whether it was hard copy files, computer hard drives, or networks vulnerable to attack from cyberspace, the firm Collins worked for held an impeccable record of success.

Collins realized what kind of fortune lay waiting for a man aggressive enough to capitalize on the opportunity. Instead of signing another employment contract, he left his job and formed Safeguard Protection Services. He offered most of the same products as his former employer, but

A **Pound** of Fur

Collins had a distinct advantage – his connections in military intelligence. Collins knew that in order to build his company he would have to cultivate those relationships and spread money around Washington like fertilizer.

He became a master lobbyist for his own company. He attended dozens of conventions, strategy sessions, and personal soirees thrown by members of the House and Senate. His company expanded quickly, he received contracts in over a dozen countries to provide select levels of personal or records security.

He hired ex-military only, even for clerical positions. His personal secretary provided the only exception; as a first cousin she offered her own brand of fierce familial protection for Collins.

Detail oriented. Protective of self, company and employees. Outstanding organizational skills.

Kitch dropped the report onto the newspapers covering his desk. Lowering his head, he massaged the bridge of his nose for a full minute. Everything he read about the man reinforced his gut feeling. Collins had to be behind the murderous spree of the vigilantes. Kitch also felt quite certain that the mess in North Carolina also sprang from Collins' deviant mind.

The problem lay in his lack of evidence. No matter where he went to investigate any of the incidents, he came away with nothing. *Because of Collins' superior planning traits, no doubt*, thought Kitch. He would have to catch him in the act. Somewhere, somehow, he would luck upon a tip concerning one of Collins' planned excursions.

Unfortunately, the raids on the dogfighting rings had fallen off considerably. Either Collins' out of state activities had replaced the local vigilante killings or he had smelled Kitch following his trail. If he had suspended the attacks for the latter reason, then the man possessed an unnatural ability to sense heat. One other supposition held true as well. Even though the raids had nearly disappeared, the number of fighting rings had decreased accordingly. Apparently, the goal of the vigilantes had been achieved; they had put the fear of God into anyone with a fondness for animal cruelty.

Kitch thumbed through Collins' pictures again, looking at the man at different stages in his life. *What could possibly happen that would turn someone so viciously against his fellow man*, he thought. Everyone loved animals, well, almost everyone. Some existed at the extreme poles of affection and revulsion. There were people who didn't care for animals at all, or thought that because they were animals, they didn't deserve a moment's consideration from human beings. Some people even tortured animals for their own amusement. Kitch couldn't understand that kind of mindset; but he could understand why a man like Collins would want to punish such people.

There were others who seemed to worship animals. Kitch's sister and her husband kept a diverse menagerie of creatures at their home: dogs, cats, ferrets, and even a dozen chickens in a fenced coop beyond their back yard. Kitch didn't understand the attraction. He neither liked nor disliked animals, but when he visited his sister's home for dinner, it was difficult for him to be comfortable. He couldn't grasp the idea of treating animals as if they were children.

A Pound of Fur

Obviously, Collins held a deep bond with animals of every sort. *Fish, too*, thought Kitch as he flicked his eyes back to the newspaper account. From the pictures, the man appeared to be born with a genuine love of animal life. Somewhere along the way that love became a twisted, sadistic desire to protect God's creatures from what he deemed was a sickened human society bent on horrific abuse. Kitch surmised that Collins anointed himself the guardian of defenseless animals. *Well*, thought Kitch, *every man finds his calling*.

He placed the report and the pictures neatly in their places, which he set on top of the computer to his right. He folded up the sections of newspaper, taking a moment to glance at the horrible machine used on the fishing champion. He felt a chill pass over the skin on the back of his neck.

He inserted the newspaper into the sleeve. Opening the drawer to his right, he found the appropriate folder and slotted the file. After making sure everything was properly situated, he slid the drawer shut.

Lieutenant Kitch picked up the phone and dialed the police department information line. "Yes," he said after the operator answered, "may I have the number of the Greenville, North Carolina State Police?"

··· 13 ···

"I recommend we lay low for a while," said Turner. "The Greenville mission roused quite a few people. There's a lot of heat."

"I agree," said Michaels. "You know we're with you one hundred percent, boss, but if we're to continue with this work, we can't afford to get arrested."

Collins held the burner phone loosely in his hand. He remembered vividly the way Jeffries had twisted and flopped while hooked up to the winch. He congratulated himself on his ability to terrify Mayfield.

A momentary wisp of remorse floated into his mind. He quickly rejected it, hammering his philosophy back in place. The only thing violent people understood was greater violence. No amount of cajoling, political pressure, fund raising, or argument would ever convince them to change their ways. He remembered the look in Mayfield's eyes, a pure message stating that he would immediately shut down his operations. The man had been so pompous up to that point, the turn-around cemented Collins' belief in his methods. Scare the living shit out of someone, assure them that they are next unless they reform, and the outcome becomes predictable.

A Pound of Fur

Collins knew his team wouldn't end up changing the world, even if they worked tirelessly seven days a week for the rest of their lives. Even with everything they could accomplish, they would only make a minor dent in the overall abuse problem. He felt it was his destiny, however, to continue fighting for the safety of animals. He would do so until he died, went to jail, or both.

"I concur," he said. "I'll be back in Los Angeles tonight. Let's meet first thing in the morning at the office. We'll set a new timeline for our operations."

"How long do you think we'll have to lay low?" asked Turner.

"Six weeks at least, but I want it to look like we're still working. There's a certain police lieutenant we need to pay attention to. I want to set up some dummy scenarios and see what kind of action he takes to thwart our plans."

"Is it Kitch?" asked Michaels. "Isn't he the one you said was sniffing around the office last week?"

"The very one, and he's smart, too. We can't make any mistakes with him on our trail."

"Tomorrow, then?" asked Turner.

"Seven o'clock in the conference room. I'll bring the coffee. Oh, and Turner, I want you to make plans for a trip this weekend."

"Where to, boss?"

"Casper, Wyoming. You'll go in, scout out an operation and leave. Shouldn't take you more than a day and a half."

"I'll be ready to go on Friday."

"Good. By the way, good work in Greeneville."

··· **14** ···

"Good morning, Mr. Collins."

"Morning, Shari. How busy are the sharks today?"

"Swirling around in big packs, hungry as ever," replied the bright, youngish looking middle-aged woman.

"Who's first up?"

"Some folks from the pentagon called twice this morning, and the engineer working on the new armored vest wants to speak with you."

"Anyone else?"

"A Lieutenant Kitch called twice while you were away. He seemed pretty eager."

Collins stood by her desk, riffling through a hefty stack of messages.

"I'll let you decide who to contact first, although if I were you, I'd give that policeman a call. He seemed anxious about something."

"Thanks, Shari, I'll do that. No disturbances for two hours, okay?"

"You're the boss, boss."

Collins closed the door to his office. He dropped his

briefcase onto the overstuffed chair and walked around the curved edge of his desk. He pushed the button on his computer, flicked on the monitor, and plopped down in his sixty-five-dollar Office Depot desk chair. As his computer hummed to life, he thought about his impending conversation with Lieutenant Kitch. His take on the man so far told him not to be to coy or flippant. No one elevates to the rank of lieutenant in the Los Angeles Police Department without showing a keen intellect and a savvy ability to solve cases. He would have to be careful from now on, gauge everything he said, and read every comment Kitch made.

The desktop on his computer came to life, showing a montage of every animal he'd ever cared for in his life. Collins took a moment to glance at each one. The largest of the images belonged to the dog Collins grew up with, a salty golden retriever named Samson. He passed away when Collins was just nineteen years old, but until that time they'd kept each other company for ten years.

Collins reminisced about the night his father had taken him to see some golden retriever puppies. They had driven about thirty miles outside the city to a modest place in the suburbs of Los Angeles. Upon entering the home, the breeder told Collins and his father that only two puppies remained from the litter, a male and a female. Even more, the woman stated that the female had pretty much been spoken for earlier that day. Collins' father had sighed, asking the woman why she hadn't spoken up earlier on the phone. She apologized, asking if they would like to look at the sole remaining puppy. Collins' father agreed, calling to his son to accompany them to the other room.

When the woman led his father into the kennel room, she found a nine-year-old Collins sitting on his haunches playing tug of war with a fat little puppy. The feisty little Golden tugged as hard as he could on the play toy, shaking the boy's arm vigorously. Every time Collins jerked the knotted cord, trying to free it from the puppy's iron grasp, the Golden would snap its head back and forth with just as much emphasis. Collins laughed joyfully, looked up at his father, eyes pleading as he gathered the plump, golden ball of fur into his arms. His father paid the breeder and off they went.

That night, Samson stayed in Collins' room. Early the next morning, the puppy woke his new master, squirming and yipping as if he were the happiest dog on earth. Collins grabbed his new best friend, hugging him and smelling the fresh fur. He let Samson go and closed his eyes again, only to be startled a moment later by the same adorable dog. He soothed Samson, petting him and telling him how much he loved him.

Poor Samson had tried everything to warn Collins. When he could hold it no longer, the cute little puppy released his bowels and laid a fine pile on the floor. The look on Samson's face told Collins everything he needed to know. The poor dog had been pleading with him to let him outside. Even at his tender age he had already been potty trained, but when Collins failed to answer his pleas, he held it as long as he could before depositing last night's dinner in the bedroom.

Samson had looked so ashamed. Collins quickly gathered him up in his arms, kissing him over and over, telling him it wasn't his fault. Like all dogs, Samson immediately returned to his playful, happy self, licking Collins' face and bathing him in puppy breath.

Collins blinked his eyes twice, driving the memory down into his soul. He'd loved Samson deeply. He was the dog Collins grew up with; very few things took the place of that kind of bonding experience.

He punched the speaker button on his desk telephone. As the dial tone droned on, he pulled up his contact list on his computer. Finding Kitch's office number, he pressed the digits to make the call.

"Homicide, Lieutenant Kitch."

"Lieutenant, this is Kevin Collins."

"Ah, good morning, Mr. Collins. Thank you so much for returning my call."

"My secretary informed me as soon as I came in this morning."

"From?" asked Kitch.

"A spontaneous but urgent business trip."

"To where?"

"Washington D.C. by way of North Carolina."

"Greenville, North Carolina?"

"Yes," said Collins, momentarily alarmed.

"So your secretary said. I was wondering if I might drop by for a cup of your delicious coffee sometime this afternoon."

"I'm sorry, Lieutenant, I've only returned this moment. I have many items to attend to, and then there's always the backup when one is away for a few days."

"I promise to be brief, maybe thirty minutes at most."

Collins scanned the calendar on his computer. "I can give you fifteen minutes at four o'clock."

"Excellent," said Kitch. "Four o'clock, then."

Collins typed in the appointment. He shot a quick e-mail to his secretary informing her that the lieutenant would be dropping by this afternoon.

He attended to his office duties; returning calls, filtering e-mails, fingering through a stack of proposals, and mostly tossing piles of junk mail into the trash. After he finished these duties, he checked his watch. He had twenty-five minutes left before his first appointment.

He stood and walked over to his mini bar. He extracted a syrup bottle filled with a bizarre looking liquid. It had the appearance of syrupy lemonade, with a strange twist. A friend of his had mastered the method of mixing grain alcohol with lemons, vodka, and a few other ingredients Collins couldn't remember. All he knew is that with one small shot of the elixir, he could focus on any project intensely.

He removed the simple screw cap, sniffing the liquid fire before imbibing. He selected a chilled port glass and poured a small amount. Cheering the ghost in the room, he threw back the delicious shot, waiting for the Everclear aftertaste. He stood with eyes closed, bathing in the rapture of expert mixology.

After returning the glass and bottle to the mini bar, he paced across the room and sat down in front of his computer. Punching up the internet, he typed the following into the search line:

Captive Hunting Casper Wyoming

A second later a list of websites appeared advertising various hunting lodges, hunting tour guide services, retail outdoor adventure stores, and a host of odds and ends. Collins scrolled through the pages until he found what he wanted.

A Pound of Fur

After he clicked the link, an elaborate web page appeared. Even with his accelerated cable access, Collins had to wait a few seconds for all of the images to load. Collins began scanning the contents. Pictures of a wide variety of African game dotted the frame of the site. There were also pictures of domestic animals as well; something Collins wasn't too surprised to see.

He fished around in the site, trying to assimilate as much as he could about the captive hunting farm called Hunt of Your Life. Rich, overweight executives, ex-athletes and entertainment industry moguls would pay handsome fees to be flown in private jets to the tiny Casper regional airport, and then driven in limousines to the facility. Deluxe accommodations awaited them at the compound. Dinner, drinks, brandy and cigars accompanied a quick tour of the facility, where the attendees would "hunt" a wild animal over the next few days. Over the course of the weekend, the men and women staying at the compound would bag a prize trophy and a host of stories to take home.

Collins had researched these types of organizations thoroughly. The "hunting grounds" were usually no more than ten or twenty acres of land. Mostly flat and barren, the facility was set up so that aging, out of shape elitists could shoot innocent animals without expending much effort. Worse than that, the animals were usually drugged to the point of stupor, so "tracking" them wouldn't be a problem. The biggest insult to humanity, mused Collins, was the fact that many of the animals were sold to Hunt of Your Life through unscrupulous brokers who collected them from zoos around the world.

The multi-line phone on Collins' desk buzzed. He

checked his watch quickly. His secretary had waited precisely two hours before contacting him. He depressed the speaker phone.

"Yes?"

"Your ten o'clock is here, sir."

"Fine, send her in. And Shari, I want you to book travel arrangements for Turner this weekend. Friday to Sunday, round trip air to Casper, Wyoming. Reserve a rental car and a hotel as well."

"Done," she said.

Collins closed the internet window and stood to welcome his first appointment of the day.

··· **15** ···

Everett Turner walked quietly along the well-maintained trail in the hills north of West Covina, California. The sun, exceptionally hot for a weekend day in May, had chased away other visitors to the outlands.

Turner walked with a measured pace, keeping his footfalls soft so he might sense other creatures keeping him company along the trail. Every fifteen minutes or so he would turn and glance back at the hastily built suburban developments. Looking ahead again, he would shake his head and grimace. Nursing a spiritual illness brought about by man's stupidity, he pondered the fate of the creature he valued beyond all others.

He stopped suddenly, listening. The cry came from far ahead, but the sound was unmistakable. A whining sound, like an infant wailing in the distance, told Turner that a cougar had risen from its slumber. He waited, hoping for another mountain lion, perhaps one closer to him to sound a reply. After an interminable silence, he heard another squeal, possibly the mate of the first cougar, giving its response. *This one is much closer*, thought Turner.

He stood as tall as he could, expanding his six feet, four-inch frame to its limit. If there was a mountain lion close by, he wanted it to see a formidable opponent should it decide to charge.

He listened, slowing his breathing to almost nothing. He heard the low, thick drone of a bumblebee, the flittering wings of a pair of hummingbirds, and nothing else. The cougar had been very close, no more than a hundred yards away. Right now it could be stalking him for all he knew. In another second he might hear the telltale scraping of the lion's claws as it launched itself toward its target.

Nothing happened, however. He heard the sounds of the desert and nothing more. He looked around one last time before deciding to press ahead.

He took three steps and stopped abruptly. A big male cougar gracefully leapt to the top of a rock outcropping less than fifty feet from him. It scanned its surroundings quickly. Satisfied about the lack of a threat, it turned its stunning gaze in his direction.

Turner didn't have to control his breathing any longer. The air in his lungs seemed trapped as he stood staring at the largest mountain lion he'd ever seen. Easily two-hundred-pounds, a size even a man of Turner's bulk had to be nervous about. If it decided to attack, he would be hard pressed to escape with his life.

The lion showed no ill intent. It made no move toward Turner at all.

It simply stared at him, showing him the teardrop markings from its eyes down to its nose. It began grooming itself, always stopping every few seconds to place an eye on Turner.

A Pound of Fur

Turner couldn't proceed forward, or he would cross directly in front of the cat. He didn't really want to end his hike after only a few miles, though. He decided to have a seat about fifteen feet back along the trail. He found a huge boulder with a flat surface. It would be comfortable enough under the circumstances.

He crouched, looking at the beautiful cougar. The lion yawned slowly, exposing the massive fangs fronting its mouth. It glanced at Turner, realizing again an intruder had entered its domain. Not only that, but apparently it had decided to stay. A nervous whine poured through its half open jaws.

"Easy, friend, I haven't come here to do you any harm. I only ask that you allow me to stay and share a little time with you."

The cougar blinked its eyes. Ignoring Turner again, it resumed cleaning itself. Before long, however, the lion's mate called out again. The male ceased its activities, standing immediately and sniffing the air for anything alarming. Then, with one last glance backward, it leapt quietly onto the ground and loped away. Turner watched it as long as he could. It seemed to melt into the desert rather than disappear into the brush.

Turner relished his good fortune. To come that close, to have an encounter like that, he felt as though he'd connected with the animal's spirit.

He turned, looking back at the homes, which sat only a fifteen or twenty-minute walk away. He marveled at the arrogant stupidity of people, or was it just the asshole developers that put people at risk by pushing this far into the wild.

Either way, the warnings had been crystal clear – spread suburban development out into cougar territory and there will be attacks. It was inevitable that when humans put homes directly in line with mountain lion feeding and breeding areas, they were asking for trouble.

Of course, only a few months after the new phases sold and families moved into their new homes, cougar attacks occurred with random regularity. *The idiots even put hiking and biking trails right in the middle of mountain lion territory*, thought Turner, *what the hell did they think was going to happen?* Two mountain bikers were attacked first. One lost her arm. The second lost her life trying to defend her friend. Then a twelve-year-old boy was attacked in broad daylight, fifty feet from his house on a hiking trail. The lions never stood a chance after that.

First the police came, then the forest service and the humane society, and finally the professional hunters. They went out into the brush, skulking through the desert looking for the culprit lion that had the audacity to defend its territory. Of course they found and killed a cougar, but they had no way of knowing whether it was the one who attacked the bikers or killed the boy. They were merely after a trophy, something to show the news media and the neighborhood, something to take the heat off the jackass developer who built the neighborhood in the wrong part of the desert in the first place. Hell, the company probably built a dozen neighborhoods just like it, suckering families everywhere to buy their crappy homes and serve their kids up to hungry lions.

Turner jumped from the rock. Landing on the trail, he walked away from the homes and deeper into the desert. He listened carefully for any sounds the cougars made while hunting or huddling together. Not wanting to disturb them, he walked softly on the deeper sand. He saw a roadrunner scamper through the brush. Lizards crossed his path many times. Even in this barren land, small finches whirred by every few seconds, on their way to a shady tree or a spot of water somewhere.

Turner took everything in, trying to blend into the natural surroundings as best he could. He felt completely relaxed in the desert, much more so than he did in the city, or around people. Nature's residents didn't understand deceit, or manipulation, or false impressions. They didn't prejudge, hold grudges, or offend without provocation. Nature simply existed, and if instinct gave animals and birds this measure of simplicity, thought Turner, he would trade logic and deduction for it any day.

It was no wonder more and more humans lost their minds every year. The high stress, fast paced, technology driven, anti-social environment served no good purpose for people. Even they knew it; they saw the signs as society progressed ever further away from spiritual wellbeing. As slaves to advertisers, however, they merely bought the same old tune and walked blissfully toward the ruination of the self. *It didn't figure*, thought Turner, *but then, it really did make sense after all*. People were stupid, arrogant, and self-absorbed, living only for the moment. No wonder they were eating bullets at a record pace. The society they bought into couldn't have been more destructive.

Turner inhaled deeply, enjoying the smells of the desert. Tomorrow he would report to Collins' office for a strategy session regarding his trip to Wyoming. He wondered what kind of games his boss had in mind this time.

He scanned the environment slowly. Crouching down, he dragged his fingers through the sand. *Someday,* he thought, *I'll move far away from this madness.*

··· 16 ···

"Come in, Lieutenant," said Collins in a stern, businesslike tone. "Something to drink?"

"Nothing, thank you," replied Kitch as he slowly sat on the bloated couch. "However, feel free to partake if you desire."

Kitch waited patiently while Collins addressed his needs at the mini bar. He took the opportunity to scrutinize the office. Strangely, everything seemed to be in exactly the same place as the last time he visited. No one was that anal, not even an ex-military intelligence officer with a penchant for torture and murder.

"Well," Collins said, now seated at his desk again. "What would you like to accuse me of today, Lieutenant?"

Kitch took a moment before responding. "An unfortunate way to begin a conversation, don't you think?"

"You're a detective. I'd have to guess that you suspect me of some crime. Why else would you be here?"

Okay, thought Kitch, *direct and to the point*. "How was your conference in North Carolina, Mr. Collins?"

"Not entirely profitable, but nonetheless an important appearance. Why do you ask?"

"I'm always interested in the health of local businesses. If your company is succeeding, then taxes are paid, and my salary is intact."

"Very altruistic."

"Yes, I believe it is. By the way, where did you stay while attending the conference?"

Collins became perturbed. "My secretary can provide you with my itinerary, Lieutenant."

"I am merely making small talk," said Kitch, preparing to fire his first salvo. "You are aware of the brutal murder that took place outside of Greenville this past weekend, are you not?"

"I'm sorry, I was ordered to Washington late Saturday night. I've been involved in a ferocious slate of meetings with the pentagon."

Kitch stared at Collins, trying to read any sign of surrender, or guilt, or perhaps remorse. He saw nothing.

"What happened?" asked Collins.

"Two men were kidnapped from a national sport fishing competition. One found himself coupled to a rather demonic piece of machinery. I get the impression from reading the reports that the winch was constructed to simulate an extremely powerful fishing pole."

Collins sipped his lemony concoction, staring at Kitch with unblinking eyes.

"Whoever tortured this man did so in the most hideous of ways. They inserted a large meat hook through the man's lower jaw. I'm sure you can imagine the effect this had on his skull."

"Probably ripped the jawbone away at the hinge."

"Precisely. We found him in a bloody heap with three bullets in the back of his head. His wounds from the winch were so severe we had difficulty determining where his face began and ended."

Collins set his glass down quietly. "I guess some people don't agree that fish enjoy being yanked out of the water by a sharp hook tugging at their mouth. Who was this guy, anyway?"

"Brett Jeffries, the winner of his weight and line class."

"No real loss to the human race, right?"

"Are you saying you approve of the way this man met his death, Mr. Collins?"

"I'm not saying anything like that, Lieutenant. Personally, I think the guy was a complete jerk."

Kitch served up his second volley. "May I see a copy of your itinerary for last weekend, right now?"

"Am I under arrest?"

"Nothing of the sort, Mr. Collins. Let us say at this point you are merely a person of interest."

"Fancy name for a suspect, don't you think?"

"Do you have anything to hide, sir?"

Kevin Collins carefully plucked the small glass from the desktop. Staring at Kitch, he drained the last of the limoncello. "I'm not sure I like your tone, Lieutenant."

"That may be, sir, but I must insist that I be given your schedule immediately. I'd like complete information dating back to the Thursday before you left for North Carolina."

"My secretary will provide you with everything you need, with the exception of my interests in Washington. You must understand the sensitive nature of those proceedings. The information is classified at the highest level."

"I shall endeavor to convince a federal judge of the seriousness of our request. I will return at a later date with the proper authoritative paperwork."

Kitch pressed his palms against the couch while leaning forward to get up. He heard Collins' voice as he balanced his weight on his legs.

"May I ask you a question, Lieutenant?"

Kitch brushed his pant legs, removing the static wrinkles. He looked up at Collins but did not answer.

"I'd really like to understand your feelings about these crimes. Please don't give me the standard department answer about how your job precludes you from any emotional involvement in the cases you're given."

"And your question?"

"What would you do if you witnessed firsthand the abuse of an innocent animal? I mean real abuse, hard core, physical abuse? Would you pass by, hoping the batterer would see the light someday? Would you step in and take the animal away from the person? Or would you pull that gun you carry underneath your jacket and threaten the man's life?"

"I'm sorry, Mr. Collins," answered Kitch, "I am not here to…"

"Answer the question, Lieutenant. I have acceded to your requests for my time, and I am very interested in what you would do. I don't see why giving me an honest reply will hurt your reputation or lessen your edge in any future interactions."

A Pound of Fur

Kitch hesitated for a moment before answering. He straightened his jacket roughly. "I believe, Mr. Collins, that I would pistol whip the son of a bitch until someone dragged me away from him."

Collins smiled. "That's all I wanted to know."

"The records?" asked Kitch.

"Shari will see to your needs. I assure you she is most efficient."

"I must insist, Mr. Collins, that you notify me immediately regarding any future out of state business engagements you may have in the future. Failure to do so again might elevate your standing downtown."

"I'll cooperate to the best of my abilities."

"I expected no less. Good day, sir."

Collins waited until Shari had the police lieutenant well in hand before turning his monitor back on. He scanned the scheduling program for the first open weekend over the next three-month period. Selecting the appropriate date, he blocked off a four-day weekend, titling the engagement, "Day Camp."

··· 17 ···

Turner and Michaels stood quietly next the nondescript panel truck. Each held a damp towel in one hand, using them to wipe blood from their arms, clothing, and shoes. Michaels selected a fresh towel to dab the chunks of blood, skin and brain matter from his face and neck. The men worked silently, glancing at each other sparingly. Their job was to guard the fighting dogs, who sat whimpering in their separate cages in the truck bed. They did so with an endearing tenderness. Underneath their silent demeanor, however, lay a blanket of concern for their employer. Tonight's mission had been unlike any other. Collins had been efficient and precise, as always, but a sizzling current of palpable savagery accompanied their raid on this particular dogfighting ring.

"What the hell was that all about?" asked Michaels.

Turner shook his head. He had worked with Kevin Collins for more than half his life. This night marked the first time he ever felt apprehensive. He stared blankly at the towel in his hand. "I don't know."

"Look, you know I'll do anything for him, but we killed people tonight who weren't exactly on our usual hit list."

Turner tossed the towel into the metal hold on the side of the truck. He looked back at the crumbling warehouse, hoping to see his boss walking toward them.

"Turner?" asked Michaels.

"All *right*." answered Turner. "Something's wrong, but neither you nor I know what's up. Let's give him the benefit of the doubt until we talk to him."

At that moment, the door to the dimly lit warehouse cracked open. Collins, standing alone in the light, looked out toward the truck for a moment. He gave the slaughterhouse one last glance before shutting the door behind him. He walked quickly toward his trusted lieutenants. He also wiped the victims' remains from his person with a filthy hand towel. When he reached the truck, he tossed the cloth into the hold, locking the door behind it. He checked the dogs one by one, cooing and kissing to each individually. He smiled as he saw tails wagging within the cages. Satisfied with the operation, he turned to Turner and Michaels.

"Pearson and the others have left?" he asked Turner.

"Yes, everyone's gone, all except us. Pearson reported no police activity in this area. Apparently, the dummy information we fed to the LAPD threw them off our trail."

Collins nodded. "We have to knock off for a while. That pesky lieutenant has a very sensitive nose. He's been by more than once for a visit. Our last one didn't encourage me very much."

"Does he know about the operation?" asked Turner.

"No. But he suspects, and he's no fool. Sooner or later he'll stumble onto something. He's ordered me to report any out of state business trips to him, preferably before they happen."

"What do we do?"

"We can't continue with the dogfighting raids. I have sources telling me the LAPD has patrol cars cruising potential sites every week."

"So we postpone activities for a while. We're young. We can always pick up at a later date."

"No, we're not stopping everything," said Collins. "I want you in Wyoming this weekend. Check out that captive hunting operation. I've already scheduled a trip for two months from now. Find out everything you can about their business. Determine the logistics of taking a team there, how long for the operation, everything. If it looks good, go ahead and make arrangements for a party of four. I'll send you the dates Monday. In the meantime I'll contact our vendors and see what can be done about shipping the supplies and equipment."

"You sure you want to move ahead with this?"

"Yes. I want you to manage the venture personally."

Turner shook his head in the affirmative. As Collins turned toward the truck, Michaels caught his right arm.

"Boss, can we talk a minute?"

··· 18 ···

Lieutenant Kitch stared at the four officers assembled in his office. On his desk lay an assortment of particularly gruesome pictures. The officers either sat in ancient metal frame chairs or stood with their shoulders slumped against the cubicle framing.

"You gentlemen patrolled the assigned areas and yet heard nothing, saw nothing that might have alerted you to this attack?"

The officers shot a series of nervous glances at each other. Harmon, the oldest of the group by three years, offered the first explanation.

"Lieutenant, we combed that area for four solid hours. We left for no more than thirty minutes to investigate a fresh lead. We returned to our original stakeout immediately thereafter. Sir, we kept our eyes on the scene and our ears glued to our radios. Nothing gave us any indication of an attack in that part of the city."

Kitch sat motionless. He stared past the patrolmen, catching all of them in his peripheral vision. He saw alarm, maybe even nervousness, but nothing more. These were good men, hand-picked by their sergeant. Collins had fooled them by feeding the department bogus information.

"Very well. You men performed admirably. Apparently, we are faced with an extremely crafty adversary. Harmon, I want you to calibrate every attack over the last three months. Note their locations and the proposed sites fed to us by our "sources." I want to see if a pattern exists. The rest of you men will spend your shifts in the neighborhood surrounding the latest attack. If anyone will come forward, I want them in this office ten minutes later. Is that understood?"

The uniformed men nodded their assent before filing out of Kitch's office.

Kitch scanned the photos again. The grisly images nearly convinced him of Collins' innocence. Three men lay dead on the ground close to the fighting pit. Two of them had nothing but scrabbled flesh, muscle and veins sprouting from spinal columns severed at the neck. The skulls had obviously been blown to bits by a powerful weapon, a twelve- or ten-gauge shotgun fired at point blank range. The third body looked as if it had been thrown into a woodchipper. Kitch winced as he looked upon the picture again; even a man of his experience wasn't immune to being rattled by the sight of such unbridled violence.

Judging by the reports from previous raids, the third man must have run the dogfighting operation. For one thing, he didn't have a shred of clothing on him. It was Collins' modus operandi to strip the site manager naked before throwing him into the pit with the most savage dog he could locate. This time, however, his mind had apparently run amok. Kitch was only guessing, but it looked as though Collins had allowed every dog at the site to attack the man simultaneously. The wounds on the body told the entire story. There must have been thirteen or fourteen dogs, a total melee. Fingers and toes were missing; entire chunks of flesh had been ferociously ripped away from the torso, legs and buttocks, and a reddish, hairy void sat in place of the man's genitals, a clear indication of where the dogs had attacked at one point.

Kitch closed his eyes. He felt nauseous. He couldn't stop his mind from presenting the imagery of how the attack must have appeared. A naked man, pulled and twisted in several directions at once, bellowing with unspeakable agony as the enraged pack tore him to pieces. Removing a handkerchief from the inside pocket of his suit coat, he dabbed the cold sweat from his forehead.

The lieutenant wanted nothing more than to drive to Collins' office and arrest him. He felt certain of his guilt in the attacks, but the man covered his tracks too well.

He had told no one in the department of his suspicions. Until he found credible hard evidence, or caught Collins in the act, he would assign his teams, collect what clues were left behind, and continue his impromptu conversations with his adversary. He had called Collins' secretary two hours ago, asking for another meeting. She politely accommodated, giving him three openings over the course of the coming week. Thanking the woman politely, Kitch settled on Friday at eleven o'clock.

He carefully gathered his pictures, sorting them into the file folder. After glancing one last time at the gruesome photo of the third man's battered body, he inserted the folder into his desk drawer. He stood, panning his eyes over his desk, making sure nothing was out of order.

As he holstered his weapon, his mind drifted toward one unavoidable fact. Dogfighting activity in Los Angeles County had dropped to almost nil. Gruesome though his tactics were, the word had definitely gotten out. Collins and his crew had made their presence known, and people all over the county were scared to death.

⋯ 19 ⋯

Everett Turner emerged from the CRJ100 jet powered aircraft. His flight, originating from Los Angeles International Airport, had stopped once in Salt Lake City before depositing Turner and twenty-nine other passengers onto the lonely tarmac at Natrona County Airport. Turner had watched the scenery every second after the pilot had announced final approach. To his amazement he saw nothing but dirt and scrub brush the whole way. Casper, Wyoming, was a smudge in the landscape of a state known for great hunting, better steaks, and constant wind.

As he walked toward the terminal, Turner noticed the absence of anything technologically sophisticated. Rounding the corner in front of the entrance, he held the door for a family of five, a husband and wife no older than thirty, herding three young children in their wake. Turner had been so focused on the safety of the kids he nearly ran smack into a mountain lion propped up just inside the terminal. When he finally looked up, he jumped back, startled by the snarling countenance of the stuffed animal. A host of other creatures, all frozen in their beautifully crafted death, glared at him as he moved by the huge display. A sign advertising a taxidermist stood proudly by the line of animals.

A man holding a sign bearing Turner's fictitious name stood next to the baggage claim checkout area. As he saw the throng approaching from Turner's flight, he raised his sign high in the air. He was dressed in the uniform of the corporate hunter: Timberland boots, Wrangler jeans, a long-sleeved western shirt, and a North Face down vest. On his head rested a ridiculous Australian hunting hat, with an even more absurd patch. It didn't even look professionally made; the insignia slumped to one side as it boasted the company name in hideous fluorescent colors.

"Mr. Jacobson?" asked the valet with the ludicrous hat.

"Yes, sir, that's me," said Turner excitedly. "Paul Jacobson, from Fresno. When can we get underway?"

"Just as soon as the luggage comes up the conveyor belt. You just relax, I'll grab your bags and we'll be off."

Turner looked back toward the small claim area. It seemed his was the only arriving flight. The luggage should come up straight away.

"How's the weather in Fresno?" asked the valet.

"Same as always for this time of year," said Turner.

"You'll like it here. This is the best time to be in Casper. Crisp, clean air, moderate wind, and not too hot."

The conversation droned on for another five minutes before the conveyor belt sparked to life. After the valet collected Turner's bags, insisting on carrying everything, the two men walked outside. A dirty Dodge Ram pickup sat in the lot, only fifty feet from the terminal door. Turner laughed quietly. After the valet queried him, he told the man that if they were in Los Angeles, the walk to their car might have taken thirty minutes or more.

"That's why we live out here," said the valet. "In Wyoming a man does what he wants."

The drive from Casper to the hunting farm took a little over an hour. Turner mentally noted potential trouble spots along the way. There were few to speak of; this truly was God's country. Moving their gear into place after the raid wouldn't be a problem.

"Don't get many folks from Fresno up here, Mr. Jacobson," said the valet. "Where do you hunt most of the time?"

"Mostly in Owens Valley, a little south of June Lake," answered Turner. "Sometimes in the desert outside of Las Cruces, depending on the time of year."

"So this is your first time in a captive hunting farm?"

"Yes. A very good friend is turning fifty soon, so I thought a trip like this for a few of us might be just the ticket."

"You're in luck," said the valet. "We just got another shipment of fresh animals. Got two lions, three tigers, and a couple of brown bears. I'm sure we'll be able to get a similar group for your party. You'll get a firsthand look at what you'll be hunting when you come back with your friends."

"Always wanted to bag a bear," said Turner, swallowing his distaste for the man driving the truck.

"You'll get your chance, Paul. You'll get your money's worth, I promise."

The truck veered off the main highway. Turner grabbed the overhead handle, bracing his body as they rumbled up a rock-strewn dirt road. The valet handled the uneven surface with sure hands; he had obviously been up and down the hill many times. Conversation ceased as the ride became bumpier. The road seemed to expand and contract at various intervals, but it never disappeared entirely. Turner made a mental note of this, filing it away for his report later that evening. He peered through the windshield as the truck crested the hill.

In front of him sat a sprawling compound. The valet pulled the truck up to a mechanized gate, where a lonely security card apparatus stood ready to examine their credentials. Turner looked at a large sign on the building closest to the gate. He winced internally, repulsed by the mission statement.

The gate creaked open. Turner examined the fence as they passed through; it seemed a simple structure, no doubt easily battered down by a good-sized tractor-trailer.

"Here we are, Mr. Jacobson," said the valet, cheerfully. Jumping out of the truck, he grabbed Turner's bags and headed toward the office at a brisk pace. Before they even reached the building, an older man dressed exactly like the valet pushed through the door.

"Mr. Jacobson?"

"Yes, sir," said Turner. "You must be Byron Forney."

"Guilty as charged. I guess you met my son, Junior."

"Yep, but I hadn't made the connection. In all the time we were driving out here we never formally introduced ourselves."

The men clasped hands all around. Turner noted that both Forney and his son had limp, lifeless hands. He tamped down his enthusiasm; he couldn't wait to meet the rest of the employees. He wanted a complete personnel assessment for Collins when he contacted him.

A **Pound** of Fur

"Let me give you a tour of our facilities, Mr. Jacobson," said Forney. "Junior will take care of your bags. After the tour, we can meet some of the current residents. If you're lucky, we might even squeeze in a hunt today."

"Great," said Turner, looking eagerly toward the hunting area. "I'd love to see how you operate out here."

"This here is our ready room," said Forney, reaching out toward a large, stainless steel door handle. "Before every hunt we all gather in this room to plan strategy. We want to make certain every one of our guests remains completely safe while at Hunt of Your Life, especially during the action."

Forney led Turner through the encampment, showing him almost everything: the mess hall, bathrooms, rooming quarters, and finally, the hunting area. Turner nearly blew his cover and slapped Forney when he saw the tiny area where the "hunts" took place. Barely twenty acres, with little brush or rock formations for cover, the "forest," as Forney called it, gave the animals little hope of survival. Add to that the fact that they no doubt were old, sick, and drugged beyond stupor, and it was all Turner could do to keep his cool.

"What do you think?"

"It's perfect," said Turner, thinking only of what would happen when Collins arrived with his own menagerie.

"Excellent," said Forney, watching the dollar signs dance in front of his face. Let me show you the animals we have in stock right now. After that we can get some lunch."

Turner followed Forney into a large utility tent, maybe three thousand square feet in area. He saw a series of cages, very small cages for wild animals of any size. As they rounded the first row, Forney pressed a button on the wall closest to the first enclosure.

A hastily erected tarp covering the front of the cages rose up from the ground. Controlled by a squeaky winch, the tarp took almost a minute to reveal the occupants. When Turner finally focused on the first of the animals, his shoulders sunk with despair.

A large but scrawny African lion lay at the back of the cage. Flies buzzed around its head, obviously an irritation, but the lion made no move to dissuade them. It looked terribly old, and seriously drugged, by the glazed expression in its large, golden eyes. Nothing moved on its body, not a muscle. One of the eyes shifted slightly, looking at Turner. Apparently, it could still sense a newcomer invading its territory.

"Beauty, isn't he?" asked Forney.

"Looks to be straight off the savannah. Seems kind of run down, though, don't you think?"

"We have to keep the animals drugged to a certain extent. The trip to Casper and then to Hunt of Your Life is kind of stressful. Once we get them here, we just continue giving it to them. Wouldn't be good for the animals to win, now would it?"

Turner smiled. "Can't have that," he said, "especially after all the money they're paying to hunt here."

Turner pointed at the lion. "Think you can save this one for my friend?"

"Afraid not, Mr. Jacobson. That animal's been spoken for already. As a matter of fact, you can watch the hunt this afternoon if you want."

A Pound of Fur

Forney watched Turner's reaction, gauging how much money he'd be able to charge the man and his friends for another African lion. "It's possible we'll be able to get another one by the time you and your party arrive. When did you say you wanted to come back?"

"Six weeks from today, if that's possible."

"I don't see why not. We'll check the schedule as soon as we get back to the office." Forney stepped over to the next cage. "Come over here, I want to show you something really amazing."

Turner looked at the lion one last time, grieving internally that they wouldn't be able to save the big cat. Waiting only a second or two, he followed Forney to the next cage. What he saw there took his breath away.

A massive, dark brown grizzly sat in the back of the enclosure. Looking like an eleven-hundred-pound teddy bear, the grizzly sat on his rump with his legs splayed out in front of him. It chewed on its right forepaw, pulling tufts of fur out from between its claws. It took no notice of Forney and Turner; instead it vigorously pulled at its fingers.

"Who gets to shoot him?" asked Turner.

"I'm saving that one for myself. We got him special from a zoo in New York. They said he killed two other bears when he was just a teenager. They couldn't control him, and he was no good to them in an enclosure all alone. Said he just slept all day, 'cept when it was dinner time, of course."

"You were lucky to get him."

"You're damn right about that."

Turner walked up to the cage. Wrapping his hands around the bars, he stared at the bear with mute fascination. *Such a magnificent creature*, he thought. Its skull was as big as a man's torso. The claws could cleave a man's head from his body with one swipe. Its overall size left Turner speechless. He leaned his forehead against the bars.

The grizzly emitted a low, rumbling growl, letting its paw fall to the ground as he did so. The massive body shifted, ready to charge if Turner made another wrong move.

"Looks like he needs a dose of the medication you're giving to the lion."

"I'm not gonna drug him," said Forney. "I'll tell you what, though, he gets all the food he wants. I'm making sure he isn't the least bit hungry when he goes into the hunting area."

"What type of weapon are you planning to take in with you?"

"What do you mean, weapon?" asked Forney, chuckling. "I'm going in loaded for bear, if you'll pardon my expression. I'm bringing in a Remington Model 700 for the kill shot, but I'll soften him up with a few clips from an AK-47 first."

"That'd be fun to see."

Forney escorted Turner around the rest of the tent, showing him a good-sized collection of wild game. Turner saw two tigers, three mountain lions, a water buffalo, a large group of coyotes, and various other native and non-native animals. He acted excited and eager at the sight of each one. Inside, however, he cringed after seeing the condition of the inhabitants. With the exception of the grizzly, every animal in the Hunt of Your Life inventory was painfully old and weak. You could almost go into the hunting area with a baseball bat and make your kill.

A **Pound** of **Fur**

Forney held the door for Turner as they exited. "Let's go back to the mess hall; I'm sure folks will be gathered there for lunch about now."

They exited through a different gate. Turner had counted five gates in all, a number easily handled by the team Collins would send. He also noticed the high walls encircling the hunting area. Once inside the enclosure, neither man nor beast would be able to escape.

"Right back in here, Mr. Jacobson."

Turner walked through the door Forney held. He felt surprised as he walked into a dark mess hall. He felt alarmed when he saw a large group of very relaxed people staring up at him from their seats around the tables. He panicked momentarily when a rucksack collapsed over his head and shoulders. A second later he felt two hard blows from rifle butts, one on the nose and the other at the base of his skull.

··· 20 ···

"Any word from Turner?"

"Nothing yet, Sir."

Collins stood just outside his office. In his right thumb and index finger he slid two quarters over and under each other, a habit he formed while still active military. He knew something had gone terribly wrong; he could feel it as if he were there himself.

"You have Lieutenant Kitch in fifteen minutes. Would you like me to reschedule?"

"No," said Collins. "Send an emergency assembly call to every team operating in the country, Code Yellow. Tell them to be ready to deploy in twelve hours. If Turner phones while I'm entertaining the lieutenant put the call through immediately."

··· **21** ···

A grimy, urine stained bucket of tepid water splashed harshly across Turner's face. Clearing his head, he held his hands up, hoping to block any more of the reeking fluid from stinging his eyes. He opened them slightly, seeing a blurry, darkened room. The blinds had been drawn to keep out the sun, leaving a hazy, sinister ambience.

From what Turner could see it seemed to be some kind of storeroom. It stank to high heaven; he didn't have to see the remains to realize that this served as the slaughterhouse for Hunt of Your Life. After the day's events, they would drag the dead carcasses into this room for a pre-taxidermy cutting party. No sense in paying someone to do what you could do yourself, thought Turner as his head cleared.

A heavy boot slammed against his rib cage. He coiled up immediately, only to feel another hard kick against his spine. When he tried to stand, he felt the pinch of the plastic cuffs holding his ankles and knees tightly together. He rolled onto his back, cradling his head in his forearms.

"Your name isn't Paul Jacobson," said a voice somewhere in the room. "It's Everett Turner, and you live in Los

Angeles County. You work for a firm called Safeguard Protection Services. It's owned by a psycho named Kevin Collins."

The voice stopped. Turner waited.

"Well?" asked Forney, after smacking Turner's right knee with a piece of rebar.

"Yea? So what?"

"You bastard," said Forney as he weighed in with the rebar. He gave Turner half a dozen strong whacks about his body. He reeled himself in, breathing heavily and sweating. "What did you think you'd find here, a bunch of country hicks without any brains in their heads?"

"Exactly," said Turner.

"Let me take a few turns with that, Pop," said the younger Forney.

Forney spat at Turner before flinging the rebar in his son's direction. Junior caught the weapon easily. Stepping forward, he bashed Turner's ribs until the skin broke. Blood poured from the wound. "Prick," he said before backing away.

To his credit, Turner hadn't made a sound. Years of military training settled in immediately, allowing him to take the punishment without calling out. He realized, however, that he had seriously erred by not checking out the principals of the organization more carefully. Forney had been right after all; he had taken them for a bunch of hicks. As he lay there bleeding, deciding whether they would kill him outright, he wondered just who he'd missed when appraising the small company called Hunt of Your Life.

"What are we going to do with him, Pop?"

A **Pound** of **Fur**

"I told him I wanted to keep that bear well fed," said For-ney. "Do you hear that, Mr. Turner? You thought you would just roll in here and scout out my camp for a hit by you and your boys, ain't that right?" Forney kicked him one last time with the steel toe of his combat boot. "C'mon, let's go tell the others."

··· **22** ···

Kevin Collins shook Lieutenant Kitch's hand as they crossed the threshold of his office. Making an offer of employment again, Collins smiled when Kitch deferred.

"Public service has been my life for nearly thirty years, Mr. Collins. I dare say I'd feel traitorous if I left the force for the private sector."

"What about when you retire?" asked Collins. "Will your conscience vote against a second career once you've completed your obligations to the city?"

"That decision will come at a much later date, and after much deliberation."

Collins shook the lieutenant's hand again. "So, I'll see you tomorrow morning at my home?"

"Apparently, the only way for me to keep tabs on you is to befriend you even more than I had initially planned. Yes, I will join you for breakfast."

"Excellent," said Collins as he escorted Kitch to the foyer of his company headquarters. "Eight o'clock?"

"I look forward to it. Please extend my appreciation to your secretary for the excellent tea."

A Pound of Fur

Collins watched Kitch walk through the front door. When he felt sure of his absence, he turned and walked back to his office. He caught Shari taking a few drags from a Winston. She put the cigarette out as soon as she saw him enter the room.

"Turner?" he asked briskly.

"Nothing, sir. I've checked every channel of communication we have. No one's heard anything."

Collins lowered his head, thinking.

"What do you want to do?" asked Shari.

"Activate all teams. Go to red sign bravo. Have all team leaders on a conference call in ten minutes. Telephone LAX and have my personal jet prepared for a quick flight tomorrow. I'll be in my office waiting for the conference call."

"Where are you going?"

"Casper, Wyoming, but that's between you and me."

··· 23 ···

Turner tensed as his body slumped into a chair. Someone wrapped a thick cord around his chest and the back of the chair a few times. He half saw and half felt a boot wedging up against his side. Then someone yanked the cord as tight as it would go.

He couldn't move his arms or any other part of his body. The plastic handcuffs still held his ankles and knees in place. The cord held him fast against the chair.

The lights in the mess hall came on suddenly. Turner slammed his lids shut, trying to keep the light away from his damaged eyes.

"Don't worry about your eyes, Turner," said Forney. "The stinging sensation should go away in an hour or two."

Turner tried opening his eyes, but the tingling singe forced them closed again. He thought about what might have been in that bucket.

"We wouldn't want you to be completely blind, now would we?" asked Forney. The others in the room laughed along with the owner of Hunt of Your Life. They all shared an equal distaste for the bruised and beaten man sitting in front of them. They had come from far and wide, spending obscene amounts of money for a sporting weekend in Casper, and the man in the chair had tried to ruin it for all of them.

"Forney, you jackass," said Turner. "You're all going to die."

"What the hell are you talking about?"

"What do you think? Collins is going to come here. He's going to bring an army with him. You won't be able to stop him. You're all dead unless…"

"Shut up!" screamed Forney's son, Junior. "Shut the fuck up! Nobody's coming here, you're just trying to rile everyone up, maybe make a case for us to let you go. Well, it ain't gonna work, Turner. Even if they did come, we have enough guns and ammunition to hold off a hundred armies."

"Don't be alarmed, folks," said Forney to his guests. "What Mr. Turner here is talking about is a raid on our facilities. You see, he and his buddies like to kill people. I heard they even lashed some guy onto a makeshift hook down in Greeneville. Dragged him around like a mackerel until his skull came apart."

Turner tried to open his eyes again. This time they felt a little better, but he still kept them closed.

"His boys are all in Los Angeles," Forney continued. "Even if they left right now, they wouldn't be able to assemble and stage a raid until long after you'll all be gone. Don't worry about a thing."

"Hey, Forney," said Lawrence Tannenbaum, one of Hunt of Your Life's guests for the weekend. "Let him heal up overnight. Maybe I'll trade in that tiger for a real live human being."

"Tempting," said Forney, "but no deal. Hunt of Your Life has never put a human being on the block, and we're not going to start now."

Jeezus, thought Turner. *The one thing that might have saved your ass, and you throw the idea away just like that?*

"I'll tell you what we're going to do. Tomorrow afternoon we're going to drop Mr. Turner here right smack in the middle of the hunting grounds. Then we're going to back that grizzly's cage up to the gate and release him. We're all going to watch while that bear chases him down and rips him to pieces. After that I'll go in and finish him off.

"We're going to take some real good footage of Turner's last stand, too. Send it back to Los Angeles with a handwritten note to Mr. Collins, telling him to keep a lot of real estate between his boys and our hunting farm. I figure that ought to do it."

The crowd in the room stirred. The excitement of future events seemed to get everyone's blood up. A small, sturdy woman stepped in front of her husband.

"I'm ready to go, now. I know we said we could wait until later in the evening, but I want that cat now. How long 'til we can set up the hunt?"

"That's what I like to see," said Forney, "a high degree of anticipation before the games begin. Okay, Gloria, we'll get set up just as soon as we can. Junior, you make sure the grounds are ship shape. I'll let Jessup and Graves into the paddock. Everyone meet in the ready room in one hour."

··· 24 ···

Gloria Dunn sat front and center listening to Forney outline the details of the hunt. With sweaty palms, she cradled her rifle. She'd spent the last thirty minutes disassembling and cleaning the weapon, as ordered by Forney. She sat, stone-faced, allowing her emotions to run freely.

She paid attention to each feeling individually. The most profound sensation running through her had to be a thrilling sense of awe. After a lifetime of hunting game in her native Montana, today she would face down a man-eater, an African lion, and a male to boot.

She had worked her way up through the ranks of her family, surpassing her brothers in accuracy and body count. After taking her first buck at fourteen, then an elk at sixteen, her father had finally recognized her abilities as a hunter. The day he took her to Alaska for a hunt was the proudest of her life.

On the first day of their trip her father had been killed by a rogue moose. They happened upon it accidentally, and consequently Gloria had been ill prepared for the confrontation. The moose tore into their dog team, killing three animals instantly and tossing the sled aside like kindling. Her father managed to get a shot off, grazing the moose's head and infuriating it even further. It charged straight into him, shredding his midsection into ribbons of muscle, bone and veins.

Flinging her father aside like a punctured tire, the enraged bull turned to face Gloria. She had gathered herself, placed one knee on the ground and carefully took aim. Squeezing off three shots in rapid succession, she dropped the moose in its tracks.

Dropping her weapon, she ignored the injured dogs and ran to her father. Miraculously, he was alive. Gloria turned him over, holding his intestines in one hand while wiping dirt and sweat from his brow with the other. Both father and daughter knew this would be their last conversation. Tears were put aside. Her father made certain Gloria knew how to contact the rangers for a rescue. She pressed a finger against his lips, telling him how much she loved him, and how she'd always wanted to make him proud.

Dunn told his only daughter how sorry he was for being harsh as she grew to womanhood. He had raised four sons; he didn't have it in him to raise a girl any differently. She had surpassed all of his expectations, he said, and he felt certain she would someday marry a fine man and raise sons of her own.

Another fit took control of him. He pressed his face to the ground, coughing up blood and dark mucus. He knew his time had come. He grasped his daughter's hand one last time, telling her with his remaining strength how much he loved her.

Gloria brought herself back to the present. Forney stood at the front of the ready room, detailing everyone's position for the hunt.

"If at any time you determine that Gloria's in trouble, you have my permission to shoot."

"No," said Gloria. "No one's bagging that lion but me. I don't care for or need your protection, Mr. Forney. Once that gate drops, I want to be left alone."

"And what if the animal charges and your weapon jams?"

"Then it jams and I'm screwed. You can all stand guard if you want, but if anyone kills that lion but me, I'll draw down and shoot that person in the ass."

"Now wait just a minute," said Forney.

"No, you wait," interrupted Gloria. "I paid fifteen thousand dollars to come here and hunt. With travel expenses it may hit twenty grand. There's no way I'm going home knowing someone else bagged my prize."

"But this is for your own protection."

"Fuck that. I can take care of myself. I don't need anyone watching over me."

"And your husband has no problem with this?"

"None at all," said Doug Chaney. "Gloria's a grown woman. Once she sets her mind to something, there's no stopping her. Hell, she didn't even take my name when I married her."

"All right, have it your way then. I'm still posting everyone on the perimeter in strategic locations. We're even bringing Mr. Turner so he can enjoy the hunt. I'm sure he'll get a big kick out of it, being a nature lover and all."

The group worked out the rest of the details in less than ten minutes. Forney ordered Gloria to report to the main gate. His son would be there to enter the code. Once inside, he would secure the lock until the hunt ended.

··· **25** ···

Gloria listened to the tumblers in the gate roll into place. She felt an exhilaration she'd never before experienced, knowing soon a man eater would be set free in the hunting grounds. She walked carefully and quietly across the hard-packed dirt, using her excellent hearing to register anything else that might be within the walls of the arena. The wind had picked up noticeably; the Wyoming weather pattern proved true again. Dust swirls danced over the hunting area.

The noise of the wind scraping across the dirt alarmed Gloria somewhat; she needed absolute quiet if she hoped to track the lion before it caught her scent. There was no use trying to stay downwind, the crazy, misdirected eddies blew everything in all directions at once.

She heard the forklift nudging up against a gate on the far side of the hunting area. The pod moved into place and the door flew up. In seconds the lion would be inside the enclosure. Gloria checked her weapon, one round chambered, twenty-nine more encased in a clip. She crouched down, listening for the telltale sound of the gate opening and closing.

■ ■ ■

A **Pound** of Fur

After clipping the plastic handcuffs from his ankles and legs, Forney ushered Turner through the door. Assuring him that he would toss him into the hunting grounds should he act up, Forney led the badly beaten man toward the main observation area. They walked up two flights of stairs, settling on a deck that overlooked everything.

Forney pushed Turner backwards into an old, rickety chair. "You should like this, being the tree hugger you are."

"Fuck off."

"You still think your boys are coming for you, don't you?"

Turner spit a tooth onto the boards. "They're coming, count on it."

"Go fuck yourself," said Forney. "You really think we can't protect ourselves out here? You think we're just a bunch of slack jawed dumb shits?"

Turner moved his head in the direction of the hunting area. If Forney wanted to sacrifice these people, then so be it. It be would be on his conscience.

■ ■ ■

He saw the Dunn woman silently moving through the thickest section of foliage in the grounds. She squatted, watching and listening for any sign of the lion. Holding her rifle in her left hand, she carefully wiped her forehead with the wristband she always wore. She seemed calm enough, but Turner could tell her senses were on high alert. For a moment he admired the woman. She took her hobby seriously. Turner almost wanted to shout down to her, tell her to run to the gate and leave. He did nothing, though, preferring to watch the hunt unfold.

The lion, an emaciated, fourteen-year-old male, took a few steps into the compound and promptly collapsed on the ground. With its tongue dangling lazily from its mouth, the abused beast gazed in one direction only, toward the gate where it had entered the hunting grounds. It looked exactly like what it was, a depleted, abused animal, thoroughly disoriented.

Forney's son stuck a shotgun through the bars of the fence. Sitting low to the ground, he took aim at the lion's rump. He shot only once, firing a twelve-gauge round of rock salt into its flank.

The cat sprang up, turning around and snarling in Forney's direction. Reaching around, it licked its hind quarters, trying to remove the stinging bits of salt. Its eyes, golden brown and filled with hatred, never left Forney, even after the barrel of the shotgun appeared through the fence again.

Junior let another round go. This time the lion forgot about its condition. It charged the fence, crashing violently into the bars separating it from Forney. One of its fangs snapped off, broken above the root by the collision with a hard metal post. It rammed his paw through the barrier, swiping at Forney viciously. Junior slapped the paw with his shotgun. Then he walked away from the fence, leaving a very angry lion snarling in his wake.

Gloria heard the commotion. She homed in on the noise, guessing it to be over the hill, a few hundred yards away. Most likely on the other side of the compound, no doubt. She checked her boundaries, assuring herself that no surprise attacks would occur before moving forward.

Still enraged but seeing no profit in staying by the

fence, the lion turned, loping toward the center of the hunting grounds. Every ten feet or so the animal would stop, squat, and lick the stinging, bleeding wounds along its flank and tailbone. After cleaning the abrasions as best it could, it gazed about the complex, sniffing repeatedly. Even in its depleted state, the lion sensed danger.

After giving its rump another licking, it padded over to the perimeter. Instead of walking aimlessly down the center of the arena, the big cat decided on a smarter course. It could do nothing to hide in the sparse conditions, but it would make itself difficult to find at least.

Slinking along the fence line, the emaciated cat stopped every few feet to take in its surroundings. After a few such attempts, the lion's body stiffened. It caught a scent it recognized from thousands of years of instinct. Somewhere close by, a human being skulked around hunting prey. The lion held its position, peering through bleary eyes, trying to catch any movement within its range of vision. It sniffed again, and then again, its fur bristling down its backbone.

Gloria kept to the center of the hunting grounds. She made a choice between trying to conceal herself or providing the most time to react in case of a charge. She chose the latter. She knew that if a large, wild cat got the drop on her she would be hard pressed to protect herself.

Walking slowly and silently, she felt the wind freshen a bit. She became nervous but quickly stifled the emotion. She summoned an image of her father, guiding her thoughts along a safe, rational path to safety. If the lion lurked behind her, she might detect it in time to turn and fire. If it was downwind, in front of her, the cat would no doubt catch her scent long before she knew it. It unnerved her, but at the same time, she felt exhilaration rushing along the pores of her skin.

About fifty yards to the left and thirty yards ahead, she spied movement along the fence line. Instinctively, her right thumb passed over the stock of the rifle. Without a conscious thought, she flicked the safety off. She felt the barrel sliding a bit in her left palm. It was then she realized how hot and dusty it had become. Grasping the rifle in her left hand, she swiped the wristband on her right forearm across her forehead.

During the interlude, she never took her eyes from the fence. She saw it now, an African lion. Skinny, yes, old, probably, but nonetheless a man eater. She sensed rather than felt her right hand gripping the trigger housing on her weapon. She peered through the scrub, finally locking eyes with one of the most beautiful and deadly creatures ever to inhabit the earth.

The lion sank languidly against the fence. It spied the woman standing on the raised mound some distance away but did nothing. It made no threatening move toward her at all. After a few minutes of non-activity from either of them, the big cat began settling down in the shade. The lion stretched its forepaws out in front of its body, preparing to lie down.

Forney's son waited directly opposite the lion, standing right outside the fence. In his hands he held a cattle prod, fully juiced with nine thousand volts of electricity. He waited until the lion had lowered its body, keeping its rear end high in the air, stretching out the way cats do prior to lying down. He jammed the prod through the bars of the fence, connecting perfectly with the lion's scrotum. Forney felt a sick sense of satisfaction as the electricity surged into the surprised animal.

The lion roared. It circled the immediate area, crying out repeatedly while scraping its rump along the ground.

Forney tried for another contact, but the lion had moved too far from the fence. In a moment of furious frustration, it lashed back at Forney, scraping the prod from his grip. It bounced on the ground inside the enclosure before settling against the fence. Hitting the bar with its charged end, the prod released its remaining energy in a shower of sparks. It shot away from the fence, sailing across the hunting grounds like a discarded toothpick.

The lion's rage poured through its broken teeth in one pathetic snarl. Unable to get to Forney, the big cat turned to face Gloria. It mattered little who stood before it now. The intense pain in its rump and scrotum fueled its desire for retribution. Slinking low along the ground, it began stalking its victim.

Gloria saw the prowling lion come over the rise toward her. When they locked eyes again, it growled a vicious warning. She knelt, taking a firing stance and breathing steadily. She wrapped the rifle strap around her forearm, hitching the weapon tightly against her body. She placed the crosshairs directly on the lion's chest, listening to her father's advice.

"Always shoot for the largest part of your prey," he advised. "Even if you don't kill it with the first shot, you can always put it out of its misery with the second."

Watching the lion prepare to charge, she silently asked her father for courage and a steady hand. Then she saw it, the telltale signs of a cat warming up for the kill. The muscles tensed along its body, the paws straightened slightly, claws penetrating the ground. Finally, the tail lashed back and forth like a metronome, giving the cat a perfect cadence with which to strike. In a puff of rising dust it exploded toward her.

Gloria squeezed off her first shot. The .375 caliber bullet slammed into the lion's midsection, spinning it around mid-stride. She barely had time to aim again before the cat, bleeding heavily from its chest, turned and charged again.

The second bullet crashed into the lion's head, sending blood, teeth and brains flying. The four-hundred-pound animal slumped down next to her. Gloria wouldn't believe it for the longest time. Afraid to stand, she squatted with her rifle pointed at the lion's back.

A round of congratulatory cheers rang out from different parts of the hunting grounds. The men stationed around the fence line, including Doug Chaney, whooped and cat-called to the woman sitting next to the carcass. The man standing next to Chaney clapped him on the back several times, sharing the joy of witnessing a successful hunt.

Panting with the exhilarated feeling of accomplishment, Gloria Dunn finally stood up. She nudged the lion with the barrel of her rifle, convincing herself the danger had passed. The lion's shoulders rolled under the weight of her weapon. The beautiful golden fur shifted once or twice, rolling over the dead bones and muscle. She looked at the huge head, the massive jaws, and the dead eyes. She couldn't wait to bring the skin home.

"Okay, Junior, you can open the gates now." The megaphone in Forney's hand blasted its message through Turner's ears and across the hunting grounds. When he heard the first of the gates being thrown up, he lowered the device and sat back down.

"Well, what did you think?" he asked Turner.

"I think you're a sick fuck."

"Come on, drop the holier than thou act for one second. What did you really think?"

"You throw a diseased, decrepit animal into an enclosed area against impossible odds, torture it and then kill it, and you want to know what I think? Isn't it obvious, you piece of shit?"

"Never could understand your type," said Forney. "That animal had every chance of winning that battle, as much a chance as Ms. Dunn. It wasn't tied down or restricted in any way. It had free run of the facility once we released it into the hunting area. What the hell's your problem, anyway?"

"You're my problem, Forney, you and everyone like you. Have you ever for one moment tried to understand the beauty of an animal like that, or the intelligence?" Turner shook his head.

Forney slapped Turner across the face. Blood dribbled from two different locations, painful wounds, reopened with the strike. Turner couldn't be sure with his swollen eyes, but for a moment he thought he saw fear in the fat man's face.

"You stay here awhile, asshole," he said. "I gotta go attend to Ms. Dunn and make arrangements for dinner. I'll come back later; lock your ass back in your hole. Maybe we'll have some more fun tonight."

"Enjoy yourself, dumb shit," said Turner. "This'll be the last time you watch the sun go down."

Forney kicked an empty beer can in Turner's direction. He turned, expelled a large fart in Turner's face, and waltzed down the stairs, laughing.

··· 26 ···

A low whistle trilled through the darkness. Three seconds later, another sound rose from the sparse shrubs dotting the hill surrounding Hunt of Your Life. Three short chirps signaled readiness.

"Nothing moving here," Jensen whispered into his shoulder mike.

"All quiet on the north slope," said Winter.

"Looks like we go from where I sit," added Sanchez.

Keller listened to his men report in. Things seemed to be going their way. They'd arrived just prior to midnight, hiking the last three miles in complete silence. Staying far into the brush, the moonless night shadowing their advance, the platoon strength squad had circled their objective without encountering a soul. After they'd moved into position, he'd instructed his men to stay low, awake and alert, for the next three hours.

Keller had positioned two men on another hill almost a thousand yards from their present position. Equipped with night scoped sniper rifles, it was their job to eyeball any movement, and if human, take out the enemy either with darts or live rounds.

"Dunhill," he whispered into his shoulder mike, "are we safe to move forward?"

"Looks quiet from here," said Dunhill in a low, even response. "There's a lot of brush in some places on the hill. That could provide cover if their men are good."

"Do you see anything moving at all?" asked Keller.

"Nothing human. Only four-footers inside the fence line. One looks like a lioness."

"What's she doing? Is she pacing by the fence or moving about aimlessly?"

"She's been right by the fence since we sat down. Just moving back and forth methodically. She seems to be staring at something. Maybe there's a rabbit or something outside the fence."

"Shit!" said Keller without turning off his mike. "Stay sharp back there."

He clicked three times in rapid succession to warn his men. He wondered if some of them had been caught already.

■ ■ ■

Sanchez watched an owl dip into the windless night from a tree a hundred yards away. The bird's flight took it directly toward Keller's team. The motionless, white face mesmerized him. The soundless flight held his eyes until he felt a circle of cold steel press against the back of his neck. He set his rifle down and placed his hands on the ground.

"Good move, dumbass," said a gruff voice above his head. "Now put your face in the dirt between your..."

Sanchez heard the sound of a rifle stock crunching against his captor's neck. He felt a body slump against him and then slide off his shoulders. It tipped over, rolling onto the ground face up.

"Boss," said Winter into his mike. "We're made. Someone just moved on Sanchez. I neutralized him, but our other positions are probably compromised."

"Check. Listen up, everyone. Move toward the compound now. Whoever you can't capture, kill."

A second later, gunfire disrupted the dark calm of the night. Muzzle flashes preceded yells and screams as men on both sides took hits from small arms fire. No longer concerned about stealth, Keller barked orders into his shoulder mike.

"Disperse! Don't group together. Give them as hard a target as you can, and fire at will, dammit. We didn't come all this way to donate body parts."

■ ■ ■

The towers around the hunting grounds served two purposes, as perfect viewing stations for the hunts and as lookout towers for miles beyond the fence line. Night-vision goggles provided excellent sightlines in all directions. Keller's men had little chance of climbing the hills undetected, and now they found themselves caught in a full-blown firefight. Forney had positioned other men on the far side of the hill. He knew the attackers would come from the direction of the airport in Casper. Protected by the men in the towers, those sneaking their way through the brush had the location of Keller's men radioed to them every few seconds.

Junior laughed like a hyena as he sprayed the north slope of the upper hills with an automatic rifle.

"What you think of that, huh?" Spittle flew through his lips as he held the AK-47 in his flabby arms. "Didn't think we'd handle your stupid little posse, did you, you assholes."

The idiot wounded three of his own men with his drunken bombardment of the exterior grounds. He managed to hit one of Keller's men as well, a superficial wound only, allowing the man to scramble away and take cover.

One of Keller's men riddled Junior's watchtower with a burst from his rifle. Wood splinters flew everywhere, but Junior had climbed or fell down the steps, escaping the barrage.

Dunhill and his mate took in the scene calmly. Shifting their eyes quickly, they located as many of their men as they could. They fired 100-millimeter rounds at the rest.

The bodies of two tower guards flew backwards over the railing of their hiding places, their heads blown apart by the huge bullets. Two more dove down the stairways before the structures sustained heavy damage.

The fight moved onto the open area around the compound. Most of Keller's men had separated and moved to a safe distance. Forney's men followed, certain of their victory. They ran out into the night, a few wearing night goggles, but most moving blindly through the darkness. Every few seconds a volley of gunfire scattered the group, but they rushed ahead anyway, unaware of what lay waiting behind them.

Dunhill raised his rifle again. He crumpled a second later. Keller's other sniper also went down, taken out by three sniper bullets, center mass.

"We got 'em, now, boys," Junior shouted, huffing and puffing as he followed a fresh pair of tracks. "Let's take these assholes and use them to warm up the animals today."

A **Pound** of Fur

"Halt!" said a voice blasting through a megaphone. "All employees of Hunt of Your Life. Stop where you are and throw down your weapons. If you fail to comply, we'll kill every one of you."

Junior didn't know what to do. One second he had everything under control, and the next...

"We won't warn you again. Give up and live. Do anything else and die."

"Fuck off!" Junior screamed. He opened fire in the direction of the voice. He lost his footing in the loose rock and fell back, smacking his head on a piece of shale. He lay unconscious, mouth open, index finger still hugging the trigger.

His men fired their weapons wildly, but after two more fell the others quickly surrendered. Collins' second platoon swarmed around them, rifles leveled. Keller brought his men forward. Jensen held Junior by the shoulder of his jacket. Having jarred him from his brief nap, he dragged him forward toward the group.

"This is the asshole that whacked his own guys trying to shoot us."

Keller looked him up and down. "What's your name?"

"Who the fuck are you?"

"Someone who's going to be alive in twenty-four hours." Keller looked around, making sure his wounded were accounted for. He wanted them to receive immediate attention when they reached Hunt of Your Life. "We need a couple of jeeps, or a truck with a good-sized bed."

"Eat my ass, fuckface."

Keller raised his rifle butt.

"Collins said..."

The stock connected with Junior's forehead. A second later Forney's son was on the ground again, unconscious.

Sanchez shook his head. "Collins said he wanted everyone healthy and ready." He looked at Junior. "Now what?"

"Fuck him. He'll be awake soon." He slung his rifle and turned toward the hill. "I should have shot the stupid prick."

··· **27** ···

"Morning, Sam," said Collins. "I hope you brought an appetite."

"I seem to carry one everywhere I go. People are often fooled by my slight physique. I assure you; however, I can eat a lumberjack size breakfast without difficulty. Everyone in my family was blessed with a hyperactive metabolism."

"Excellent. I'll tell the staff to cook for six."

Collins led Lieutenant Kitch through the foyer of his expansive home. They passed through an immaculate living room, then through other less appointed but well used dens and family rooms. The home looked to be well kept but extremely comfortable. Kitch noted the expensive lounging chairs and generous sectional couches. Collins opened a door at the far end of the floor plan, showing Kitch into his study.

Floor to ceiling windows made up the entire east wall. Thick, masculine blinds shaded the intense sunlight trying desperately to enter the room. Perfectly varnished, rich, mahogany stripping covered the other three walls. An assortment of well-placed shelves, subtle light boxes, and bookcases lined the wooden walls. A simple chair and ottoman sat perched by the towering glass. An even less imposing floor lamp seemed to spring from nowhere behind the chair, arching over the backrest to provide the perfect amount of light for reading or relaxing. Kitch wanted to walk over and plop himself down. He stood quietly, however, glancing at the final piece of furniture. A modern desk, huge and reassuring, braced the west wall of the office. And there, smothering the contents of a wooden inbox, was the grandest cat Kitch had ever seen.

Collins walked over to it, holding his index finger forward so the huge feline could have a sniff. After identifying his master, the cat turned its head, dropping its cheek into Collins' rolling knuckles. A resounding purr emanated from the huge body. Kitch clearly heard it, even while standing on the other side of the office.

"A remarkable cat in an even more impressive home," said the lieutenant. "I congratulate you on your success."

"Thank you. I've been fortunate."

"I must say, that's the largest cat I've ever seen."

"The breed is called Maine Coon," said Collins. "They're exceptionally large, very low key, and extremely loyal."

"The dog of the cat family, you might say?"

"Well said. This particular cat weighs almost thirty pounds. His name is Chambers. He's been with me six years. Ah, here comes his little playmate."

"Little?"

Kitch gazed upon the strangest cat he'd ever seen. It looked like a smaller version of a wild animal. As a domestic cat, the animal was huge. Looking at its body composition, Kitch estimated it tipped the scale at the same weight as the Maine Coon.

A Pound of Fur

This one had short fur and a very distinct musculature. The coloring seemed entirely unique, almost like an ocelot or a jaguar. Its eyes shone like the purest gold; when it looked at Kitch the lieutenant felt like genuflecting. Without a doubt it was the most mesmerizing creature he had ever seen.

"My God," he said. "What is that?"

"It's a Bengal Cat, Lieutenant, and a very rare one at that. It is the product of decades of selective breeding, using the rarest and most beautiful of all domestic cats. This particular animal came about from crossbreeding with an African Serval. That's what gives it its immense size."

Kitch walked over to the gorgeous feline. He could do nothing else after it had stared at him so fondly. When he came within three feet, Collins interjected.

"I wouldn't hold my hand out to him if I were you. He's not exactly tame."

Kitch looked at the Bengal, watched it curl its lip and raise one of its sturdy paws, preparing to strike. Collins moved quickly to intercede, putting his body in between the Bengal and Kitch.

"There, now, Galten," Collins cooed. "This is a guest in our home; I expect you to treat him as such."

Remarkably, the Bengal's mood shifted noticeably. It became almost docile; friendly even. It sauntered over to Kitch; curling its head as it approached him. A luxurious purr emanated from its insides.

Kitch looked to Collins for his approval and upon receiving it, bent down and allowed the Bengal to inspect him. He held his hands in check at first, but after sensing nothing but a loving curiosity in the animal, he reached out. Cupping the silky fur in his palms, Kitch began scratching the glorious creature. He felt overwhelmed, as though he was in the presence of royalty. The Bengal accepted Kitch's attention as his due and nothing more. After a few moments the big cat removed his jowls from Kitch's embrace. It rubbed against his body, nearly bowling Kitch over with its weight and coordination. Then it sauntered away, jumping up onto the desk to sit close to its companion.

The Main Coon raised its head slightly, saw who was invading its space, and then lowered its cheek onto its paws. In moments it fell fast asleep again.

"Extraordinary creatures, Mr. Collins."

"Call me Kevin."

"And you may call me Samuel."

A soundless alarm illuminated Collins' study.

"I believe breakfast is served," said Kitch's host, "if you'll follow me to the solarium."

Kitch took one last glance at Collins' feline children. He felt a pang of envy, even jealousy. How someone could amass such wealth and live contentedly with only a few companion animals was beyond his capacity. Family had always been his first priority.

They sat in a room surrounded by creature comforts of every sort. A simple but sturdy dining table centered the room perfectly. Along each wall in the solarium stood cat trees of all sizes, spaced between pillows, blankets and toys of every description. Some looked to be quite new; others had lost their original design long ago. It seemed a bizarre place to entertain a guest for a meal.

He sat in the chair furthest from the doorway, guided

there by Collins. As soon as he slid his chair in and grasped his napkin, two uniformed waiters entered the room bearing steaming plates of crepes prepared from scratch, containing the freshest blackberries and sour cream. Kitch's stomach growled noticeably as the pleasing aroma entered his nostrils. Even in his euphoric state, however, he noticed the men serving the meal didn't exactly have the look of everyday waiters. They were powerfully built, extremely coordinated, and they no doubt took orders from Collins.

"Thank you," he said as the man deftly set his plate in front of him. After responding that orange juice would suit him nicely, the uniformed server placed a glass of fresh squeezed juice along with an additional glass of ice next to his right hand. Another server attended to Collins' needs at the same time. After adroitly presenting the first course, the two men stood silently side by side.

Collins and Kitch ate in silence. Each subtly eyed the other as they consumed the delicious crepes. After scooping the excess blackberry juice from their plates, Collins finally broke the silence.

"How is the investigation coming along?"

"Unfortunately, clues have been hard to come by of late."

"Perhaps the perpetrator is laying low, or your attention has caused him to rethink his priorities."

"What makes you think the murderer is male?" asked Kitch.

"Do you think a woman would be capable of the type of brutality you've seen during your search?"

"In my profession, Mr. Collins, anything is possible."

The waiters re-entered the dining room. With little

wasted motion, they cleared away the crepe plates, replaced Collins' coffee with a fresh cup, topped off Kitch's orange juice and set a new glass of ice before both men. Satisfied at the condition of the table, the men left the room as quietly as they entered.

"Just a patriarchal blunder," said Collins.

"Perhaps," answered Kitch. "We haven't yet discovered any hard evidence that might result in an arrest."

"What service can I offer to assist you?"

Kitch smiled. "A confession would do nicely."

"Believe me, Sam, if I was the one behind these heinous acts, I'd save you the trouble. In a way I wish it was my work. As you can see, I love my cats, as I love all animals. I donate considerable sums to a great many shelters every year. I haven't lost any sleep over the conditions in which these abusers have met their deaths."

Kitch almost responded but held his tongue when the uniformed men returned. Instead of carrying plates, they rolled a sterling silver cart into the room. One of the men looked over the table, making sure every aspect of the breakfast service looked acceptable. The other man opened the serving tray's sliding window, revealing an assortment of side dishes surrounding two perfectly prepared dishes of eggs Benedict. Together, the two servers arranged the main plates and the side dishes on the table. With a glance at Collins, they closed the serving cart and quietly left the room.

"The meal is exquisite," said Kitch.

"I take pleasure in very few things," said Collins. "One of them is food, as you can see by my ample midsection."

"For an ex-military man, you've kept yourself in better shape than most."

"I don't remember ever telling you of my armed forces background."

The two men ate under a strained silence. Kitch had blundered by revealing his official interest in Collins. He tried his best to conceal it by thoroughly enjoying his eggs. They were, without a doubt, the best he'd ever tasted. The aroma of the accoutrements was enough to hinder rational thought.

Kitch looked at Collins through veiled eyelids. He saw the man eating contentedly, so he decided to follow suit. It would give him a chance to regroup as well as enjoy his food.

After a few minutes of softly clinking silverware, the two men pressed their plates forward a bit. Each finished their remaining orange juice, and then wiped their lips with napkins retrieved from their laps. Neither seemed eager to continue the conversation. Kitch waited for some explanation for Collins about his military years. Collins, ever the chess master, sat patiently, at ease with the lieutenant's discomfort. At length, Kitch spoke while Collins' men cleared away the table settings.

"Tell me, Kevin, if you love animals as much you say, why not devote some of your considerable resources to aiding the courts?"

"To what end?" asked Collins.

"Why not form a foundation to fund a special task force to find and prosecute animal abusers?"

"Similar to that which presently operates downtown?" he asked. "You must be joking."

"I never joke about the law."

"I also view the law very seriously. It's the adjudication I find sickeningly humorous."

"For example?"

"I could cite a dozen cases with little effort," said Collins. "A man beats a helpless puppy because of his insecure jealousy over his girlfriend. He stabs one of its eyes out, breaks both of its forepaws and all of its ribs. Do you know what his sentence was? Two months house arrest with six days work at an animal shelter."

Collins continued, clearly agitated. "A woman, high beyond belief, puts a litter of kittens in a microwave oven, turns it on for five minutes, and then stands there ignoring the screeching wails of the helpless, innocent animals. They die, one by one, exploding from the inside. Her sentence? Three months in county jail. She got out in eighteen days.

"Then there's this asshole assistant parks and recreation director up in San Jose who likes to kill neighborhood dogs. He weighs two fifty, maybe two sixty-five, and he attacks and kills a four-month-old Golden Retriever puppy without provocation. Then he has the balls to go on television and say the dog bit him and that's why he had to kill it, in self-defense.

"Any kindergartner would know that if you try to kill an animal, he'll bite you to save his life. But they'll let this guy off, just wait and see. He won't even lose his job or do any jail time. If there is a God, then these vigilantes as you call them are going to catch up with this guy real soon."

"You'd consider that form of street justice acceptable?"

"Goddamn right. Just take them around the back of the courthouse and put a bullet in their brain. End of story. One less asshole in the world."

"You seem rather distressed about official court proceedings against such people."

"Aren't you? It took you assholes five convictions to finally send a guy who was heavily involved in dogfighting to jail for any considerable stretch – five years – and we both know he'll be out in less than two."

"All the more reason for an expert team of vigilantes to take matters into their own hands, eh, Kevin?"

"I'm rooting for them all the way."

"Is that why you invited me to your home for this delicious breakfast?"

Collins cut a freshly baked cinnamon roll in quarters. He forked one of the steaming, syrupy sections into his mouth. He chewed for quite some time, savoring the delicious taste. After adding some ice to his refreshed orange juice, he took two measured swallows before setting his glass quietly on the table.

"I asked you here this morning to tell you I'm leaving shortly for Washington. I've been summoned to the pentagon for a briefing about a new crowd control product our engineers have been working on. I'll be gone until Tuesday."

Kitch stared at Collins. The man's face seemed to be etched in stone.

"And if I asked you to come downtown this second to answer some questions while tethered to a polygraph machine?"

"I'd have to respectfully decline."

"On what grounds?"

"I'm not exactly sure," said Collins, "but my lawyer would beat us to the station with a briefcase full of complaints regarding my illegal detainment."

As if on cue, the stunning Bengal walked into the breakfast room. It jumped onto the table with the grace of a ballerina. It sat, preening itself and looking at Kitch and Collins in separate turns. Yawning widely, it finally settled on a choice. It turned toward Kitch, striding carefully through the breakfast implements. Upon reaching him, the huge feline began purring loudly while pressing its cheek against Kitch's outstretched hand. It meowed lightly, as if talking to him.

"You have a gift, Sam," said Collins. "He rarely speaks to anyone outside of his immediately family."

"A stunning animal, if I may say so."

"I agree. Exactly why I chose him to come here and live with Chambers. I felt any less of a companion wouldn't complement him. I'm glad to say they get along famously. There were a few tussles at first, mostly just getting acquainted. After that they became fast friends, and now they defend each other against the staff and even me. If I raise my voice at one of them, the other quickly jumps in to protect his sibling. It's quite amusing. If I weren't such good friends with both of them, I doubt I'd have the courage to continue with the stern warnings I'm forced to give them from time to time."

"This cat," said Kitch, "would be a handful if irritated."

"And he's the weaker of the two," replied Collins. "Chambers may seem docile, but when the two of them wrestle, he usually gets the better of Galten."

Collins uttered a soft command, followed by the squeak that came from between his lips. The sleek Bengal leapt from the table immediately, darting out of the room without a backwards glance. He stood, waiting for Kitch to follow his prompt. When both men had left the dining area, two attendants swiftly cleared away the remaining plates, glasses and silver.

"You'll telephone when you return?" asked Kitch.

Collins nodded. "My driver will take you back to your office."

"Be careful, Kevin."

"I'm sorry?"

"I enjoy our conversations. But I caution you, I'll issue an order for your arrest the instant I feel it's warranted."

"Goodbye, Lieutenant."

When Collins closed the door, he turned to find one of his attendants waiting.

"Is my driver ready?" he asked the trim, clean cut man.

"Waiting in the garage, sir."

"The flight, and the helicopter?"

"All pre-arranged. The Lear is topped off and waiting at your private hangar. One of our choppers is already on the tarmac at the Casper airstrip. You should be at the compound in less than four hours."

"What is the status of the raid?"

"Hunt of Your Life is under our control. Turner has been freed and treated. They beat him pretty badly, but he'll survive. Everyone's waiting for your arrival."

"Our animals?"

"Stationed just down the hill from the compound. Three cages, all on one trailer. Along with their transport, we should be able to safely remove all the animals once our mission is complete."

"Any trouble from local law enforcement?"

"None. The area is so obscure I doubt any rangers or

highway patrol will happen by accidentally. Everything appears to be in good order."

"Good work, Clark," said Collins. "Put yourself in for a bonus at the end of the month."

"Take me along, sir. I'd be satisfied with that."

··· 28 ···

Byron Forney turned his ample head toward the valley below him. He heard the chopper charging up the hill before he ever saw a wisp of sand or flurry of wind. The silent, disciplined band of men had only moments before hustled him, his workforce, and his guests into the hot, dry sun outside the administration building. His parched mouth had nothing to do with the weather. A rank fear roiled in his stomach, a physical certainty telling him something horrible was about to happen. He glanced over at Turner, who stood talking to another man, obviously one of the leaders of the highly trained group of soldiers.

The helicopter exploded over the hillside in a fusion of noise, fluid motion, and purpose. Forney realized it was too late. He had acted foolishly by underestimating his opponent. With the cache of weapons he had at his disposal, he didn't think anyone would have the nerve to attack them.

With its rotors thumping loudly, the helicopter hovered over the center of the compound. Everyone except for Forney, his son, and a belligerent guest shielded their eyes from the whirling dirt and sand. They pressed their chins to their necks while straining against their handcuffs, then slammed their eyes shut, twisting their heads as the hard grains pelted their eyelids.

The chopper touched down. The pilot quickly shut down the engines, securing the cabin for departure. When the rotors had reached a manageable tempo, he gave his commander thumbs up.

A man in aviator sunglasses exited the passenger seat of the chopper smoothly. He reached back into the cabin for a hat and a weapon, the shotgun he always carried during a raid. Ignoring the people crowded around him, he walked directly over to Turner.

"Okay?" he asked, nodding once.

Turner nodded. "Nothing that won't heal. Thanks for getting everyone here so fast, boss."

Collins nodded. He held out his hand, shaking Turner's lightly. He then took Michaels' hand, grasping it firmly.

"Excellent work. I heard you had some trouble with the raid. Everyone okay?"

"Thanks, boss. Two of our men are injured badly. Two died in the firefight."

Collins nodded dispassionately. "Where's the grizzly?"

"Inside that tented structure," said Michaels. "He's wide awake and pissed off. We haven't fed him today."

Collins smiled, turned his gaze to the owner of Hunt of Your Life.

Forney shook his head, blinking sand from his eyes. He shouted at Collins.

"I know who you are, asshole. You have no right to come

here and interrupt my business. This is private property; I'm ordering you off the premises, and I mean now."

Collins shook his head, looking at the man who had nearly killed his associate. At times his distaste for people made him ill. Forney looked exactly like what he was, an amoral, non-caring, disgusting mistake of biology. Collins felt half ready to turn the shotgun toward him and fire both barrels at the fat, sweaty belly. Instead, he slowly strolled over and confronted him.

"Is this your son?" he asked, waving his shotgun at the younger Forney.

"If it's any business of yours, yes, he's my son."

"I'm in a charitable mood, Forney, so I'll make you a deal. The first hunt today will pit one of you against that grizzly. I'll let you decide, you or your son, one-on-one against the bear."

"What the hell are you all about, anyway?"

Steely eyed, Collins responded. "Stopping assholes like you. Now pick. You've got five seconds."

Forney stared at Collins, hatred streaming from his eyes. He waited, one second, then two, until it seemed he would refuse.

"M-me," he finally stuttered. "I'll go in, on one condition, though. Let my son go free."

Collins spat on the ground at Forney's feet. He turned to the three men standing guard by the large tent. "Let's see the bear."

··· 29 ···

It took a twelve-ton forklift to lift the massive cage containing the grizzly. The bear growled menacingly at the man driving it. When the forks had been inserted all the way underneath the cage, it charged the bars closest to the driver, crashing against the cage wall. An immense, hairy paw shot through an opening, the huge claws swiping within inches of the metal housing protecting the driver. As the bear struggled to reach his quarry, clouds of metallic flecks mixed with dust drifted in the wind.

Collins' man hoisted the cage. The grizzly backed away from the bars, suddenly fearful. The teetering floor of its enclosure became its primary focus. It settled back down on all fours, still baring its huge teeth.

When the forklift passed under the roof of the tent structure, the bear reacted to the first daylight it had seen in weeks. It raised its huge nose to the sky, squinting under the piercing Wyoming sun. It blinked its eyes, trying to block the sand carried by the stiff wind blowing through the compound.

As the forklift approached the hunting arena, the huge bear gazed at the people gathered outside the main gate. The engine quieted, the wheels slowed and then stopped. The bear looked up and saw Byron Forney standing less than ten feet in front of him.

Swiftly, violently, and without regard for pain or punishment, the grizzly charged his captor. The momentum of the impact against the bars nearly knocked the heavy cage from the forks on the lift. If Collins' man hadn't left them tilted slightly upward, the enraged animal might have driven the huge enclosure onto the ground in front of Forney. Held in place by elevation and gravity, the cage nonetheless buckled and shook as the grizzly tried to reach him.

"Looks like he remembers you," said Collins.

Forney's skin sagged around his skull. Ashen and quivering, it revealed exactly what rushed through his mind as he watched the bear lunging toward him. His eyes, bigger than billiard balls and filled with horror, stared at the gigantic creature. It seemed as though everything around him had disappeared. Only the grizzly bear remained, filling his world like a nightmare he couldn't dismiss.

"You men know what to do."

With eerie military precision, Collins' men ushered everyone but Forney up onto the observation decks. No one voiced any objections. They walked timidly up the creaking steps, their fear silencing any challenge against the strange man in the aviator sunglasses.

When the employees and guests were situated at different points along the multi-acre spread, Michaels gave Collins a sign of thumbs up.

"Mr. Forney," said Collins, "I want Turner to escort you to your gate. Before you go in you can shout apologies to your guests, and to your employees, for sentencing them to death."

"Where's my weapons?" asked Forney.

Collins stared silently through his sunglasses.

"Give me a Goddamn weapon!"

"How does it feel, Forney?" asked Collins. "How does it feel to suddenly realize you're being hunted, and you have no chance of survival?"

"We're human beings!" Forney shouted. "They're just animals! We have a God given right to hunt them down if we want!"

Collins spit in Forney's face. He slapped the whining fat man hard across the cheek. "Take him up to the north gate."

Collins looked back at the man driving the forklift. He twirled two fingers in the air before pointing to the south gate. As the machine growled smoke, pushing its way toward the fence, he walked alongside it. The grizzly, somewhat calmer now without Forney in the area, sat in its cage eyeing him calmly.

Collins marveled at the size of the beast. The huge snout, filled with heavy, sharp teeth, and the massive paws containing the largest claws of any land mammal in North America, gave the bear its frightening look. By contrast, the rounded ears and the gorgeous coat made the grizzly look like an oversized teddy bear.

Collins changed direction, walking a little closer to the cage. Instantly, the grizzly assumed an offensive stance. It growled menacingly, challenging him to move closer.

"Alright, friend," said Collins, moving away again. "You win."

A **Pound** of **Fur**

The forklift clanged up against the gate structure. Collins released the chain locks, letting the bars connecting the gate to the fence fall inward toward the hunting grounds. The gate followed, crashing to the ground in a spray of rocks and dirt.

"Don't open the cage just yet," Collins ordered. "I want to wait until he enters the hunting grounds."

Turner walked Forney up to the north gate. The closer they got the more belligerent the man became.

"You'll all hang for this, I swear it!" he shouted through the spittle dangling from his lips. "This is my company; it's all legal. We have every right to be here doing what we're doing."

"You don't get it, do you, Forney," said Turner, calmly. "When the sun goes down today, Hunt of Your Life will no longer exist. Everyone here will be dead, the entire complex burned to the ground. The only items we'll take with us are the animals you'd planned to kill."

Turner kicked the gate open so hard it slammed against the fence line. He shoved Forney through the opening.

"Don't you eat meat from the grocery store?" Forney cried. "You're a fucking hypocrite, Turner. You're just a piss poor liberal who can't stand the fact that some people have the balls to hunt wild animals."

"Yea, that's it. Maybe you can explain it to the bear. He should be up here in about five minutes." Turner waved to the man guarding the nearest tower. Immediately, the man grabbed his shoulder mike, signaling Collins that all was ready.

··· 30 ···

Like a drawbridge with its restraints severed, the door on the grizzly's cage crashed down on top of the prone gate. It bounced a little, wobbled, and then settled, leaning slightly to the left. The bear, concerned about its newfound freedom, sat unmoving, looking at Collins and the man driving the forklift. The huge nose went into overdrive, sniffing in every direction. It seemed to sense something compelling in the direction of the north gate but preferred to wait a moment longer.

"See how smart he is?" said Collins. "Even with a clear path to freedom, he won't venture out of that cage until he's sure it's safe. What a magnificent animal."

Slowly, methodically, the giant grizzly stepped toward the open doorway of his cage. Snuffling every inch of his path, the bear never once looked at Collins. When it reached the opening, it stood still, sniffing vigorously.

In an explosion of fur and muscle, the grizzly ran through the opening. It galloped about thirty feet, stopped, and turned back to look at the cage. The men who'd released it languished quietly on the other side of the fence line. In the bear's estimation they constituted no threat. It turned, raising its nose high in the air. Inhaling and exhaling rapidly, the bear took stock of its surroundings.

"The grizzly is loose in the hunting grounds!" shouted one of the observers. He and another guest stood with two of Collins' men on the viewing platform closest to the south gate. "The bear's loose!" he shouted again, trying to relay the message to the next platform.

When Forney finally heard the muted warning, he went berserk. It seemed as though he didn't really believe Turner and his friends would do such a thing. Slamming up against the gate, he shouted at the men blocking his way to safety.

"Let me out! Let me out, Goddammit! You can't do this!"

In the midst of his rant, Forney heard his son calling to him. He looked over to his left, at a viewing platform where Junior lay prone on his stomach. He held his arm over the side. Waving his hand up toward the platform, he called to his father.

"C'mon, Dad, over here. I'll pull you up."

The grizzly showed great interest in the raucous shouting. In an instant, it forgot all about the two men who'd set him free. The wind brought a host of smells into his nostrils. It trotted through the sparse brush toward the north gate.

Panting and sweating, Forney reached his son's platform. He looked up at the outstretched hand, a good four feet beyond his reach.

"Can't you bring yourself down any farther?" he asked his son.

Junior locked his ankles together around a fencepost. He dangled his body precariously over the edge, cutting the space between his father and his hand by another two feet.

"You'll have to jump for it," he said. "I can't go any lower. I'm barely hanging on as it is."

"Damn it, Junior, when…"

"Hurry, Dad, I can see it."

Forney forgot his protests. As much as an out of shape, sixty-two-year-old man could, he jumped again and again, trying to grasp his son's hand. He had nearly lost hope when he heard the horrible growl of a grizzly bear on the hunt. Miraculously, with one heaving effort, he lunged up, grabbing his son's hand in an iron grip. Pulling with all his might, he yanked Junior over the edge of the platform. Both men fell hard onto the caked dirt and rock of the hunting area. Initially stunned, father and son rolled over, holding their backs, knees, and whatever else took a beating in the fall. The sound of heavy footfalls brought them back to reality.

"Stop this!" Gloria Dunn shouted from her viewing platform. "You've got to stop this right now!" She yelled into the impassive face of one of Collins' men. "What kind of people are you?"

The grizzly crested the final hill fronting the north gate. It took one look at Byron Forney and launched into a full gallop. A low, menacing snarl kept pace with the huge strides. The bear focused entirely on Forney, ignoring Junior completely.

Forney knew he couldn't outrun it. There were no trees to climb. He had no option except…

He grabbed his son by the shoulders, shoving him into the path of the charging bear. Even while hearing his son's terrified screams, he ran in the opposite direction as fast as he could. He had gravity on his side at least; the south gate was nearly fifty feet lower in elevation than the north.

A Pound of Fur

Junior threw his hands up as he fell into the arms of the grizzly. He felt his left shoulder crumple with a sickening echo of bones cracking as the bear pounced.

Instead of mauling him, the grizzly lifted Junior into the air, violently flinging him aside. Blood splattered everywhere as the inert body slapped and rolled against the hard-caked dirt. Junior lay motionless, whimpering like a child.

The bear's left ear twitched, the head turned, the black, moist nose lifted into the air. It took two quick sniffs and bounded toward the south gate. A blast of rage poured forth from its throat as it chased after Forney.

"Someone go to him!" Gloria screamed. "He's badly hurt, can't you see that?" She looked across the hunting grounds at Collins. "Shoot that bear before it kills them both!"

Collins watched Forney struggling over the last two acres toward the south gate. He could tell the man's hysteria had pushed him beyond all physical endurance. He had nothing left. He looked across the arena at the screaming woman. He barely heard her.

With a snarl boiling from venomous hatred, the grizzly charged over the hill. When it saw Forney again, it vaulted over a large rock, launching himself at his quarry. With outstretched paws, he knocked Forney flat on his stomach, gouging a huge swath of skin from the man's back.

Forney screamed hysterically, the shriek of a man who knew a horrible death loomed only a breath away. He rolled over, bellowing anew as the deep gashes on his back chafed against the hard dirt and rock. He rolled again and again, smelling the grizzly's rancid breath every time the sun warmed his face.

The bear paced itself, following Forney's twisting body along the ground. With a monstrous lunge, it lashed out with its mighty jaws, catching Forney's right shin in its teeth. It clamped down, shook its huge head.

Gloria Dunn screamed frantically. Forney's foot tore loose from the cracked shin bones in the bear's mouth. The man summoned strength available only to those fueled by panicked terror. Forgetting about his back and right foot, he rolled over onto his stomach. Planting his hands, he pushed himself up on his knees. He began screaming prayers to his God, pleading with him to save his humble servant from the growling giant facing him.

Seething with desire to kill the man who had shot his mate and taken his cubs, the bear lashed out at the ground in front of Forney. Striking again and again while roaring ferociously, it finally charged.

With one mighty swipe, the grizzly decapitated Forney. The man's head flew thirty-five feet through the air, bouncing at the base of the platform where Gloria Dunn knelt, vomiting over the railing. Forney's body slumped to the ground, lying still before the head came to rest nearly fifty feet away.

The grizzly pounced on the body. Thinking of its lost family, it tore the remains to shreds in a fit of vicious rage.

"Shoot the bear," Collins ordered into his shoulder mike.

Instantly, four rifles arose from different locations around the hunting grounds. With perfect precision, four darts zipped across the arena simultaneously. They found their target together in the rump of the grizzly bear.

The sedative worked extremely fast. The bear stumbled

about for a minute before falling over on its side. It lay there, breathing evenly, blood and skin draped around its teeth.

The guests and employees of Hunt of Your Life stood or sat on the observation platforms, scared beyond sanity. Every one of them knew the horrific scene with the grizzly would not be the day's final act. They bellowed at Collins and his men, pleading with them to stop the killing.

Junior rolled up on his fat rump, holding his shoulder and sobbing like a child. He wailed, calling for his Dad to help him. He looked around the hunting grounds, dazed. He couldn't even recall how he'd found his way inside the fence line. He swallowed, hard, feeling the parched Wyoming wind draining his body of fluids.

He focused on one of the observation towers. He saw men standing atop the boards, looking at him. He stumbled in their direction, asking for help in a weak, scratchy voice.

Collins tapped his mike. "Bring up the tigers."

In the time it took for his men to lift the bear with a winch and place it back into its cage, a Kenworth W900 hauling massive, custom built trailers slowly climbed the hill toward the entrance of Hunt of Your Life. When it passed through the gates and parked next to the hunting grounds, the closest observation platforms went eerily silent. Even those at the north end of the compound could see the immense bodies stalking back and forth within the bars. Gloria Dunn's blood ran cold when she looked into the cages and saw what prowled within.

Three massive Siberian tigers, young, male, and ravenous, paced back and forth behind titanium bars. Every few seconds a hollow howl squeezed through the railing, a signal from the inhabitants of the cages that they felt apprehensive, if not downright incensed about their situation.

Each of the tigers weighed over six hundred pounds. All three looked fit, fierce and anxious to be released.

Collins walked toward the trailers. He eyed the cats as they stalked the perimeter of their cage. Every few seconds one would stop, turn its great head and stare at the strange man strolling toward the truck. Then it would resume its pacing, chuffing every few seconds.

Collins sensed the tigers' uneasiness. After surviving quite a trip, they had waited impatiently at a complex outside of Casper for weeks.

"It was worth it," he said. "Now you can avenge your brothers and sisters."

The tigers paced back and forth, calling out to each other quietly.

"Alright," said Collins into his shoulder microphone. "Move the rest into the hunting grounds. Leave the woman on the platform. She's not to be harmed during this hunt."

Without answering, Collins' men ushered the guests and employees of the captive hunting complex toward the gates. Many of them fought back, swearing at the men, trying to swarm them and take their guns. They had to shoot one of the employees; the man had nearly ripped a weapon from his guard and broken free.

Gloria Dunn slapped, scratched, and screamed at the men escorting her husband to the east gate. She spat at them, finally jumping into her husband's arms, clinging to him so forcefully it took three of Collins' men try pry her away. Two remained behind, holding her arms while deflecting her kicks. Her husband passed through the gate. She called his name frantically, shouting her love and support through lips stained with sweat and bile. Her husband looked back only once. His eyes revealed two emotions, love and terror.

Collins' men began positioning the tigers in front of the south, east, and west gates. The forklift trundled back and forth, carefully lifting each cage from its trailer and depositing them gently in front of the entrances. As they arrived, other men secured the locking mechanisms.

The tigers could sense the anticipation of everyone around them. The men working on the fence line exuded tension in the beads of sweat inching down their foreheads. Those gathered inside the enclosed area radiated raw fear. The cats became animated, agitated even. They seemed to understand their roles in the strange scenario. Their pacing increased; their vocalizations grew louder. They spoke to each other, calling out to the other gates.

Collins watched closely as the operation commenced. They had already been at the hunting camp for four hours. So far, their luck had held as far as law enforcement. Their radios showed no signals whatsoever. It would be tragic if a lone trooper happened by, deciding on a whim to drive up the mountain for a casual look-see. He checked his watch. With luck they'd be finished, have all the animals loaded onto the trailers, and away in another six hours.

When all the cages were secured, Collins stepped onto the south platform. He could see the captives milling about at the top of the windblown arena. One of his men handed him a megaphone. He depressed the trigger while pointing it toward the north gate.

"You chose this destiny the day you took up arms against defenseless, terrified animals. It makes no difference whether you took part in the hunts or helped initiate them. All of you are guilty, and today you'll die facing cousins of the very creatures you tormented."

Collins looked at his victims. Five guests and nine employees, and somewhere at the top of the arena sat Junior. Badly hurt and weak from loss of blood, he didn't stand a chance against the tigers. No one did, but Collins figured they would collapse on the wounded man first. As with all natural hunters, they would cull the old, sick and weak from the herd before turning on the others.

Fourteen against three, thought Collins. He wondered for a moment what would happen if he gave the guests their weapons. The massacre would still occur, but one of the tigers would be injured or even killed. He wouldn't allow that.

"Open the gates."

··· 31 ···

The tigers surged out of their cages the instant the doors fell. From the south, the largest of the three dashed straight ahead, meeting the other two at the intersection of the east and west gates. A rumbling growl accompanied the immense cat as he ran to meet his brothers. They sniffed each other for a bit, even sparred a few times.

The wind shifted, bringing the scent of terror to their nostrils. Prey, they intoned to each other. At six hundred eighty pounds, the dominant tiger bounded up a rise, hopping soundlessly onto a rock. The new vantage point gave him an unobstructed view of the hunting grounds. A second later he dropped to his stomach. The other tigers immediately followed suit.

Collins watched in utter fascination. Tigers hunted mostly by themselves, but present circumstances had coerced these animals into a loose alliance. He wondered what would occur the moment they attacked.

With muscles tensed, they crawled silently up the hill. Their heads never rose more than an inch above the ground. The dirt beneath their noses shot forward as they exhaled.

The eyes, wide open, never left their prey for an instant. Only the ears moved, catching every sound. Mostly, they pointed backwards, an attack position on any big cat. They twitched forward or to the side every few seconds, hearing everything. The hair along their spines stood straight up.

"They're coming," said Agosto Capuana, standing next to the north gate. "One straight for us and the other two from the sides." The Italian seemed calm, but his quivering hands gave him away.

"That's crazy," said Doug Chaney. "Tigers are solo hunters. The males never band together like that."

Lawrence Tannenbaum, a former NFL all pro tackle, looked at the cats. "Well, they're doing it now."

"Fuckin' A," echoed Sid Felton, an industrial contractor from Denver. "If they're not working together then I'm back home dreaming."

Gloria called out to her husband. "Doug, Look at the workers! Maybe you can escape by copying what they're doing."

All four men looked to their left. The employees, men obviously familiar with the hunting grounds, had formed a human chain against the fence between the observation platforms. Four of them had secured their bodies on each other's shoulders, creating a serviceable ladder. If they could get one more man atop the others, they would be able to scale the twenty-foot fence line to freedom. Once one man held the top of the fence, the others could scramble up and over. Collins' men could do little to stop them. Without the platforms, they had no leverage to drive them back into the arena.

A **Pound** of **Fur**

The tigers saw the men clinging to the fence. The fur on their backs flared.

"Watch out!" Gloria screamed.

The cat on the right flank shot forward toward the line of employees. The men had time only to turn before it launched itself into the middle of their makeshift ladder. With a vicious snarl, the tiger crashed into two of the men.

The others fell from the fence line, too terrified to scream. They collapsed in a heap of broken bones, their eyes darting in every direction. Ignoring the stabbing pain of their injuries, they sought only to locate the enraged animals.

The charging tiger collapsed onto the men taken in the charge. The huge body crushed one of them, immobilizing him completely. The other fared even worse, for the tiger's jaws had found his throat before they even hit the ground. The fangs closed around the man's neck, shattering his larynx.

With the limp body still dangling from its mouth, the tiger turned toward the other man. It dropped the first carcass before pouncing on the second worker. A shriek of unspeakable agony hurtled around the grounds, sending goose bumps along the skin of almost everyone present.

Collins watched dispassionately. What happened next no one would ever forget, but in his mind the slaughter represented justice. Anyone who would partake in the brutality these people engaged in deserved what they got. He removed his sunglasses, wiped the bridge of his nose with his fingers, and replaced them.

Upon witnessing the blood and death before them, the other two tigers reacted brutally. The dominant male galloped through the running bodies, striking anything that moved.

With claws fully exposed, it launched itself from victim to victim, fiercely slashing at their backs, legs, and buttocks.

One by one the people in the hunting grounds crumpled. As well as they could, they watched the tiger chasing the others, knocking them askew as blood exploded from their wounds.

Turning toward safety in the opposite direction, they locked eyes with the third tiger. This animal, unlike his larger brother, had no desire to rush through the killing grounds indiscriminately. It walked toward them slowly, determined, waiting to pick a target. It eyed Sid Felton, especially his shredded pants and the equally mauled legs. Having made its judgment, it charged without mercy.

The few that remained hurled rocks, plants and dirt at the tiger as it approached Felton. Like a locomotive, the tiger slammed into the man's midsection, twirling his body and knocking him face first into the dirt.

In a feral rage it slashed Felton's throat, sending blood and flayed skin flying. The big cat sniffed his kill for a moment, verifying the man's death. Then it moved on, searching for another victim.

The first tiger joined the third, slowly pursuing prey. Both cats' faces shone crimson with the blood of their victims. They cornered three of the Hunt of Your Life employees by the fence. Each held out hope that he would be the one they spared. One actually tried climbing the wood paneled fence. The last thing he heard or felt were his bloody fingernails scratching in vain against the weathered wood.

They attacked as one, tearing the man's legs from his body. As he bellowed hideously, they bit into his midsection, ripping him in half. The other two employees, initially too shaken to move, took off running toward the south gate.

The tigers sprinted away from the dead carcass. In an instant they wrestled them to the ground. The terrible screaming began anew as the cats tore into their bodies. Both tigers collapsed on the throats of their victims. A sickening gurgling sound rose from the dirt. The tigers stood again, sniffing the air for fresh prey.

The dominant male chased Doug Chaney relentlessly, pushing him toward the south gate. Although badly injured, Chaney managed to keep a steady stride through the hunting grounds. He kept enough of the rocks and brush between him and the tiger to slow it down, or so he thought. He could hear Gloria somewhere in the background, yelling, giving him instructions, relaying the location of the tiger.

As he loped over the final mound, Chaney saw the south gate. The gate and the cage door lay open on the ground. As he ran, he wondered if he might be able to jump into the cage and close the bars behind him.

He heard the pounding feet beside him on his left. Gloria screamed, telling him to run faster. His mouth and throat throbbed. He ran as well as he could, twenty more steps, fifteen, ten.

Chaney leapt for the cage. He flew through the doorway, crashing onto the bars at the rear of the enclosure. Up quickly, he turned and limped toward the entrance. As he bent down and grasped the rough metal bars, he yanked the door with every bit of strength he had. After trying again, he lifted his eyes. The tiger had placed one massive paw on the far end of the gate.

Chaney locked eyes with the animal. It didn't approach right away, and somehow Chaney understood.

Perched on an observation deck close by, Gloria screamed for her husband's life. She begged and cursed the men who'd taken them all prisoner. She pleaded one final time, looking directly at Collins' aviator sunglasses.

"Stop this!" she shrieked. "Shoot the tigers now. Spare my husband. You heartless bastard, do you have one selfless bone in your body?"

Collins said nothing. He locked eyes with Gloria Dunn as she demanded a reprieve for her husband. As the wind swept her last question away, he turned and looked toward the south gate.

Gloria shifted her gaze as well. What she saw caused her to squeal like a newborn sow.

Chaney braced himself against the back of the cage. His heart stopped when the tiger stepped forward between the bars. He lashed out with his booted foot, kicking toward the striped face. The tiger backed away a step, evaluating. Then it moved carefully forward, this time countering with its massive paw every time Chaney attempted to connect with his boot.

With claws extended, the tiger caught hold of Chaney's leg, pulling its prey forward. It yanked tentatively, without success. Then it raised its eyes, watching the man's knuckles grip the bars desperately.

Chaney knew his time had come. The tiger had played with him to this point, but very soon it would tear into him as his brothers had ripped into the other guests and employees. With his last breath, he understood the panic and despair felt by a hunted animal.

A Pound of Fur

With one mighty heave the massive tiger pulled him completely underneath its body. It chomped down on Chaney's face, crushing most of the bones. The muffled screams of the dying man could only be heard by those close to him; his wife, Collins, and a handful of Collins' men. The tiger wrenched the skull back and forth, breaking Chaney's neck.

Gloria snapped. She had gone utterly mad watching her husband die. She tore herself away from her captors, jumping down the stairs a flight at a time. As she reached the dirt at the base of the observation deck, Collins signaled two of his men. They joined those who had been guarding Gloria. They caught her ten feet from the south gate.

She peered anxiously through the bars of the cage. Her husband's head dangled to the side, held onto the body only by a few strands of muscle and sinew. The tiger never looked up; instead it lay across Chaney's body, tearing away chunks of flesh.

Gloria's face became a freakish mask of horror and disbelief. She stomped her feet, trying to crush the toes of her captors. She swung her elbows wildly, hoping to connect with a nose or an eye socket.

"You bastards! You heartless, fucking bastards! I'll see all of you hang for this!" The four men wrestled against her tirade; they had a difficult time restraining her.

Collins radio sparked. "Go ahead," he said after depressing the switch.

"Only one man left, chief, aside from Junior."

"Where are they?" asked Collins.

Michaels looked down into the hunting grounds. "Junior's wedged into a shady corner about a hundred feet west of the north gate. Capuana's giving the two cats up here a run for their money. I'm not sure if they're tired, sated, or bored, but the Italian's got them guessing. Every time they get ready to attack, he uses whatever foliage he can find to dupe them. He can run like the wind, too."

"Where is he right now?"

"He's between the east and north gates."

"Shoot one of his legs out."

"Say again, boss?"

"We don't have all day. We've been lucky so far as it is. Put a bullet in one of his knees and let's finish this."

"Understood."

Reluctantly, Michaels relayed the order. He almost suggested they spare the man. Everyone else, including the employees, had run wildly about the grounds. The tigers had dispatched them easily. Capuana had stayed behind, coyly fading into the fence line. He made himself as insignificant as possible. Had he not run out of comrades, the ploy might have saved him. After the tigers had killed everyone else, however, two of them came looking for him.

He was bracing himself against a tree trunk when the shot rang out. The bullet entered the back of his leg, shattering his kneecap. Even through excruciating pain, he held his place behind the tree. Lifting his leg, he lessened the sting of the bullet.

The tigers sensed a wounded animal. One broke away from the tree, taking a wide arc to the rear. The other kept Capuana occupied, lunging side to side and striking with an unsheathed paw.

A **Pound** of Fur

Crouching, the first tiger stalked the limping man. When its counterpart caught hold of Capuana's sleeve, it charged.

Capuana never saw it coming; his attention lay solely on his shredded jacket and how to release it without giving the animal an edge.

The six-hundred-pound body flattened him against the tree. The impact knocked him cold, a fortunate occurrence. In a feral rage, the two tigers slashed at the body mercilessly, dismembering it.

They stood there, sniffing what remained.

The dominant male appeared, climbing over a boulder to address his brothers. Lifting its striped head, the dusky nose began quivering. Chaney's blood dripped aimlessly from its chin. It chuffed, and then sniffed again. It gazed down at Capuana's broken body. After looking at his brothers one last time, it sprang away in a shower of pebbles and dust.

The other tigers followed. The silent signal given to them by their leader gave them no alternative. They marched uphill through the hot wind, toward the top of the hunting grounds. The leader changed course slightly; his compass directed him to a spot directly west of the north gate.

After seeing his father mauled to death by the grizzly, Junior had crawled into the shade of the northern fence line. He sat favoring his left shoulder, keeping it away from the coarse wood. He had wailed like a baby when he saw the bear chasing his father. After hearing of his death from the other guests, he moaned and sobbed, but held his position. Never once did he venture away from the shaded barrier.

Even when everyone entered the hunting grounds, he kept quiet, motionless. When the tigers charged up the ridge, beginning their attack, only his heartbeat and breathing quickened. He stayed still, letting the cats focus on the chaotic sprinting of the others. As the cats disappeared through the acreage, he felt a moment of relief; perhaps he would be spared after all.

He heard the dominant male coming before he saw him. The heavy footfalls and low grunting jarred him from his mental stupor. Without moving his head he opened his eyes. Looking up through half closed lids, he saw it walking calmly toward him.

Thirty paces before reaching Junior, it stopped. The great striped head turned, checking on the progress of his brothers. One by one, the two other tigers came abreast of their leader. They, too, sniffed deliberately, wary of the grizzly bear's scent. Watching, sniffing, listening, the three cats coolly evaluated the scene before them.

Junior's body began shaking uncontrollably. He looked at the tigers, watching them preen themselves. Intent on their task, they seemed to be in no hurry.

An eerie calm had settled over the arena. Only the sound of the wind and the few leaves dancing with it disturbed the stillness. Collins and his men stood motionless. They had planned the raid on Hunt of Your Life meticulously. In seconds it would be complete.

Turner occupied the west platform with Michaels. He looked out onto the hunting grounds. Mangled, blood-soaked bodies lay everywhere. A few unsullied hairs fluttered in the wind; other than that, human life in the compound had been stilled, all except Junior.

A Pound of Fur

Turner felt nothing for them. Junior, however, held a special place in his heart. It was he who had inflicted most of his injuries. Every so often Junior had visited him in the slaughterhouse, tormenting him by re-opening wounds or placing a foot on his broken bones. It didn't seem so much like torture, not in a military sense. Junior enjoyed inflicting pain as any psychopath would, the perfect offspring of a man raised with no moral compass.

Junior sneezed. He tried his best to disguise the reflex by not moving, but the tigers needed no other incentive. All three rose as one, their lips curling back. Junior looked at the huge fangs, sobbing as quietly as he could. As the tigers marched toward him, he broke, screaming a rebellious curse in Turner's direction.

"What you're doing is worse than anything we've ever done! You bastards will pay for this! God's going to condemn you to hell!"

As he spat out his last remark, he felt the bones and muscles of a burly paw crushing his foot. He tried contorting his body, keeping it in line with his revolving ankle. Forgetting where he was for a moment, he swung a fist at the offending limb. The pain increased as the tiger's paw suddenly carried more weight. He whimpered.

The three cats smelled fresh blood. They moved in, slowly, the lead male in front, the other two on either side. The beautifully colored faces sank, sniffing the last living body in the hunting grounds. Tongues appeared, licking the sweet blood.

The last joyful moment of his life occurred when Junior felt the tongues tickling his body. His respite turned to horror as the lead male bit down. The other two tigers settled in, crouching on their forepaws. Each of them chomped on Junior's torso, feeling flesh and muscle flay between their teeth.

After a moment of harrowing agony, the silence of the Wyoming wilderness returned.

··· 32 ···

"Michaels," said Collins, "Dart the tigers. I want every animal in this compound loaded onto the trucks in two hours. Proceed to the shipping terminal at the Casper airport. There'll be four choppers waiting to take the cages to their respective locations. They'll only be there for an hour after you inform them you're coming. I know that's tight planning, but we'll be drawing enough attention as it is. Get the cages loaded onto the choppers as quickly as you can and then get to your transports."

"On it, boss," answered Michaels. "What about the compound?"

"Burn it. Set the timers for five hours. Everyone should be long gone by then." Collins looked at Turner and then at Gloria Dunn. "Let's go."

"I'm not going anywhere with you, you murderer."

"That's right," said Collins. "You're not."

Gloria swallowed the next invective. She suddenly felt a cold fist gripping her heart. She looked at Collins, seeing him in a new light. Murdering her husband was bad enough; she wondered about his plans for her.

Turner motioned for her to follow Collins. She did so, understanding that the men surrounding her would just as soon kill her as take any more of her insults. She also knew that resistance would gain her nothing. Try as she might, she'd never overpower a group of strong men, even if they didn't have weapons.

The small group walked past the office and down the driveway about fifty yards. As she walked, Gloria felt the ground under her feet vibrate as a helicopter began turning its rotors. She looked back at the chopper. The man working the controls had the same stoic expression as all of Collins' men.

"So, what now?" she asked the man walking in front of her. "Dodge ball?"

"Not exactly," said Collins. He came to a halt about half-way down the driveway. Raising his arm, he pointed to a Range Rover parked less than a few hundred yards away. Still residing on Hunt of Your Life property, the vehicle would be hard to see from the main highway.

"That's yours, isn't it?" he asked.

"So?"

"Watch the front passenger window."

Collins raised his rifle, peering through the scope. After aiming for less than a second, he squeezed off one round. The window of the Range Rover silently shattered.

"When you get to the jeep," said Collins, "you'll notice the driver's side window shot out as well. The keys are in the ignition."

"You're letting me go?" asked Gloria, wide-eyed.

"That's entirely up to you."

"So I just walk down there, turn the keys and I'm gone, right?"

"I'd run if I were you."

As Collins chambered the next round, Gloria Dunn's skin crawled. From where she stood, she had perfect line of sight to Collins, his hunting rifle, and the helicopter. She watched him turn his attention to the pilot. After receiving thumbs up, he turned back to Gloria.

"Nice meeting you, Ms. Dunn."

She ran down the driveway as fast as she could.

··· 33 ···

Collins hopped into the back of the helicopter. The runners had already left the ground as Turner and Michaels took their seats. The pilot increased power, sending sand and debris flying in all directions. Collins looked out the nearest window, checking the progress of his team. One truck had already been loaded; the second trailer had two cages aboard. They'd be gone in less than an hour.

"Take a wide circle before returning to the compound," he said to his pilot. "Then head straight for her."

Gloria jogged toward the Range Rover as best she could. Her feet already screamed from the abuse they were taking in the loosely tied military boots. She might have taken a moment to lace them up tighter had she not been so terrified.

Her musings ended when she heard the chopper rotors explode over the hill. Turning, she saw the helicopter's nose drop as the pilot accelerated toward her. Three hundred yards away, it would be on top her in seconds.

She had no idea what to do. No one could outrun a chopper on foot. Even the fastest land animal in the world wouldn't have a chance. Turning her head forward again, she focused her eyes on her vehicle. Every step she took brought her closer to freedom.

A Pound of Fur

The first bullet slashed into the ground six feet to her left. Her body jerked to the right, a spasm in response to the proximity of the shot.

The chopper roared by her right ear, driving dirt and rocks into her body and face. She threw her hands up, trying to cover her eyes. The dirt flew in every direction, stinging her neck, cheeks, ears and eyes.

Another shot rang out. Gloria felt the ground explode underneath her right foot. Even with the protection of the heavy boot her foot cried out from the stinging impact. She stumbled, but rose quickly, stubbornly determined to make her goal.

Before she even looked up, the helicopter zoomed by her left flank. She ran to the right, hoping to protect herself. The chopper arced swiftly, coming around again. It raced directly over her head, causing her to stand still in the midst of the whirlwind. After it passed, she looked up.

The third shot spun her around two hundred seventy degrees. Blood and skin flew away from the flayed wound in her left arm. She hit the ground, hard, and could not keep herself from rolling. When the wound smashed against the hard pebbles she cried out. Half frightened and half furious, she found the strength to stand and run.

The chopper passed directly over her again, blinding her. She ran without direction, hoping only to keep moving. It roared overhead, again and again, stirring up whirlwinds of dust and debris. Soon the confrontation became the pilot's to control; Gloria merely dodged the wind from the rotors.

She stumbled again, falling hard on her left knee. She crawled on her hands and knees until she could rise again.

The chopper filled her world; the powerful engine, the spinning rotors, the men she glimpsed every now and then as the machine sped by her.

A piercing realization suddenly dawned on her. She suddenly knew exactly how the wolf had felt. Driven by an overpowering, frightening object, it had run for its life. Terrified beyond belief, it ran helter skelter, trying desperately to escape the horrible ending to the strange dance thrust upon it. If it ran east, a shot rang out, driving it in the other direction. After heading west, the chopper bore down on it, burying it in dust and debris.

The helicopter had unlimited resources, but the wolf eventually became fatigued. After twenty minutes, the animal crouched down, breathing heavily, drool dripping from its jowls. That's when Gloria, her husband, or their guide would take the kill shot. The wolf had no chance. It wasn't hunting or a remedy to a problem; it was murder, pure and simple.

Without having any idea of her whereabouts, Gloria ran as straight as she could. Limping noticeably, she peered through the murky dust. Trying to find her vehicle, she lurched ahead, staggering badly.

The roar of the chopper consumed everything as it sailed over her head. As it passed, a strong gust of wind quickly cleared the debris. Remarkably, Gloria saw the Range Rover less than fifty yards away. The proximity gave her newfound hope and strength. With a rush of adrenaline she hadn't thought available to her, she surged forward.

A bullet crashed into her left leg, blowing through her hamstring and thigh. The bullet slamming into her bicep had been painful, but this injury punished her senses. Nearly blacking out, she fell hard to the ground face first. Nothing, not the impact on her arm, her nose, her forehead or anything else registered. The nerves in her leg commanded every ounce of attention. She reached down to the wound. When her hands touched the bloody mess that used to be her thigh, she bellowed in frustration.

"You bastards! You fucking bastards! You killed my husband and now you want me? You don't have the right…"

Somewhere within the pain the truth bore through the madness. They don't have the right. *They don't have the right.*

The chopper appeared out of nowhere, hovering over Gloria Dunn. The brutal wind from the rotor pounded her face. She didn't move. She stared straight up at her tormentors. She watched Collins level his rifle, as she had done so many times in the past.

"*I* didn't have the right," she whispered.

Collins peered through the scope.

··· 34 ···

Collins checked his watch after boarding the Lear jet. It was the newest of the Bombardier Aerospace line, and Collins had ordered one the second he saw the plans at the company headquarters. The model wouldn't be available to the public for another year. His connections in the pentagon allowed him to purchase a prototype for a considerable discount. He agreed to serve as test passenger while his pilots put the aircraft through its paces. After the first run, Collins' flight captain signed off on the magnificent aircraft.

Five forty-five. With luck he would be back in his office by nine-thirty. No doubt Detective Kitch would be sniffing around the next morning. Collins gave ten to one odds that an unmarked car would be stationed somewhere within a city block of his building. Five to one there'd be another one down the street from his home.

He had just begun reviewing a file from his briefcase when the radio on his shoulder buzzed quietly. He glanced up at the cockpit door. Seeing no lights indicating the pilots wished to speak to him, he waited for a message from Turner or Michaels.

"Yes," he said after depressing the switch.

"Turner, boss."

"How are you feeling?"

"Sore."

"When you return to Los Angeles, I want you to pack a bag and stay at my home for a couple of weeks. I'll have a nurse on site to tend to your recovery."

"What about Buck?"

"Bring him along, of course. The place is big enough. He'll never find the boys."

"Okay, boss," said Turner. "One thing to report."

"Go ahead."

"The smoke from the compound attracted a state trooper. He caught us heading back to the airport just as we turned onto the main highway."

"How did you handle it?"

"We flattened his tires and destroyed his radios. We left him in the shade with plenty of water and food."

"And his disposition?"

"Not too happy, but when he realized we worked for the feds he eased up a little. We told him we'd send a car for him in a couple of hours."

"Okay," said Collins. "Doesn't sound like anything we have to worry about."

"Boss?"

"What is it?"

"Appreciate you activating the team so quickly. Another day and Junior might have killed me."

"You're a valuable asset, Turner, and a good friend. I'll see you tomorrow night at my house."

"Out."

Collins looked out the starboard window. Peering directly into the falling sun, he pondered their next move as he lifted the file again.

··· 35 ···

Hunted

"Everything you have told me is true?" asked Cosimo Capuana. "There is no mistake?"

"None," said Capuana's oldest brother. "Although badly burned, the body has been identified. Agosto's remains are en route to New Jersey as we speak."

Cosimo's insides shriveled. His only son, murdered through some bizarre act of violence, mutilated by wild animals. He couldn't stomach the visions his mind entertained.

He had fought bitterly with Agosto over his decision to travel halfway across the country to take part in his latest escapade. Cosimo had offered to send him on Safari anywhere in the world, with all the finest trappings.

He'd felt terribly unsure of Agosto's decision, and told his son about his misgivings. Surely something terrible would happen. He'd argued, pleaded, and in the end, he forbade Agosto from going.

The prideful young man had stormed from the room. Although he had the fine, Sicilian features of his father, he'd inherited his mother's violent temper. Throughout his teen years he and his father clashed over everything. Their love for each other was never in question, but the younger Capuana also possessed his father's insatiable ambition. He lusted after every aspect of life. He used his family's great wealth to challenge the world at every turn. While his body was young and strong, he pushed himself to the limit in every way.

The Hunt of Your Life affair had been a whim, a dare thrust upon him by a close friend. He had looked at the materials, boasting wildly that he would return from Wyoming with the largest trophy ever collected.

In the early morning hours after the fight with his father, Agosto Capuana left his family home for the last time. Like a wraith he'd crept soundlessly through the rooms of his father's house. He wanted to be on a westbound flight long before his parents awakened. He'd left a small envelope by the coffee maker containing a brief letter. He thanked them for their concern and assured his father he would be home in less than a week.

"Who else knows of this?" asked Capuana.

"No one in New Jersey, not yet anyway. The state police in Wyoming, of course. The medical examiner, by now, perhaps a few reporters."

Cosimo winced. He would have to tell his wife today, before the vultures descended upon their home. His sweet Fiorella; her pain coursed through his body. If she survived the blow, she would never be the same. She loved Agosto more than life itself.

He looked out his office window at the repulsive scene in front of him. The filthy docks, the machinery, the men moping around their jobs, the spirit sucked from their souls long ago. He realized suddenly that what he saw before him mirrored his own life. Without his son, everything he owned, everything he had accomplished meant nothing. He let the anger seethe, then boil. Closing his eyes tightly, he uttered a silent farewell to Agosto.

"Tell me again what happened," he said.

"Cosimo, please."

Capuana looked at his brother. He didn't speak another word, but Arrigo understood the command.

"Agosto signed a contract to hunt a lion at a place called Hunt of Your Life in Wyoming. He stayed the weekend with the other guests. Apparently, a group of men raided the compound. They put the guests and the staff in the hunting arena. Then they released the animals."

"What kind of animal killed my son?"

"Two tigers. They ripped his body in half at the waist."

Cosimo grimaced at the thought of his son being mauled. He tried to picture the type of man who would order such a slaughter.

"I don't care what you do," he said. "Find the men who took Agosto from me."

"And when we do?"

"Bring them to me, or me to them, I don't care which. They took their pound of fur and it cost Agosto his life. The only demand I make of you is to be certain they're alive when I confront them."

"And if I can't?"

"Then throw yourself from the top of this building, brother, for anyone who keeps me from avenging my son's death will find themselves next in line."

··· **36** ···

After dismissing his advisor, Cosimo Capuana sagged in his ancient leather chair. He stared through the filthy windows out onto the New Jersey docks. The Port Newark Terminal loomed in the distance, its tired horn periodically sounding shift changes.

He had arrived in New York with his parents and brothers more than fifty years ago, fresh faces in a strange land. His father humped freight during the day and cut fish at night. His demanding schedule overtook him in his thirties. He died a pauper, but in a free land.

Cosimo and his brothers left school to provide for their mother. At first, he followed his older siblings as they scrabbled together a living on the docks. Soon, however, he realized that in America one had to create one's opportunities. He fell in with a gang of capable young men; from that moment forward Cosimo Capuana abandoned the idea of an honest day's work.

He didn't go hungry by any means. In a few months' time, he organized the ragtag bunch of hooligans into a sophisticated crew. They stole everything; clothing, jewelry, meat, milk, fish, and even toys. Cosimo's strategy kept them all from getting arrested; he would always fence the items the same night they pulled a raid. Since they never kept any inventory, the police had no place to search for stolen goods.

Capuana stayed away from the action, always keeping himself in the public eye while the jobs commenced. He provided solid alibis for the men under his command. They came and went like ghosts; no one ever saw them. The next morning the goods would be missing and the crew would be hanging around the docks with other day laborers. Of course, due to Capuana's influence, no one ever picked them for a job.

The coronation occurred without any fanfare. The young men he ran with recognized him as their leader without a word spoken. He took to the role comfortably, a man at ease making decisions. Soon, in addition to their weekly robberies, Capuana's crew branched out into the docks. They ran everything: payday loans, prostitution, gambling, even bootlegged liquor. If someone had a problem and they had money to pay Capuana, the difficulty disappeared overnight.

He bought the main terminal building at the Jersey docks. Hiring most of the laborers over the next three months, he transformed it into a base of operations any military officer would admire. No one could approach from the west except by boat. That meant anyone hoping to attack Capuana's operations had to enter and exit by the same path, a suicide mission at best.

The building looked dilapidated from a distance, but upon closer inspection one would notice a few subtle improvements. The men Cosimo hired at the docks had spent weeks refitting the interior walls with enough plating to repel more than a few rounds of hefty ordnance. Numerous windows, all armor plated, afforded his men ample lookout stations. No one would ever approach the terminal without being spotted by Capuana's men. Fake shipping crates had been attached to walls and placed at various locations on the warehouse floor, providing machine guns, shotguns, even grenades if one knew how to release the latch under the lid. As long as Capuana's men remained in the building, they were as safe as gold bars in Fort Knox.

Before he turned thirty years old, Cosimo Capuana controlled an empire worth more than fifty million dollars. He dominated the ports in New York and New Jersey and ran a complex organization that stretched from the east coast all the way to Kansas City. He felt proud of what he had accomplished, even prouder of the fact that he had taken his brothers into his organization. He placed them in important positions, knowing they would die before betraying him.

He lacked one essential item: an heir to continue his legacy. Cosimo hadn't been able to watch his father grow old, a loss that pained him deeply. Through all the trials he had experienced in his young life, family still meant everything to him. How he would have loved taking care of his father, providing him with a comfortable home, grandchildren even. He would not allow his children's children to grow up without a grandfather's weathered face and smile.

He met Fiorella Bellezza at the spring festival in the Bronx. He had been asked to attend as the major sponsor of the event. At first, he declined, citing business matters occurring the same week. Something made him reconsider, however, and as he walked the beautifully decorated streets, visiting with each vendor displaying their wares in the extensive farmer's market, he bought dozens of trinkets, passing them over to his men as he shook the hands of hundreds. A tightly packed crowd followed his every step, hoping for a taste of his generosity.

The first time he saw Fiorella, her hands and arms were filthy. She had been assigned the duty of cleaning the onion bulbs from the family farm. A dirty job on most days, but nearly impossible on festival day. Hundreds of bulbs, caked with crusted soil, had to be cleaned and presented for sale to passersby. Fiorella had been arguing with her mother at the moment Cosimo arrived. Both she and her mother stood face to face screaming and gesticulating wildly at each other.

Cosimo's heart thumped in his chest as he watched the beautiful young woman rant. Her fiery rage provoked every feature to its fullest expression. Her eyes, black as a moonless night, glittered fiercely as she returned her mother's insults. Her glorious chocolate hair, tied back in the morning but presently slashing back and forth, captivated Cosimo. He remained transfixed mostly because of her lips. Full and pink, they jutted out as she yelled, stirring his loins in a way he hadn't felt in years.

Waving his bodyguards back, he approached their canopied market space. The fight thundered on, both women so intent on their arguments they never saw the well-dressed man standing just beyond the printed banner strung across the front table. Finally, Fiorella's father stepped around the warring women. He addressed Cosimo politely. When he couldn't hear the young man's reply, he turned, roaring his displeasure. His voice, long the authority in his home, penetrated the battle between mother and daughter. Her father admonished them for ignoring a customer, obviously a man of importance.

"Si?" he asked the man in the expensive suit. "How may I serve you?"

Cosimo held the man's gaze. In his peripheral vision he caught Fiorella straightening her dress and apron. She brushed her hair back with her fingers before retying it. Her mother, the argument forgotten, helped her daughter look her best for their handsome customer. She looked at Fiorella's hands, a crusted, dirty mess, and shook her head.

"The onions," said Cosimo, pointing to the burlap sacks. "How many do you have?"

"Today, one hundred twenty pounds."

"A fine harvest."

"Si, we always work hard for the festival."

"How much for a pound?"

Fiorella's father gazed at Cosimo for a moment. A Sicilian could spot one of the friends easily. He did not want to offend this man. Too high or too low a price might be seen as an insult. He exhaled roughly, taking the straps of his apron in his thumbs and fingers.

"For you, twenty cents a pound."

Cosimo stared at the man, taking his measure. Silence had always served him well; most men were unnerved by quietness in another man. He decided he liked Bellezza. He would do as a father-in-law.

"I'll take them," he said, shifting his eyes to Fiorella.

The young woman smiled before hurrying to collect

a pound of onions. She reached for a sack and suddenly stopped. She looked up at Cosimo, confused.

"My apologies, Signorina," he said softly. "I would like all of the onions you have today."

She looked at him, still unsure of his intentions. When her father rattled off his instructions, she stood, beaming like the sun.

Cosimo nearly collapsed at the sight of her smile.

Holding himself in check, he paid her father twenty-four dollars and an extra six dollars for delivering them to his home, under the condition that he promised to bring the onions himself and stay for coffee.

Fiorella's father eagerly accepted the invitation. He thanked Cosimo profusely, shaking his hand over and over again. His plump, pretty wife hugged their benefactor, refusing to release him until she kissed his cheeks a half dozen times.

Through all the well-wishing and blessings, Cosimo kept glancing at Fiorella. She did her best to act demure, but the eyes of the strange man held her heart captive. She smiled coyly as she handed one bag of onions to each of his men and smiled again. Cosimo finally gave her a wide grin, tipped his hat and walked away.

They married a year later. The wedding took place at the Gardens of St. Francis outside Atlantic City. The patron saint of animals always held a special place in Cosimo's heart. He often recalled his mother keeping a stone statue of St. Francis in their small courtyard when he was a boy. She would go out each morning and place fresh breadcrumbs in the statue's basket.

"Now, watch, Co Co," she would say. "Stay very still."

As if by magic, birds began appearing in the courtyard. They flittered down the passage, timidly flying around the statue. They stopped every few feet, twitching their heads to and fro; making sure it was safe to proceed a little further.

Finally one would land at the edge of the basket. After another quick look around, the beak disappeared into the slate colored basin. A second later it reappeared, holding a crumb or seed. In the bat of an eyelash, the bird disappeared to enjoy its breakfast.

After seeing their comrade come to no harm, other birds quickly flocked to the statue. Soon as many as a dozen finches took their place on the rim of St. Francis' basket. Cosimo hid in the kitchen, giggling at the sight of so many birds darting around their protector. He heard their small wings fluttering as they bounced around the basket. He listened to their sharp, high pitched cries.

He held his place, silent as a shadow, watching the birds for nearly a half hour until the last of the meal had been eaten. Then, one by one, they left the little courtyard.

"Remember St. Francis, Co Co. He is the kindest of all saints."

Three months after the wedding nuptials, fortune smiled upon the Capuana family. Fiorella announced she was with child. Cosimo was overjoyed; he flooded the street vendors with money and favors. His men had never seen him so generous. One by one he sat them down, asking if they or their families had want of anything.

He walked on air during the entire pregnancy. He showered his wife with expensive gifts. Baskets of fresh flowers arrived at their home every morning. A nursery fit for royalty sprang up in the Capuana residence. He bought everything he could think of; his wife even admonished him at one point.

"Cosimo, you'll spoil the child before he is born."

"It is a boy? You know this?" he would ask.

"No one knows the will of God, mi cuore."

Cosimo would not be dissuaded. He thought of nothing else. For a man to sire a son was the premier honor, a testament to his life on earth. If he was blessed with a boy, he would raise him in the old Sicilian way. The boy would carry on the Capuana name. His sons and his sons' sons would make sure their family continued forever.

On the day his wife gave birth Cosimo looked like a man suffering from the plague. He brought in the finest doctors and nurses, paying them all to perform the procedure at his home. His men stood or sat close by their boss, equally as befuddled and nervous as him.

Each time his wife cried out, Cosimo's strength withered. He wanted more than anything to rush to Fiorella's side and comfort her, but the doctors had strictly forbidden his presence. He felt anguished that he could do nothing to ease her pain. At the same time he harbored a terrible fear for the health of his child. Boy or girl, he said to his God, it didn't matter, as long as the Holy Father gave them a healthy baby.

When he heard the doctor's footsteps in the hallway, he marshaled the last of his reserves. He stood as the rigid man wearing the white coat over his scrubs approached him. Cosimo could read nothing in his eyes; this worried him.

"Mr. Capuana," he asked, holding out a recently washed hand.

"Si, I am Cosimo Capuana."

"Please, follow me."

"I must know. I'm afraid I won't be able to take even one step. Please, my child."

The doctor smiled. "You have a fine, healthy boy, Mr. Capuana."

The weight of a hundred worlds fell from Cosimo's shoulders. He followed the doctor into the nursery. At the sight of the empty room, he became alarmed again.

"My wife, I must see her."

"There is something I must tell you before we join your wife in her bedroom."

Cosimo stared at the doctor, clamping down on frayed nerves.

"Your wife's pregnancy became quite complex. The breach birth damaged her reproductive passage. She is in no danger, but she will never give birth again."

"Have you told her this?"

"Of course not. She is weak and tired. I will tell her during the post-partum consultation."

"No," said Cosimo. "I will tell her."

"I'd advise against that, sir. It would be better if a medical professional delivered the news."

"Then bring me a Sicilian doctor. I know my wife, and I will be the one who delivers this terrible blow. We will weep together; we will heal our hearts together."

The doctor looked into Cosimo's eyes. He knew better than to press the issue further. He nodded to the man, and then motioned for him to follow. He led him to the master bedroom, where his wife, weak from labor, lay in bed clutching her son.

The instant Cosimo saw his baby boy, his worries fell away. He rushed to wife's side, kissing her repeatedly. Every second or so he stopped to look upon his son, but always he returned to his wife.

"I wish to call him Agosto," he said softly to Fiorella. "After his grandfather, if you don't object, of course."

"It is a strong name, like you, mi cuore."

··· 37 ···

Kevin Collins arrived in the parking garage of his building at seven o'clock on Monday morning. Dressed in a crisp suit and wearing a brand-new pair of dress shoes, he looked less like a man who had spent the weekend on a killing spree in Wyoming and more like the chief executive of an expanding security services company. Holding his briefcase with three fingers, he reached across and pulled up his left sleeve. Checking his watch one last time before entering the building's foyer, Collins riffled through a mental list of his morning's activities.

The elevator signal illuminated. A moment later the door opened silently. To his great surprise, Collins looked into the car and saw lieutenant Kitch.

"Good morning, Kevin."

Collins walked into the car, unperturbed.

"I felt it might benefit us to have a private conversation before the day's business distracts you."

"Be my guest, Sam. I'll give you the ninety seconds I have available to me. Unfortunately I have a rather important conference call with the pentagon at seven fifteen."

"I suggest you postpone it."

"I'm sorry, Sam, that's not possible. We're in negotiations for a new piece of riot control equipment. A competing company is close to stealing our contract. Since this particular piece of business is worth more than fifty million dollars, I'd like to take that call."

Kitch calmly walked over to the elevator control panel. He pressed the stop button. A second later a loud bell sounded throughout the building.

Kitch took a ring of keys from his coat pocket. Selecting the appropriate one, he inserted it into the panel, turning it clockwise. The bell ceased, its last toll fading away in the elevator shaft.

"Just what do you think you're doing?" asked Collins.

"Since you're the principal stakeholder in the conference call, I presume we can speak for a few moments."

"Make it quick."

Kitch removed a newspaper from under his arm. "Have you seen the front page of the Times this morning?"

"No, I haven't."

Unfolding the paper, Kitch handed it to Collins. When he refused to take it, Kitch dropped it on the floor at his feet.

Collins couldn't help but glance at the headline. In the media's customary fashion, an account of his weekend lay splattered across the page. GRUESOME MURDERS IN WYOMING splashed across the entire top fifth of the page. Photos of Junior and Chaney, the most horrific deaths by far, lay silently before Collins.

"Lieutenant Kitch, I have work."

Kitch simply met Collins' gaze.

"I suppose you think I flew to Wyoming, mutilated a group of people and then returned to Los Angeles, all in less than forty-eight hours?"

Kitch kept his silence. He watched Collins closely.

"Please turn the elevator back on, Lieutenant. Your games are irritating me."

"I haven't come here to arrest you," said Kitch. "I merely wanted to share a small piece of information our department has discovered."

Collins checked his watch again. "And that is?"

"Quite an anomaly, really. Most of the people killed in Wyoming were those one would expect to encounter in such a place."

"Assholes?"

"If you will, but one of the unfortunate individuals had no business being there at all. In fact, if he didn't have such name recognition, I'm sure their coroner might have tagged him 'John Doe' and forgotten all about him."

Collins said nothing.

"Have you ever heard of the Capuana family?" asked Kitch.

"Of course," replied Collins. "Who hasn't?"

Kitch couldn't believe his eyes. Collins had twitched. At the mention of the Sicilian's name, his eyes darted back to the newspaper. A second later he regained control. Kitch had seen the man flinch, however, and it confirmed something he'd assumed for some time. Collins had orchestrated the attack on Hunt of Your Life, most likely the Greenville episode, and the local fighting rings.

"Agosto Capuana was killed over the weekend, Kevin. He was the only son and heir to Cosimo Capuana, a very powerful Mafioso in New Jersey. Mr. Capuana will never have another child with his wife, I'm afraid, due to complications during her pregnancy. That adds a little sting to the elder Capuana's pain, wouldn't you think?"

"You said you weren't here to arrest me, correct?"

"I dearly wish I could, Kevin. At least with you in custody I could protect you. Without the proper evidence to back up my allegations, however, I can't see the case gaining any traction. For the moment, anyway."

"Then we're finished?"

"Yes," said Kitch as he reinserted the key into the elevator panel. After restarting the car, he turned and looked at Collins. "I admire you, sir, so I will only say this once. If it was you who led the attack in Wyoming, I would find a secure place to hide myself."

The elevator slowed as it reached the top floor. Kitch continued. "It is my understanding that Cosimo Capuana's wife has entered a psychiatric hospital. She broke down immediately after hearing of her son's death."

The bell sounded for Collins' floor.

"Capuana has offered ten million dollars for the man who murdered his son. Not only is his family actively pursuing the identity of the killers, but so is every other crime organization on the East coast."

Collins stood ramrod straight, staring at the seam in the elevator doors. When the car finally opened, he gave Kitch a curt farewell.

"Good day, Kevin."

··· 38 ···

"Good morning, Mr. Collins," said Shari, cheerfully.

Collins brushed past his secretary's desk without acknowledging her salutation.

"Your conference call is waiting. Is there something wrong?"

The door to Collins' office rapidly opened and closed.

Collins tossed his briefcase onto the worn cushions of his couch. Ripping his suit coat from his shoulders, he tossed it over the back of a client chair. As he walked around his desk, he slapped the intercom.

"Shari, ask the conference call attendees if they'll wait ten minutes. Give them my apologies and tell them I'll be with them as soon as I'm able. Say I got held up in traffic."

"Mr. Collins, what's…"

He cut her off. "Find Turner and Michaels. Get them in here in five minutes."

"Mr. Turner is convalescing at your home. I can find Mr. Michaels for you if you like."

"Shit," said Collins. In his panic he had forgotten all about Turner. "Alright, tell Michaels I need him to drop what he's doing and report to my office pronto. Is that clear?"

"Yes, sir," said Shari. "Mr. Collins, may I ask what's happening?"

"Follow your orders, Shari. Find Michaels. Do it now. Make sure he comes here immediately."

It seemed only a second had gone by when the door to Collins' office burst open. Collins looked up, controlling the reflex to jump when he heard Michaels enter the room.

"What's up, boss?" Michaels took a chair opposite the one containing Collins' coat.

"We've got trouble. I want you to locate the security services training squad, the one we used to prepare our guard forces for the embassy in the Emirates."

"Nielson's men?"

"Yes. I want them here in twenty-four hours. I haven't got time to explain. I promise I'll do so later today. Plan on coming to my home for an hour after work today."

"Anything else?"

"Send a dozen professionals to my home; they're to leave immediately. Make sure they're armed to the teeth."

"What's their function?"

"Detain anyone who comes within fifty feet of the house, unless they have credentials. If they put up a fight, they're to be captured or killed."

When Collins picked up his phone, Michaels got up from his chair. He walked to the door and opened it. As he swung it wide, he heard Collins call out to him again.

"Michaels, keep your eyes open today. Wherever you go, don't let your guard down for a second."

··· 39 ···

"It's all there, Mr. Capuana, names, home addresses, employment, work schedules, even the cars they drive."

Cosimo Capuana stared into the eyes of Kevin Collins. The photograph showed him standing with a group of high-ranking army officials, obviously in Washington, D.C.

"This is the man who led the operation, this Collins?"

"Si, Capo."

Capuana slowly riffled through the pictures. He looked at Turner, Michaels, and an assortment of other men. All military, he suspected, by the look of them. He came back to the picture of Collins, leaving it on the top of the pack. He never again took his eyes from it.

"Safeguard Protection Services," whispered Capuana, "his company?"

"Collins owns a big security training house in Los Angeles. "Deals in weaponry, protection, small force training, off-site installations, the works. Big connections in Washington. Lots of money."

"Are we going to be able to deal with them?"

"Together, no, but if we find them alone, unaware, then yea, sure, we'll take 'em down."

"I want Collins brought to me personally."

"What about the others?"

"I could give two shits about the others. Shoot them, stab them, bury them for all I care. Just make sure someone finds them eventually. I want the world to know what happens to those who hurt my family."

"We'll take care of it, Capo."

Capuana nodded his head, his brow creasing. "Where did you get this information? Are you sure it's dependable?"

Antonio Moretti smiled. "Couldn't be any better. I got it from our man in the Los Angeles Police Department."

··· 40 ···

"Are you shitting me?" asked Turner, sitting up in bed holding his ribs. "That crazy Italian kid was Cosimo Capuana's son?"

"Sicilian, and yes, it was him," replied Collins. "What the hell he was doing at a two-bit junk store like Hunt of Your Life is beyond me, but it doesn't matter, now. His old man knows we murdered his son. I'm sure he's got every hitter in New Jersey on their way to the west coast right now."

"Jeezus," Turner said. "We knew the kid's name. How could we have missed that?"

"You have to get lost, boss," said Michaels. "Go to Washington, hell, go to China and lay low for a while."

"It's worse than that. Capuana's after revenge. He'll kill half the population of L.A. just to get to me."

"Nobody's got that much juice," said Turner. "The heat'd be all over him if he started a bloodbath like that."

"Not the way he'd do it. Besides, he doesn't give a shit. I killed his son, and if I know him, he's pushed everything else out of his mind. To him this is a Sicilian vendetta. He won't care if he gets arrested or killed. His son is gone and I took him."

One of Collins' men quietly entered the study. "Telephone call, sir."

"We're busy."

"Cosimo Capuana wishes to speak to you, sir."

Collins looked at Turner and Michaels. Both men stared blankly back at him, nervous sweat tickling their nostrils. Collins leaned over his desk and hit the speaker phone.

"Kevin Collins speaking."

"This is Cosimo Capuana."

"How did you get this number? No one knows..."

Capuana interrupted. "I want to assure you of one thing, Mr. Collins. No matter what anyone does from this moment forward, you are a dead man."

Silence.

"I'm giving you an opportunity to save your friends, your family, the people who work for you."

"Continue," said Collins.

"Nothing you do will save your own life, but if you promise to come to New Jersey and give yourself up to my men, I will put a stop to the carnage that will overtake Los Angeles."

"I'm sorry about your son, Mr. Capuana, but he deserved to die just like the rest of the people in Wyoming."

"My son was a willful boy; it was hard even for me to contain him."

"Mr. Capuana..."

"Right now my wife is lying in bed in a psychiatric hospital, strapped down so she will not take her own life. Even I cannot see her for seventy-two hours. The doctors say if she does recover from the shock it might be years before she resumes a normal life."

"Sir…"

"Make your choice, Collins. You, or you and everyone you know. I am a busy man; I have a great many details to attend to."

"I assume I can phone you at this number when I arrive?"

"Call me the moment your plane touches down. And Collins, don't deceive me. I'm angry enough."

"I'll see you in two days. I don't want anything to occur here in California, do you understand? If anyone gets hurt here, the deal's off."

"Agreed."

Collins reached for the speaker button to end the call.

"Mr. Collins?"

"Yes. I'm still here."

"You are a brave man. No one would give himself over so easily under these circumstances."

"Goodbye Mr. Capuana."

Collins pressed the button.

"Are you nuts, boss?" asked Turner. "They'll cut your heart out and make sure you live to see it before they stuff it in your mouth."

"He's right, Kevin," Michaels added. "You may think you're going to walk out of here and take the Lear to Jersey, but we have other ideas."

"Good, because so do I. I may have just bought us two days. We have that long to plan our strategy."

"You going after him, boss?"

"No, he'd never be that stupid. Besides, I'm sure his people told him everything about us; military background, weapons ratings, counterintelligence and anti-terrorism training, the works. He's got his people armed with anything they need."

"They're not dumb, boss," said Turner. "They're coming for blood, and you can bet they know what they're doing."

"There's something else. Those hitters are most likely going to land at LAX tonight. Capuana might hold them off for another day, but he sure as hell won't call them back to Jersey."

"How can you be sure?" asked Michaels.

"If we had just killed your only son, would you be in the mood to offer concessions?"

"I guess not."

"All right," said Turner. "What are we going to do?"

Collins exhaled. "Hope like hell we get to them before they get to us."

··· 41 ···

A crew of seven casually dressed men strolled through the main terminal of the Los Angeles International Airport. They spoke little, ate and drank nothing, and walked straight past the baggage claim carousel. As much as they tried to go unnoticed, however, nearly everyone they passed stole a glance at the small group.

Once outside the terminal, three of the crew immediately withdrew cigarettes from their coats. Lighting up, they took a few hasty pulls. The large plumes of smoke leaving their bodies ended the drought from the interminable six-hour flight, increasing the pleasure of the first cigarette since disembarking. They looked infinitely more relaxed; they began scanning the oncoming vehicles for their ride.

A white Ford Excursion cut across three lanes of traffic. It swept forward into the loading curb, nearly knocking the first man in the group over and ignoring the bleating horns of the frustrated drivers behind it.

The driver stayed put, engine running. The men climbed into the vehicle, shutting the doors behind them. A thick coat of smoky black tint protected them from prying eyes. As it had before, the large, imposing Excursion pushed its way into the flow of traffic. The security guard on patrol at the curb started to wave the driver over, angry at his impertinence. After the vehicle disappeared around the corner, however, he forgot about it.

"You're late,' said the man riding in the front passenger seat.

"Fuck off," replied the driver. "How long did you have to wait, a minute?"

"I don't like to wait at all. Gives me the creeps; the L.A. cops probably knew we were coming before we got on the plane in Jersey."

"So what? The boss set you guys up real good: safe house, weapons galore, food, drinks, women, what are you crying about?"

Teddy Sacco peered through his sunglasses at the driver. He'd never met the man before. After five minutes with him he felt like putting a bullet in his ear. Capuana had called in favors from a west coast family, however, and Teddy wasn't about to piss off the chain of command.

"Yea, you're right," he said, "what the hell am I worried about?"

The other six men rode in silence. Bumping along in the back seats, each reviewed his assignment, thinking through the steps over and again.

"How long until we make the house?" asked Teddy.

The driver checked his watch. "Half hour."

"Good. We haven't had a decent meal since we left Jersey. Fuckin' airline didn't have anything besides peanuts."

Sacco opened his folder. He flicked through the pages quickly, taking only cursory glances at their overall assignment. He wanted to examine the immediate task.

"Michaels," he said. "Andrew Michaels – married, no kids in the home, pets galore. Dogs, big dogs – shit."

"They got a fuckin' malamute over there," said a man in the back of the vehicle.

"What the fuck's a malomar?" asked another.

"You dumb shit, that's a cookie. I'm talking about one of the biggest, baddest watch dogs you'll ever see."

"How big can it be? A couple a bullets'll stop it."

"You better hope so. As a matter of fact, you can go in the yard first. I don't want to go eye to eye with a hundred eighty pounds of pissed off sled dog. And don't miss when you shoot it; you'll have one shot before it rips your throat out."

"Yea, yea."

"Okay, shut up and listen," said Sacco. "We go to the house, eat a quick meal, and then go get this guy Michaels. The boss wants the whole place burned to the ground, with Michaels, his wife and all their animals in it."

"Pissed off or what?" said the man in the back.

"Scare tactics," said Sacco. "It'll make the others think too much about what to do or where to go. When they make a mistake we'll get 'em easy."

The Excursion rumbled up the 405 freeway toward Santa Monica.

··· 42 ···

Collins sat at the desk in his study giving orders into a telephone. All around him, men busied themselves packing his essentials. He had told them to be ready to leave in two hours.

"That's right," he said into the receiver. "I want precision timers on everything in our building; lights, computers, sound system, everything. I want the sequencing to be completely random, as if the workday and the nightly watch were occurring normally. I want it up and running within four hours."

Collins had already telephoned his secretary with orders for her to contact everyone in his employ. They had all earned a week's paid vacation, he instructed. She was to e-mail every employee, and personally telephone every executive. No one would arrive at the building for a solid week. He made certain she understood his orders.

He hung up the phone and addressed Turner. "How're you feeling, Ev?"

"Tight, sore, but I can be mobile if you need me."

"I just want you to be ready to move if we have to leave in a hurry. I've no doubt Capuana's boys are on their way."

"I'll be ready."

"Good. Any word from Michaels?"

"Nothing yet. He's home gathering up his family and whatever belongings they think they need."

"I hope he doesn't take too long."

Collins nerves were firing on all cylinders. He hated to send Michaels out alone, but he needed his guards where they were, at his home. He picked up the phone again, dialing quickly. The receiver chirped and his man answered.

"Status?" he said sharply.

"The weapons are loaded, boss. We'll rendezvous at your residence in one hour."

"Negative," said Collins. "There's been an adjustment."

The man on the other end of the phone waited patiently. He knew his boss too well; asking for what would come next made no sense.

"Take the weapons to the Safeguard Protection Services hangar at LAX. When you get to the gate, give the guard the password, canine-feline. He's one of our men; he'll let you in without question."

"Right."

"We'll be there inside of an hour, so we all should arrive together. I'll set our strategy at that time."

Collins' man hung up the phone.

··· 43 ···

Michaels hurried his wife along. He checked his watch constantly, knowing that every minute they delayed could be costly.

"Everyone caged that needs to be carried?" he asked his wife.

"Yes, all the cats are sitting by the front door."

He didn't have to ask about the dogs. Patrolling the back yard, they ran around wildly, as if knowing something was amiss. Tank led the charge, checking the fence perimeters every few seconds. Hoss followed closely, sniffing the grass at the base of the fence line. If he noticed anything peculiar, he would announce it instantly. Pip ran briskly along, keeping up with her brothers. After a while, however, she settled down in the middle of the yard. Looking this way and that, she watched the shadows beyond the fence and the lights that created them.

"Got everything?" asked Michaels.

"Yes," said his wife, "for now."

Michaels grabbed an armful of suitcases, hustling them through the kitchen toward the garage door. He dropped two on the floor so he could turn the doorknob. He wedged his foot into the space before picking up the bags again. He pushed through the door into the garage with his shoulder. The light automatically came on as he worked his way around the Ford King Cab pickup. Tossing the bags into the back, he moved toward the driver's door. He opened it, leaned in and inserted the key into the slot. He fired up the truck, rolled both windows down, and slammed the door. On his way back into the house, he wedged a jamb underneath the kitchen door, keeping it open.

As his wife picked up two of the cat carriers, Michaels rushed into the living for the remaining bags. He grabbed everything and told his wife to follow him out to the garage. She complied without question. She had seen Andrew in this state only twice before. A gentle man, he would not act in such a manner unless the situation was dire.

"Okay, go back inside and get Kitty," said Michaels after securing the other two cats. "I'll get the leashes for the dogs."

As he fumbled with the leads, Michaels spied something he hadn't seen on his last trip to the truck. A white Ford Excursion with tinted windows sat on the road across from his home. It looked completely out of place. People in their neighborhood drove SUVs, but not any that looked so polished. The vehicles here were work trucks. Rarely washed due to the rural environment, none of them would be foolish enough to apply any type of cosmetics like tinted windows.

Michaels heard his wife cry out. He dropped the leashes, turning back toward the kitchen door. He met the cold muzzle of a Glock G35 pistol, pressed against his nose by one of Sacco's men. He looked past the pistol and saw five men standing next to his truck. Every one of them had similar weapons, all drawn.

"Inside," said the man cooling Michaels' face with the gun. Michaels heard his wife cry out again. He obeyed their command quickly, leading the man through the doorway. As the rest followed, Michaels heard one of the cats in the truck whimper.

··· 44 ···

Collins and Turner sped past the checkpoint for the private planes at Los Angeles International Airport. Having been forewarned of their arrival, the security men waved them through without delay. Shooting past two dozen hangars housing the private jets of the most influential people in the city, Collins slowed only when they were a hundred feet from their destination. Finally slamming on the brakes, he left the vehicle before it stopped. He hustled around to the passenger side, helping Turner exit the truck.

Three Bell 407 helicopters stood just outside Collins' private hangar. Men were busy loading supplies and weapons into the aircraft. One of those present seemed to be in charge of the logistics. When he saw Collins drive up, he shouted a few orders to his men. He turned and ran toward the vehicle.

"Glad you made it, sir," he said, helping Collins remove some bags from his truck.

"Give me an update."

"There's enough food and water for six men in each chopper. We've also stocked them with weapons galore."

"Specifics, please."

"Twelve machine guns in each chopper, with twenty

extra clips per weapon; a dozen Colt pistols. We also threw a case of concussion grenades in each bird, under the passenger seat, of course."

"So don't land too hard, right?" asked Collins.

The man nodded his head once.

"Any word from Michaels?"

"Nothing. We've called his cell phone and home number, no answer at either extension."

Collins pondered that last comment. He didn't like the way he felt at all. Michaels' habits were legend. He never left himself out of touch for a second. To hear that his phones were inoperative disturbed him.

The man in charge of loading the choppers stood patiently while Collins came to a decision. He glanced twice in the direction of the aircraft, making sure his men needed no further instructions.

"Jimenez," said Collins, "I need the two best shots you have and the best pilot available in a chopper right now."

"Wallace, Franklin," shouted Collins' man. "You're off the line. Go to active duty immediately, under Collins' instruction. Is that clear?"

Both men answered without hesitation. They dropped the cases of water at their feet, grabbed two helmets and ran toward Collins.

The supervisor pointed toward the helicopter to their left. "That's McNeil, in the lead chopper. He's the best pilot in the game, flew reconnaissance and rescue missions in the last three major skirmishes. Your biggest problem will be staying in the chopper."

"Load up, you two," said Collins.

The men double-timed it to the helicopter.

··· 45 ···

"Get your fucking hands off my wife," said Michaels after entering the kitchen. One of Sacco's men had Darla's arms pinned behind her back. At the sound of Michaels' voice, the man squeezed her elbows together. Darla cried out again; this time Michaels saw the pain in her face.

The fist flew so fast the man holding Darla's arms didn't have time to duck. One second he was up, laughing with the others, the next second he lay at Darla's feet, out cold.

A gun barrel slammed into Michaels' kidney. Remarkably, he stayed on his feet. Stumbling over to Darla, he fell in next to her by the sink. She threw her arms around him, frightened beyond sanity.

Tank and Hoss were throwing a fit in the back yard. Even through the tall bay window by the sink, everyone could see the fur standing straight up on Tank's back.

"Go out and take care of those dogs," said Sacco to the man who'd been flattened by Michaels. The unfortunate soul sat on the floor rubbing his jaw.

"Alone? Are you nuts?"

Sacco growled at the man. "Aren't you good for anything?"

The man said nothing. He glared right back at Sacco.

"Jesus! Ritchie, Angel, go with him!"

"I wouldn't do that," said Michaels, holding a smirk inside his teeth.

"You afraid we're gonna hurt 'em, asshole?" asked the man with the swelling jaw. "You're damn right we are!"

"Yea, that's it," said Michaels. "Go ahead, see what happens."

The three men exited the kitchen. Checking the silencers on their weapons, they walked briskly into the family room. The wounded man glared at Michaels as he walked by. Michaels shook his head, turning to Sacco. "I'd call them back if I were you."

Teddy Sacco looked under the cabinets into the family room. Although he couldn't pinpoint it, something felt terribly wrong. He almost did as Michaels suggested, but shook off the inclination. Three men armed with Glocks should be able to handle a couple of stupid mutts.

"I'll be damned," said Ritchie, tapping the barrel of his gun on the sliding glass door. "They just up and disappeared."

Michaels squeezed his wife's hand.

"Holy fuckin' shit!"

Before the last word left his lips, the family room door shattered in a devastating explosion of glass, fur, and pissed off malamute. The massive dog took Ritchie and his unfortunate cohort to the ground easily. Tank raked Ritchie's eyes with his huge claws while snapping his frothing jaws around his gun hand. The man with the swollen jaw could do nothing; he lay buried under three hundred sixty pounds of squirming man and snarling beast.

Angel was so shocked by what happened it took him a few seconds to collect himself. As two more of Sacco's men rushed in from the kitchen, he raised his gun. He never even saw Hoss vaulting toward him from the yard. At the last second, he turned, but he was desperately slow compared to the dog's lithe movements. Hoss grabbed his gun hand in his mouth and bit down with everything he had.

"Aowwwww, FUCK!" screamed Angel.

Amidst the tumultuous din, with men shrieking painfully and huge attack dogs taking vengeance on those who had threatened their parents, Michaels knew this would be his only chance to survive. He charged Sacco like a madman, hitting him bodily, slamming him up against the granite sink. He saw Sacco's gun wobble in the man's hand. He reached for it, driving his knee into Sacco's solar plexus at the same time. He had no time to think about Darla; if she could get away, great, but his primary concern lay with Sacco's gun.

The family room sounded like a horror movie gone terribly wrong. Snarls, growls, and yips of canine pain pushed through the opening above the counter toward Michaels, Darla, Sacco and the man now holding Michaels' wife. Without the benefit of sight, Sacco had no idea what kind of mayhem the dogs were causing. Even with Michaels drumming him into the counter and going for his gun, he couldn't take his mind off of the madness in the next room.

Silenced shots rang out. The muzzles of the Glocks flashed as round after round flew about the darkened room. The haunting sound of dogs in great pain followed by the terrible whimpering of dying animals poured into the kitchen.

A **Pound** of Fur

Sacco's men swore repeatedly, mostly at the dogs, but a few remarks fell toward their fellows.

Sacco's man had released Darla. He brought the butt of his Glock down on Michaels' head. As he crumpled to the ground, Sacco regained himself. He took hold of his gun and ran into the family room. He listened as his men argued over the course of events.

"You stupid fuck, why didn't you kill that crazy dog before it jumped on me?"

"What are you talkin', Angel, I guess you didn't see I had two guys and a dog as big as a truck lying on top of me."

"Go fuck yourself. You're useless."

"Fuck you, asshole!"

"Shut the hell up," shouted Sacco, now standing in the family room. "You wanna get us popped because everyone in the neighborhood can hear you idiots screaming at each other?"

For the first time since the madness began, Teddy Sacco took a good look at his men, or what was left of them. Ritchie wasn't going anywhere but back to New Jersey; the giant malamute had almost torn his arm clean off. He was bleeding from multiple wounds on his head, face, neck, and chest. Angel's hand looked bad, but Sacco figured he'd recover soon enough. Tootie, the man Sacco initially ordered in the room, seemed unscathed, except for the ration of crap thrown at him by the others. The Scully brothers had killed the dogs as they attacked the other men. They at least were good to go. The only one unscathed, besides him, still held Michaels' wife in the kitchen.

On his knees, Michaels keened loudly. Darla crumpled to the floor next to him, screaming as well; she had lost her beautiful sons.

"You bastards!" she yelled. "Get out of here. Get out of my house!"

Michaels seemed to be in another world. "Tank, Hoss, oh God, why didn't you assholes listen to me!"

Tank, lying on his side with six bloody bullet wounds, cried out to Michaels. It was the soft whimper of a creature about to die and yet worried for his master.

"Get out of my way, Goddamn you!" Michaels shouted as he tried to run from the kitchen.

"Let him go," said Sacco. A confused subordinate stared at him.

"Let him go, jerkoff! His dog is dying!"

Michaels rushed into the family room. He first caught sight of Hoss, splayed out in front of the plasma television. Two bullets had slammed into his jaws; what remained of his face confirmed his death. He almost went to seize the dead animal; he turned when he heard Tank cry out again. He looked over and sprang toward him.

"Oh, Tank, you good boy, you're a good, good boy!"

The huge malamute responded with kisses and eager whines.

"Don't worry, boy, We're right here."

Darla ran into the room, crying loudly. Reaching out to clutch some of Tank's fur, she fell onto her husband.

"My baby, oh my baby, don't you worry. We're here with you."

Tank struggled to reach and kiss his mother. The effort seemed to weaken him; both Darla and Michaels pushed him back down.

The sound of the shot shocked both of them. It ripped into Tank's skull, killing the massive dog instantly. Teddy Sacco stood over the dead animal, holstering his Glock.

Michaels threw his wife to the side, lunging toward Sacco with murder in his eyes.

"Easy, boy," he said. "You got four guns trained on your wife. You really wanna be the reason she dies?"

Sacco turned to his men. "Tootie, get Ritchie into the truck, then get on the horn and have a doctor waiting for us back at the house. We'll be there in a few minutes. Scully, you and your brother bring in the rope and fuel. I want these two strapped together in five minutes." He turned to Angel. "How you holdin' up?"

"Hurts like hell, but I'll be all right." He stared at Michaels and his wife. "Who gets to do them?"

Sacco said nothing. He watched the two brothers binding Darla and Andrew Michaels solidly, hands and feet together behind their backs. When they finished, they made a quick trip to the truck. They returned with a rolling cart balancing four twenty-five gallon containers of gasoline. They emptied two in different rooms of the house. One they set down on the floor next to Michaels, they took the other down the hall to the master bedroom.

"Two minutes," said Sacco. "Get those timers set fast; we've been here way too long as it is."

Michaels had been positioned with his face looking in the direction of the back yard. He nearly cried out when he saw Pip hiding in the bushes next to the pool. Her stubby tail wagged furiously; Michaels could tell she wanted to run to the door and greet him. He made his sternest face, telling her with his eyes she wasn't to move an inch.

"Ready, boss," said one of the Scully brothers.

"Angel?"

"Let's get the fuck outta here."

"Hey, 'boss'?" asked Michaels.

"What do you want?"

"There are three cats in our truck in the garage. They don't deserve to die. I'm asking you man to man to take them with you and drop them somewhere safe. That's my dying wish."

Sacco lit a cigarette. "Tell you what," he said. "I'll take one of them with me. You choose and choose quick."

The pain coursing through Michaels' mind nearly blinded him. He couldn't think straight.

"The big one, take her. Promise me you'll see she arrives safely, wherever you drop her."

Sacco took a pull on his smoke.

"Promise me, asshole!"

"Okay, I promise." He turned to his men. "We're out of here."

Sacco ran into the garage. He took a quick look at the cat carriers behind the front seat of the truck. He saw a huge tortoise shell in the middle cage, so big it barely fit in the box. He grabbed the handle and yanked it out of the compartment. After making certain the cat couldn't reach through the screen and scratch the hell out of him, he ran through the kitchen and through the family room.

A Pound of Fur

"Okay, Michaels, I have your cat. Satisfied?"

"Boss," said Tootie, his head stretched around the corner of the living room wall, "we gotta go, now!" The two men ran out the front door as the flames danced in the hallway.

The Ford Excursion rumbled up the 405 freeway on the way back to the crew's base. Everyone talked at once, blaming, assessing, expressing their opinion about how things might have gone better.

"We shoulda gone over the fence and shot those dogs before we ever went into the house," said Tootie.

"Oh, yeah," Ritchie shouted, now in deep pain. "Great fuckin' plan. By the time we put enough bullets in those dogs to slow 'em down, that Michaels guy would have been outside with a couple shotguns. There'd be a lot more than one fucked up arm in this truck."

"Shit," said Rollie Scully, "a couple a poisoned steaks over the fence would have downed those mutts in no time."

"Shut the fuck up!" said Sacco. "It didn't go good, all right? It's over; save your energy for the next guy's house."

The men were silent for a minute. Angel finally noticed the cat cage sitting in between Sacco and their driver. "Hey, Boss, you startin' up a shelter?"

The men laughed together, finally letting loose.

Sacco turned to the driver. "Where's the control for the sunroof?"

The man pointed a stubby finger at the dial. Sacco pressed the switch, holding it until the sunshade had disappeared under the car's roof. He held the cage up and looked at the huge cat. It eyed him warily but gave a quiet greeting to the stranger holding her aloft.

"Hey," said Tootie, "I think he likes you."

Sacco pushed the front end of the carrier through the opening above him. As the Excursion sailed up the freeway, he tossed the cat carrier into traffic. He turned around, pressed the sunroof switch and quietly looked at his men in the rearview mirror.

"Teddy," said Angel. "You are one sick son of a bitch."

··· 46 ···

Collins' chopper flew low along the coastline, north from the airport toward the San Fernando Valley. When they reached the Getty Center they'd head east over the pass and into Tarzana. He only hoped they weren't too late.

"Time to target?" he asked McNeil.

"Thirteen minutes." The pilot flicked his mike again. "Sir? I've been contacted twice by the airport tower and once by the Coast Guard. Up to this point I haven't responded, but they're apt to get edgy."

"Forget it. By the time they scramble anything we'll have reached our objective. Just the same, let me know if they order any pursuit."

"Copy that. Heading east now."

The chopper made landfall in seconds. Soaring over the multimillion dollar homes in Malibu, it took to the foothills between the beach and the valley. As it descended on the far side of the mountain the 405/134 interstate merge came into view. McNeil expertly steered the chopper low and tight along the base of the mountain, following the Ventura freeway north.

"Getting a boatload of chatter, now, sir. Sounds like a big accident, or a fire, maybe."

"What's your frequency?" asked Collins, watching the traffic on the Ventura freeway race by underneath them.

"Six-six-seven point two."

A full minute before McNeil buzzed Michaels' neighborhood, Collins knew something horrible had happened. His fears were confirmed as the chopper banked hard left around a massive fire, one that had engulfed one home and singed two others before the ladder crews had arrived.

Collins swore under his breath. He said a quick prayer for Michaels' family. He took in the scene completely before giving the next set of orders.

"Let's get out of here. Proceed…"

"Trouble, boss," said McNeil. "Two police helicopters coming in on our six. One of them is hailing me. They're ordering us to land."

"Are they local police?"

"Yea, unless they're lying about their origin. If they're highway patrol we're in trouble."

"Head to the next objective, Mack. Full speed. Give me everything you can. Start out going north. Keep that heading until we'll certain they've had enough time to radio their base. We'll head east in a minute or two. We've got to get to West Covina in the next ten minutes."

"You don't think those birds can catch us?"

"Not the local police."

"Heading north for two minutes," said McNeil.

"Good. Just haul ass and hope we get to Turner's place before those assholes that killed Michaels."

McNeil leaned into the controls. He checked his mirrors every second or two. Sure enough, the local choppers didn't have the power to keep up with them. In a minute Mack couldn't see them anymore.

"Turning east, speed one hundred forty miles per hour. West Covina in sixteen minutes."

Collins turned to the men holding firing positions in both doors of the chopper. He punched his headset.

"You men brace yourselves against those flight doors. Put a couple boxes of ammunition close by, just in case."

Both men nodded, fully prepared to execute his orders.

"No one aboard fires without my authorization, is that clear?"

The two men stared at Collins, signaling their agreement.

"If we do come into contact, we'll engage only after I determine they're the men who killed Michaels. No one fires until I give orders, and that means who, where, when, and how much. Clear?" Collins didn't even wait for a response before turning around.

The men held their GAU-21 machine guns close. They owed everything they had to Collins; they would certainly fight for him.

Satisfied, Collins turned around. He scanned the ground underneath the chopper, looking for familiar landmarks.

"ETA four minutes, boss," said McNeil. "I managed to squeeze a little more juice out of this bird."

"How are we on fuel?"

"Three quarters full. We should be fine unless we have to chase someone all over the canyon."

"I don't think so. Just be ready in case I call for evasive maneuvers."

McNeil smiled.

··· 47 ···

Detective Kitch sat at his desk listening to a series of bizarre calls from the police dispatch system. A bonfire where one of Collins' men lived, units dispatched all over the valley, and an unmarked helicopter zooming all over the county. He knew the main passenger in the chopper had to be Collins. Unfortunately, he had no idea of their present whereabouts. The last report had them flying north along the 405 freeway at a speed none of his choppers could match. No doubt the initial direction served as a ruse; Collins could be heading anywhere.

To make matters worse, apparently three crews had arrived on different flights during the day; two from New Jersey and one from New York.

"Great," he hissed. "A maniac who tortures people to death, a bunch of mob hitters running loose in the county, and to top it off, I haven't the slightest idea where any of them are at the moment." His only lead came from an eye-witness, one of Michaels' neighbors. He'd given a clear description of a vehicle he told dispatch, *had no business driving around our streets*. The suspect vehicle was a white

SUV, Excursion or Expedition, with tinted windows all the way around, even the windshield. Kitch exhaled again. "In Los Angeles," he said, "there are about ten thousand vehicles fitting that description."

His telephone rang. The sound almost jarred him out of his chair, he'd been concentrating so hard. He snatched up the receiver before the next ring.

"Lieutenant Kitch speaking," he said, tersely.

"Sam, this is Collins."

The lieutenant pulled the receiver away from his ear for a moment. "Where are you?" he asked after cradling it against his head again.

"Forget that for now. I want to talk about a deal."

"Suddenly motivated, Kevin?"

"Not for me, Lieutenant, for my men and their families."

"Very altruistic."

"I don't have much time, Sam."

"What are you offering?"

"Me, in exchange for protection against the crew that just fried my man Michaels and his family out in Tarzana."

"It seems a little late to try and save him, don't you think?"

"Do we have a deal?"

"What is my part in this exchange?"

"I give you names and locations of all my key personnel. You send units to their homes. They get police protection until this is over."

"I don't believe you have the time."

"I'm faxing the information as we speak. You should receive it any second."

As if on cue, the fax machine near Kitch's desk came to life. One sheet emerged. The personal information for eight of Collins' key employees lay before his eyes.

"All right, I've received it. If I agree to this deal, where will you be waiting?"

"You'll know soon enough, and thanks, Sam."

"A pleasure, Kevin," said Kitch. "And by the way."

"Yes?"

"You're under arrest."

Kitch rolled his chair over to the dispatch exchange, depressed the toggle switch and started issuing orders. After instructing the black and whites to proceed immediately to the noted locations, he keyed in the exchange code he had only used once before in decades of police service.

"Special weapons and tactics, Sergeant Cronin speaking."

"Sergeant, this is Lieutenant Samuel Kitch down in metro."

"Go ahead, Lou."

"How quickly can you have a team in West Covina?"

The line lay silent for a moment. "Forty-five minutes to an hour, sir."

"What will it take to shave thirty minutes from that estimate?"

"Team has to be called in, sir. Then weapons check, vehicle prep, it'll take more time than that, sir."

"Sergeant, one private home has already been attacked this evening. The occupants were tied up and burned alive. I have good reason to believe the same outcome will be achieved at another home in West Covina. The assailants are most likely already on their way."

"Regular squads might be able to handle this, sir."

"I don't share your enthusiasm, Sergeant. The men involved are dedicated professionals. I wouldn't want to put a first-year rookie up against them. However, if you don't think you can help me tonight, I'll do the best I can by myself."

"SWAT team B-1 is on their way in as we speak, sir. They all live close, so they should be prepped and ready in less than ten minutes."

"How is it they heard the call so rapidly, Sergeant?"

"Cell phones were dialed the second your call came in. Protocol, sir."

"I see," said Kitch. He gave the Sergeant Turner's address and the description of the Ford SUV. "I doubt they'll be using the same vehicle, but you never know."

"Any special orders, sir?"

"The team is to stage out of sight of the main road leading to Turner's residence, at least a half mile away. I don't want the attackers running smack into a SWAT vehicle in a congested neighborhood. When I give the signal, they are to move in and contain the suspect vehicles by any means necessary."

Sergeant Cronin tapped the toggle carefully. "I read by any means necessary per your orders, Lieutenant. Have I copied correctly?"

"Affirmative, Sergeant," said Kitch. "Any means."

"SWAT desk out."

⋯ 48 ⋯

Teddy Sacco looked at what remained of his crew. Tootie and the Scully brothers seemed good to go. Beckett hadn't taken a scratch; neither had he said anything throughout the entire scene at the Michaels' house. Sacco watched him take a drag off a cigarette. A good man; quiet, but he did his work efficiently and without feelings.

Angel's right hand looked like he'd crammed it down a garbage disposal. Very little of the skin had a flesh colored tone; it mostly looked reddish with a sickly, dark blue tint. Huge gashes had been ripped away from the fingers and knuckles.

Sacco had argued with him at the safe house; he hadn't wanted him to come on this job. Angel had insisted, however, waving around his left hand as proof he could still shoot and be an asset to the crew. Sacco knew what his real motivation was: he believed that if he didn't fulfill his obligations completely, he might not get paid the full amount. At the end of their argument he had called Angel a stupid shit and waved him off. If he wanted to go to war against a highly trained military assault team, he could go ahead and get himself killed.

A Pound of Fur

The white excursion had been left burning in South Central Los Angeles. Beckett had set a timed charge; there wouldn't be anything left but a charred frame. The California contact sent two Range Rovers to pick them up and bring them back to the house. They had seen to Ritchie's wounds, regrouped, rearmed, and left as quickly as they could.

Sacco rode shotgun in the first vehicle, running east on the Santa Monica freeway at better than one hundred twenty miles per hour. Chocolate brown with cream interior, at a glance no one would identify the Range Rovers as transports for a mob hit team. Sacco kept his eyes pinned ahead of them; Tootie watched behind in the rear vehicle, and the Scully brothers manned the police radios. If a highway patrol unit, car or helicopter came within ten miles of them, they'd know it with plenty of time to reduce speed.

"There it is," said Sacco. "North Sunset Avenue. Get off there and take a left."

The wheelman glanced over at his passenger. "Save your strength for the job, Sacco, I'll get you there with time to spare."

"Sorry, just a little jumpy. Something feels wrong."

"I thought you Jersey boys were tough."

"We are, asshole," Sacco snarled. "Tough *and smart.* Definitely smart enough not to roll into an ambush."

The vehicles raced up North Sunset for three miles. They took a series of quick turns before the last street dissolved into a meandering dirt road. The lead driver slowed his Range Rover to a crawl.

"I don't like it," he said to Sacco. "If they've planned an ambush, this would be the place for it."

Sacco let the comment fall away as he surveyed the wilderness in front of them. "This guy Turner is no dummy. He could waste a small army before it ever got to his house."

Just then, the home came into view. It was a simple place, one story, Southwestern style, lots of adobe. A three-foot-high wall surrounded the front yard.

Two cars sat in the driveway. There were enough lights on in the house to give the impression of someone being home. A small wisp of smoke trailed upward away from the top of the chimney.

"Stop," said Sacco. "Stop right here." The vehicles slowed, tires softly crushing the sandy drive.

Sacco turned to his men as he activated the radio. He wanted everyone to hear his orders. "First team takes the left, second team on the right. Check all windows for any movement; I want to be damn sure there's somebody in there before we go inside." He opened his door and jumped out. As his men followed, he leaned into the passenger side window. "Turn these heaps around. If you see us running like hell, get ready to drive over anything in the way to get outta here."

The driver nodded his head. He tapped his radio and gave his partner the orders. The two vehicles quietly turned around.

Sacco put Beckett in charge of the second team. He took his men around the perimeter wall to the left. They squatted after reaching the first window. Sacco motioned for his men, the Scully brothers, to stay low while he crawled over the dusty pink fence. He ran crab-like over to the window. Crouching underneath the sill, he looked across the yard for Beckett and saw his men peering over the wall toward the house.

A Pound of Fur

One of Beckett's men cupped his hands behind his ears for a second. After that he dropped them and shook his head from side to side. Sacco understood. He pressed his body against the wall under his window, closing his eyes. He heard the low drone of a television set and nothing else. Pulling his head away from the wall, he gave the same signal.

Sacco and Beckett held their men back. They didn't believe anyone was home, but they wanted to check things more closely before issuing orders. Sacco motioned for Beckett's men to stay back until they saw their leader wave them forward.

Teddy Sacco checked two windows and saw nothing. He began to relax slightly; he didn't think they'd have to do anything except torch the house and leave. He was just about to grab his radio when he peered into the third window.

Ritchie, the man they left back at the safe house, sat in the middle of the living room. He was gagged and tied with duct tape to a massive pile of explosives.

Ritchie shifted his gaze, looked over at Sacco. Terrified, he struggled against the duct tape with his good hand. His mouth worked furiously against the gag, but his bonds held firm. He was trapped. He was going to die, and he knew it.

"Beckett," Sacco whispered into his radio.

"Here," answered Beckett. "What the hell's going on?"

"It's a set-up. Get your men back to the jeeps."

Sacco motioned to the Scully brothers, pointing them toward the driveway. He twirled his index finger and then dragged it across his throat. His team understood perfectly. They backed away toward the Range Rovers.

Sacco inched his head up again. He peered over the

windowsill, seeing the identical scene. Ritchie, deflated and beaten, sat awkwardly with his head slumped forward. Sacco listened again and then ran to the front door.

Not surprisingly, the door sat ajar, an invitation to enter the house. Every instinct in Sacco's mind told him to turn around and run like hell. One of his men was inside, though, and he would at least try and save him.

Ritchie's expression lightened when he saw Sacco walking down the hallway toward the living room. As if Sacco couldn't see the obvious, Ritchie motioned behind him, to the large pile of explosives.

Sacco ran over to his man. He looked at the duct tape first. His switchblade would never cut through it. Possibly a carving knife or some utility scissors, but he had no time to search. He might be able to slide Ritchie out of his shirt and slacks, bypassing the tape completely. He was just about to suggest it when he saw the fuse to the ordnance wound around and through the duct tape.

"Fuck," he said through clenched teeth. He looked for a timer on the mechanism but saw nothing identifiable. A small box with circuitry running through the interior seemed to be controlling it. Charge wires led to a primary detonator and to the heavy clay blocks. He'd never seen anything like it, so he didn't dare try and defuse it.

He examined the stack of explosives. It was C-4, without a doubt, enough to blow up the entire block.

"Hold on, Ritchie," he said. "I'll go into the kitchen and see about getting you home."

"Fuckin' hurry, man."

Sacco ran across the room, passing into the dining area

A **Pound** of **Fur**

and kitchen. He began throwing drawers out of their runners. Glancing quickly at what hit the floor, he moved from one to the next looking for a serrated butcher knife, something that would cut the thick wrapping of duct tape, if he could find some without the wiring running through it.

A phone rang. Not the house phone. It was a cell phone, with a bizarre ring tone. Sacco listened to the first ring, intent on his task. In the middle of the second ring he looked up.

Ritchie squirmed as hard as he could, trying to turn and see the ringer attached to the detonator. He couldn't. His eyes filled with tears.

Sacco punched his radio as he raced for the dining room window. He didn't even try for the front door. "Get those jeeps moving. Get out! Get out now!"

··· 49 ···

"That's the signal. Let's go."

After racing into West Covina, Collins' helicopter crew waited quietly over the hills from Turner's house. Collins had kept in contact with the other two teams while waiting for Cosimo's men to hit their next target. The third chopper reported heavy activity on the police scanner, especially in their area. Collins was told to expect company from his friend Lieutenant Kitch.

The chopper heaved off the ground, heading straight up into the sky. McNeil guided the helicopter over the hills toward Turner's home. Collins turned and addressed his men, speaking loudly into his radio.

"There's bound to be police activity down there. Make sure you fire only on the vehicles closest to the house. We'll go in low enough so you can get clean shots."

The pilot pointed out the front window of the chopper. He didn't have to report what he saw. Collins watched the flames shoot up over the canyon wall. He gave a non-verbal instruction to his pilot, telling him to step on it. When they crested the last hill before the house, Collins heart jumped into his throat.

"Jeezuz," he said under his breath.

··· 50 ···

Except for the flaming, crumbling garage, the home had disappeared entirely. Ritchie and Teddy Sacco had been blown into oblivion, vaporized by over a hundred pounds of C-4. Sporadic fires burned everywhere, some from combustion, and others from blown gas lines and electrical components. Any foliage within two hundred yards of the blast zone lay flat on the ground, smoking or already burned to a crisp.

Beckett barely got out with his life. As soon as Sacco had yelled the warning, he waved his men off the property and ran like hell. Had he not been trained to run like the wind in college, he might have joined Sacco on his wild ride into the netherworld.

Tootie and Angel grabbed Beckett as he scampered up behind the fleeing Range Rover. With strength amplified by a massive influx of adrenaline, they lifted Beckett through the back window and over the seat. A chorus of filthy exclamations bounced between the three men. Only the voice of their driver called them back to the present.

"Wake up, girls, we got trouble."

"Shit," said Angel, "I dropped my fucking gun back there."

"Pull the back seatback forward, jackass," said the driver. "Grab something and get ready!"

The Scully brothers beat everyone back to the vehicles. They jumped in and pulled weapons from beneath the back seat. Both men sat rigidly, listening for the slightest sound. Wide-eyed and ready, they searched the small canyon for movement.

"Step on it!" shouted the one by the left window.

A blaring roar and a powerful blast of wind carried Collins' chopper into the canyon. Lines of automatic gunfire scorched the ground in the direction of the two Range Rovers.

Collins tapped his headset. "Hold that line of fire. We'll get them racing toward the road and then come around in front of them."

"Boss," said the pilot. "Our man in chopper three reports a SWAT team in the vicinity. They can't be behind us, so if we drive those jeeps out toward the freeway, won't Los Angeles' finest have to deal with them?"

Just then, a stinging round of gunfire rattled against the chopper's skin. The man behind Collins leaned out for a few seconds. A report buzzed in Collins' headset a moment later. *Only surface damage, we're good to go.*

■ ■ ■

"Get this fucking heap moving!" Tootie screamed from the back seat of the Range Rover. "That's a goddamn fully loaded chopper behind us. If you don't get us out of here pronto, they're going to cut us to pieces!"

The driver swore under his breath. Trees had flopped all over the road like drunks after last call. He could barely pick his way through, and he couldn't go any faster because of all the debris.

"Just keep shooting," he shouted. "Blast those fuckers out of the sky and let me worry about the road."

■ ■ ■

While Collins' men reloaded, the chopper banked around Turner's property in a tight arc. It came out from behind the flames like one of Revelation's seals, screaming toward the jeeps again. As soon as the men pulled back their firing pins, their quarry lay right beneath them. Sacco's men hadn't made it to the surface street yet, so the fight was still in Collins' hands.

The pilot balanced the helicopter seventy-five feet above the Range Rover, behind the vehicle so the gunners would have a perfect, forty-five-degree angle. They riddled the jeep, shooting out windows and drilling holes through the top of the roof. When the Range Rover rolled up against a large tree trunk and stopped, Collins turned and looked at his men. They both nodded once.

Seconds later, a brace of automatic fire tore through the cabin of the chopper. The Scully brothers had waited, biding their time so Collins' attention would be focused on the other vehicle. When they saw the opening, they fired everything they had.

"Fuck!" Collins shouted. He ducked low into the floorboard of the helicopter's front seats. His pilot twisted the command stick, initiating every maneuver he knew to the extreme. He couldn't fly away from the relentless barrage of bullets, however. When Collins sat back up, he turned quickly toward his men in the back by the windows.

The gunner behind the pilot lay awkwardly in his seat. If not for the harness, he would have been blown clear of the chopper. A line of bullet holes ran from his crotch to his neck. Blood poured from the wounds, a ghastly river of death.

Collins' gunner had taken a few hits, but he had nowhere near the damage his mate received. His injuries were located in his legs, in the thigh and calf only. The femoral artery had been spared. The man was in agony, though, leaving Collins no choice but to back out of the fight. He looked back to the road, watching the remaining Range Rover as it sped out of the canyon toward the paved highway.

"Chopper One to Birds Two and Three, come in."

"Two here, sir."

"Three ready, sir, over."

"Proceed to final checkpoint. Secure area before landing. Remember, only the bad guys get shot."

"We're on our way. ETA, twenty minutes."

"Right behind Two, boss. You might want to know that the LAPD has spotted the second vehicle. They're preparing to intercept."

"Copy that," said Collins, wondering what the men in the Range Rover would do once they rolled up on an armed platoon of experienced SWAT officers. "Continue with the operation. Out."

··· 51 ···

Safeguard Protection Services was located on Wilshire Boulevard near Fairfax Street. Collins purchased the building after securing his first pentagon contract. When he told the commercial real estate representative he intended to pay cash the woman nearly fainted. He bought the building, paid twice the amount for refitting and remodeling, and promptly relocated his small staff.

The six-story building served two purposes. Primarily, it housed a legitimate business. Its secondary function was the main reason Collins bought it. It sat almost exactly halfway between downtown and west Los Angeles. That gave Collins options should he ever need to make a quick exit.

The address on Wilshire was the only part of the boulevard without a solid stretch of high rises. Collins' building stood alone for almost two city blocks on either side. This made for excellent sight lines and outstanding lanes for helicopter flight. As he grew wealthier, Collins secretly purchased the adjoining properties, leaving them as they were, thereby guaranteeing his protection.

The interior of the building served Collins and his employees well. Although it looked somewhat unkempt and old fashioned, behind the walls on every floor loomed a security system so sophisticated even the spooks at the pentagon couldn't touch it. Clients came and went, checking in with a lone guard at a small kiosk on the first floor. Every executive had an office fronted by an administrative assistant, looking very much like any other office arrangement in the city.

In truth, anyone visiting Safeguard Protection Services had an eye on them as soon they turned down one of the streets servicing the building. Security cameras recorded digital images and video twenty-four hours a day. Cars were scanned for weapons, civic or military connections, even body chemistry of the occupants. Before anyone left the parking lot, Collins and his senior executives knew who they were, where they came from, and any type of threat they posed.

The building's architecture would have brought a smile to the designers of medieval castles the world over. With the insertion of secret hallways, elevators, and false walls on every floor, Collins and his men could easily overcome a small battalion strength force using self-taught urban anti-terrorist warfare. Collins would allow nothing to interrupt his true mission in life. If enough force had ever been brought against him, he would kill whoever stood in his way, have dinner, and then move his entire operation to an identical building he owned in Miami.

About the same time the Scully brothers and their driver ran smack into the SWAT team, Capuana's second crew pulled into a deserted parking lot at Safeguard Protection Services. The guard shack was empty, the gate stood straight up. It was a sight that unnerved Nicky Falo. In his experience an open door always meant trouble.

The local driver assigned to his crew crept forward toward Collins' building, eying everything in front of him carefully. If a gum wrapper had danced across the asphalt, he would have gripped the steering wheel that much tighter.

The building looked completely abandoned, except for the lights flicking on and off at random intervals. The driver and the crew had seen many computer controlled electronic displays during their years. They spotted this one immediately.

"What do you think?" asked the driver.

"Could be empty," said Falo. "Could be a trap."

"So, what's it gonna be?"

Falo turned in his seat. He looked at his crew huddled in the back of the extended Ford E Series van. "Let's go in," he said.

■ ■ ■

Forty miles north and west, an identical van turned onto the private street where Kevin Collins lived. The driver, one of Los Angeles' oldest and most capable wheelmen, killed the headlights after making the turn. He heard the men behind him shuffling, not nervously, but rather with anticipation. They had flown to Los Angeles from New York after hearing about the bounty for Capuana's son. With only four men in their crew, each would receive over two million dollars for Collins' head.

"Let us out here," said the team leader.

"How do you know he's even home?" asked the driver.

"I don't give a shit either way. If he's here, we'll take

him down. If he isn't, we'll stage an ambush and wait for him."

"Just like that, huh?"

"What about it?"

"You Bronx idiots are all the same. Don't you know who this guy is? He owns one the biggest and most sophisticated security companies in the world. You think you're gonna walk right up to that house and ring the doorbell?"

"Look asshole," said Marcus Manning, the leader of the New York crew. "You drive the damn car. We'll handle the real work."

"It's your funeral."

"We'll radio when we're clear for pickup," said Manning as he opened the passenger door. His crew pulled the sliding door back, revealing a very businesslike assortment of duffle bags. Manning counted them before throwing two over his shoulder. His men exited the van silently, grabbing their share of the hardware.

■ ■ ■

Falo walked his men to the utility door by the dumpsters. He looked at the keypad on the wall and signaled one of his men. In seconds, the man had removed a silent charge from his vest, placed it neatly within the crack in between the two doors, and detonated it. A silent hiss accompanied a small shower of sparks as the charge did its work. Falo's man backed away.

Another man stepped up and cracked the door slightly. The entire crew held their breath as they waited for some type of defensive crossfire. Nothing broke their concentration, not even an alarm. The lights in the first-floor hallway even flicked on.

"Guess we're in," said Jack Vinitelli, Falo's right hand.

Falo nodded his head, looking at two of his men in the rear of the group. They walked forward, guns tightly braced against their hips. Vinitelli held the door wide, looking into the stairwells and waving the men through.

They entered the building without incident, quickly motioning for the rest of the crew to follow them. Seconds later, guns drawn, the men quietly climbed the stairs to the second floor.

■ ■ ■

Manning sat on his haunches staring at Collins' house. His men crouched next to him like a row of gargoyles, silently waiting for their boss to make a decision. No one spoke, stirred, or entertained any thoughts of a quick assault on the property. Manning had a reputation for an uncanny sense; he could smell a trap faster than it could be set.

He snatched a twig from the dirt between his feet. Rolling it over in his hands, he watched the property for any sign of movement. Finally satisfied, he slowly stood and addressed his men.

"Snooker, you're with me. Adam, you and Binney take the back door."

The men rose, the only sound coming from the weapons they held. Safeties clicked off, magazines were secured, and guns were deliberately cocked.

"I know someone's in there waiting for us," said Manning. "There can't be more than four, though."

"How can you tell?" asked Snooker.

"I can smell 'em."

The pairs split up, moving down the slope through the glistening evergreens. The scent of fir invaded their nostrils, giving them a slight pause from the severity of their task. After leaving the cover of the huge trees, Manning stole a look back at Binney. Confident his men would perform, he followed Snooker to the front door.

■ ■ ■

"Collins' office is on the sixth floor."

"Let's get up there and set the charges. This place gives me the creeps."

"No shit."

Falo signaled his men. The six of them sprinted up the stairwell. Had they been briefed about Collins' building, they might have noticed the microscopic filaments lining the steel bars of the railing. Every time one of them grabbed the rail to pull himself along, a signal shot forward into the computer mainframe in the basement of the building. The men stationed below knew precisely where Falo's crew was at every moment. The lack of reconnaissance cameras in the stairwells had fooled Cosimo's men completely.

"Lieutenant?" said one of Collins' trackers. "They've made it to the access door on the sixth floor. Do you want us to lockdown the stairs?"

Samuel Kitch stood behind the massive array of computer equipment. He had watched Collins' men efficiently lure the Jersey crew farther into the building. Without showing themselves or firing a single shot, they had them cold. "Thank you, but no, Mister Gideon," he said, eyes still glued to the monitors. "Six floors of open space would be a slaughterhouse for both teams. Let them trap themselves in Collins' office. We'll take them there, where they have no choice but to surrender."

■ ■ ■

Binney peered around the corner of Collins' home. Everything seemed to be set up for a party; patio furniture arranged, pool nicely lighted, soft music even played through speakers installed throughout the landscaping.

Sliding his body backwards along the wall, he turned and looked at Manning. His boss had the identical look on his face, one of irritated confusion.

A telephone rang inside Collins' home. Manning looked through an open front door and down a lengthy hallway. The phone continued ringing, seven, eight times, finally stopping at ten rings. No voice mail or answering machine picked up the call.

Manning backed away. Turning, he looked down the wall, trying to find Binney. After seeing nothing for five seconds, he assumed his other team had gone inside. He looked at Snooker, holding his index and middle fingers in a wide peace sign. His man shook his head once and hustled toward the far window at the front of the house.

Manning ran to the front door. He saw a sheet of paper with a dozen name tags stuck to it in their original layout. They were the tags people gave to guests when they arrived for a party. Manning clearly saw the phrase "Hello! My name is…" at the top of each sticker.

"Damn," he said under his breath. *Either this Collins guy is totally flipped, or someone's playing a really sick game.*

He didn't know what else to do, and there didn't seem to be anyone around, so he signaled Snooker to cover his back as he ran into the foyer. He heard silent footsteps behind him. Trusting that anything following him would soon be dead, he moved into the great room at the end of the hall.

He saw Binney moving through the backyard, checking every possible hiding place for a counter insurgency team.

"You want me to check upstairs?" asked Snooker.

"Hell no," replied Manning. "We stay together. I'll let Binney and Adam search upstairs. We'll search down here and watch each other's backs."

The telephone rang again. From inside the house the sound seemed deafening. It kept on, interminably, until after the twelfth ring when it finally stopped.

Manning looked visibly shaken. He felt like some unseen presence was playing with him. It seemed like Collins was inside the house, somewhere, screwing with him just for the fun of it.

As Binney appeared in the hallway Manning almost shot him. He exhaled roughly, pissed at himself for being such a pussy. He pointed to the second floor.

"You guys search the bedrooms. We'll cover the downstairs. Be thorough but do it quickly. I want to get out of here as soon as we can."

"What if the damn phone rings again?"

"Don't answer it, no matter what. I got a weird ass feeling about those calls."

■ ■ ■

One of Falo's men opened the access door to the sixth

floor. The rest filed in quickly, passing by without so much as a whisper. Their boots, heavy and lined with poly carbon alloy, silently crept by the door.

From the reports, Falo knew the blueprint of Collins' building intimately. He led his men straight to his office, walking down corridors and turning corners as if he were in his own home. Nothing impeded his progress. It seemed as though no one was in the building at all. *Dumb*, thought Falo, *if I was Collins, I'd have men staked out on every floor.*

He reached the corner of the hallway. Collins' door stood ten feet from him. It seemed odd that it lay in total darkness; the rest of the lights in the building came on periodically, why not the boss's office? He checked his watch – three fifteen in the morning.

"Let's go," he said, clapping the explosives man on the shoulder. "Get that door open and set the charges. Make sure you don't move anything and forget to put it back exactly where it was."

After shoving the heavy door inward, Falo's man shot a hand through the empty space, sliding it along the wall, trying to find a switch. The lights came on, but not because of any human action.

"Motion sensors," Falo whispered, and with those two words, he realized they might all end up dead. In his eagerness to please his boss, Falo had forgotten the golden rule of his trade – what appears perfectly safe most times isn't.

■ ■ ■

Manning and Binney led the search on their respective floors in Collins' home. Every room they checked yielded the same result – nothing. They met at the midpoint of the stairwell. Binney shook his head.

"Fuck," said Manning. He'd wanted a clean job, in and out and then back home to collect. Now they had to pull more exposure by setting a trap. He looked around the empty house, waiting for someone to jump out of a closet.

"Alright, let's…"

The telephone rang again. That piercing, irritating, grating sound tore at Manning's nerves.

"Dammit, where the hell is that thing?"

The phone rang only three times.

"This is Kevin Collins. Leave a message and the time you called."

A few instructions regarding faxing and other options followed Collins' message. After that a loud beep almost pierced Manning's eardrum.

Snooker and Adam joined their comrades in the great room. All four men stood stock still, waiting for the caller to speak. After fifteen seconds, Manning relaxed, letting his shoulders slump. He let his MAC-10 machine pistol fall to his side.

"This message is for the goon squad occupying my home. Throw down your weapons and proceed through the front door. Keep your fingers laced behind your heads."

Adam looked at Manning. Manning looked at Snooker. Binney looked for the phone. He wanted a few words with Collins before the fighting began.

"Right now a helicopter with four of my best marksmen is approaching the house. They have my home in sight. They'll be landing in seconds."

Manning started giving hand signals. He didn't trust anything about the house anymore. For all he knew Collins was watching them on a remote video feed. Gesturing quickly, he told his men to scatter in four different directions and then meet up at the van. Manning himself would call the driver.

"By the way, in case you intend to make a break for it, your driver is on his way downtown with a couple of private security escorts."

"FUCK!" Manning screamed.

"That's right," said Collins. "You men are fucked with a capital F, and if you have any brains, you'll drop your gear, walk out the front door, and cooperate. If you do, I promise they'll be no gunfire. I'll make another promise, though. If you try and fight your way out, you'll all be dead men."

"The hell with this shit," said Snooker. He bolted for the door leading to the backyard and the swimming pool. He half opened and half smashed his way through it. Without even knowing the layout of Collins' back yard, he ran wildly in random directions. He changed course at the pool, running left toward the fence line.

A single shot rang out. Snooker's head snapped back before erupting in a hail of flesh, hair, brain matter, and blood. His body slumped right and forward, slapping dully against the coping at the edge of the pool. The momentum propelled the body forward just enough so the shoulders slid into the water. The legs and left arm came to rest awkwardly on the ground, with the upper body wafting in the water. Blood and body fluids created a hideous discoloration as they seeped into the pool.

■ ■ ■

"Assemble your men," Kitch ordered as soon as Falo and his crew entered Collins' office. "This is the best chance we'll have."

The men in the security center broke from their routines, acting immediately after hearing the word from their superior. They disappeared silently from their posts, so much so that within seconds Kitch found himself nearly alone in the computer room.

"If you'll follow me, sir."

Kitch looked at the man holding his arm out toward the door. "Of course," he said.

■ ■ ■

"Anyone else want to run for it?" asked Manning. His senses had failed him. This was the first time he had ever been trapped by his quarry and it pissed him off something fierce. He wasn't stupid, though, or pissed enough to walk into an ambush.

"You guys can do what you want," he said to Adam and Binney. "I'm going to take my chances with the front door."

"This is fucked up, boss."

"Fuckin' A," said Adam.

"Tell that to Snooker."

■ ■ ■

Collins' man guided Kitch through a series of false walls, narrow, hidden staircases, and an elevator of sorts. They reached the sixth floor in seconds, stepping through a plain door marked "engineering." Half of the security team had gathered in the hallway ahead of them. The other half, Kitch surmised, had entered the opposite hallway, cutting off the crew's escape.

A **Pound** of Fur

Falo's men had nearly completed their work. A series of shape charges, expertly disguised as file folders, trash can bases, and false drawer bottoms, had been installed at different locations in Collins' office. If they set all of them off at once he would be ripped to shreds by the shrapnel.

Falo lit a cigarette. The momentary flash from the lighter flame caused his vision to fade for a moment. At that instant, two stun grenades rolled into the office. His men were so intent on their work, none of them sensed the intrusion. As Falo took a hasty drag on his smoke, his eye caught the wobbling movement of a grenade coming to rest.

"Get d…"

The flash blinded everyone in the room. The detonation induced temporary hearing loss. None of them saw the teams of soldiers and police officers creeping down the hall toward them.

Jack Vinitelli had been to prison earlier in his life, five to ten for armed robbery and aggravated assault. After his release he told anyone within earshot that he'd never go back. He would die first, he repeatedly boasted. Now blinded and half deaf, his mind restated those words over and over. He gripped his MAC-10, squeezing his right index finger around the trigger housing.

A voice called out from the hallway. "This is Lieutenant Samuel Kitch of the Los Angeles Police Department."

Vinitelli re-gripped his machine pistol.

"You men are hopelessly surrounded. You have only one way out, and that, unfortunately, is through us. On this floor alone we outnumber you three to one, and we have reinforcements waiting outside. We have superior weaponry on our side as well as unlimited ammunition."

Falo looked over at Vinitelli. What he saw in the man's face scared the shit out of him.

"We have you bracketed in a closed room, gentlemen, and I will not hesitate to use lethal force if it will save one of…"

Vinitelli's MAC-10 opened up, spewing bullets into the hallway. Lieutenant Kitch, surprised that anyone would fight against such overwhelming odds, had been standing in front of his men as he spoke to the crew. Four of the bullets ripped into his midsection. Two whizzed by his eyes, close enough to shave the lashes on the lids. He crumpled to the floor, turning over to protect his riddled stomach.

Both hallways and Collins' office exploded with gunfire. More flash grenades were thrown through the door. Tear gas canisters followed. The office resembled a bedroom with a hyper-active strobe light.

The men in the hallway fired continuously, giving their comrades cover so Kitch could be dragged away. After moving the lieutenant into another office and signaling for a medical unit, the first team moved quickly back into position.

"Wait!" Falo screamed. "Wait a fucking minute! Hold it, Goddammit!"

Kitch's second in command ordered his troops to comply. Falo kept screaming at his men, ordering them to stop firing.

"We've got explosives in here," he yelled as soon as he could hear himself. "One misfire and this whole floor will go up in a ball of fire they'll be able to see back in Jersey."

"Are you ready to surrender?" asked Kitch's man.

"You stupid fuck," said Falo. "Didn't you hear what I just said? Any more gunfire and we can kiss our asses goodbye!"

"We're prepared to accept that loss. You've seriously wounded our commander. That gives me the right to order any outcome I desire. You can save us all a lot of grief by laying down your weapons."

"No fuckin' way, boss," said Vinitelli. There's no way I'm letting anyone lock me up again."

"Look Jackass, if you keep this up there isn't going to be anything left of you to lock up."

Vinitelli slapped a new clip into his MAC-10 and pulled back the hammer. He peered over the broken glass on the windowsill. Finding his target, he lifted his weapon over the ledge.

Three rounds from a nine-millimeter ended Vinitelli's plans. Falo dropped his weapon after killing his longtime friend. He looked around the office, gauging the responses to what he had just done. The rest of his men lowered their weapons as well, dropping them softly onto the carpeted floor.

"Hold your fire," he yelled into the hallway. "We're coming out!"

■ ■ ■

The beaten men at Collins' office walked meekly into the arms of the authorities. As Falo felt the cold, smooth steel of the handcuffs pressing against his wrists, he stared blankly ahead, knowing what awaited him back in New Jersey. Capuana would order his execution immediately. He had missed his target and killed one of the best contract men in the organization. It wouldn't matter if he was free or in prison, Cosimo Capuana's reach extended everywhere.

They marched the crew out of the office building at four fifty-five in the morning. Falo looked at the sky, noticing the very first hint of dawn. He heard trash skipping across the lot, propelled by an early morning breeze. He watched two homeless people across the street raise their heads a little and peek at the activity briefly before rolling over and shifting their blankets. He looked up and saw a lone seagull, floating in the wind, coasting effortlessly on its way to the ocean.

"You were right to shoot Vinny," one of his men said as they stepped into the police van. "That asshole was going to get all of us killed."

■ ■ ■

Marcus Manning walked through the front door of Collins' home, hands raised in silent submission. He also saw the break of dawn, but his view was infinitely superior. As the police patted him down, he stared at the dark, unmoving ocean. The horizon, a soft pink from the sun's first rays, seemed tranquil, totally unconcerned about Manning and his crew.

Adam and Binney shuffled out behind their boss. All three men entertained the same thoughts – how could a successful crew like theirs botch a job so badly and end up in the arms of local authorities. The job seemed so simple, fly out, hit Collins, fly back, and get paid. They'd done dozens of tougher jobs in the past. It just didn't make any sense. The two men followed Manning into the van, taking seats opposite their boss. They looked at him, trying to find some solace from their leader. Manning stared at them for a second before looking down at the grimy floor of the police transport.

··· **52** ···

Sam Kitch hated hospitals. They smelled. They were bad luck for law enforcement, and sick or dying people lay everywhere. The doctors had said he could go home in ten days. He'd been out of surgery for a day and a half and already he was climbing the walls.

The surgeon who removed the bullets proclaimed him a miracle patient. Three of them had entered Kitch's torso without piercing or puncturing an organ. Another grazed the skin outside of his rib cage, doing little damage. The doctor brought the bullets back to Kitch in a plastic medicine container. He shook them before handing them to his patient, saying that anytime he felt overburdened by life he could shake his new rattle and remember how close he came. He checked in two more times that day, pronouncing Kitch alive and well and giving him the grave news about his extensive hospital stay.

On the third morning of his post operation imprisonment, Kitch sat up in bed glaring at a crossword puzzle. He had three answers remaining, but he knew he would never solve them. *These people are sick,* he thought, *they always find a few completely obscure clues.*

"Good morning, Sam," said Collins. He stood half in the hallway and half in the room, his hand pressed against the heavy door.

"To what do I owe this honor?" asked Kitch.

"A promise is a promise."

Collins entered the room and sat in the only chair available. The hard-plastic shape seemed to be the opposite of comfortable.

"I wanted to personally thank you for protecting my people."

"I seemed to be mostly a bystander, until my unfortunate encounter in the hallway."

"You took a bullet for me, Sam," said Collins. "Why?"

"I was serving the city of Los Angeles during that moment."

"Bullshit."

"I beg your pardon."

"You heard me. You could have sent any number of detectives down that hall, yet you chose to lead the team yourself. I'd like to know why."

"Perhaps I share a measure of sympathy for your cause, Kevin."

"That's good to know. Is there anything I can do for you?"

"Will you dynamite this hospital so I can go home?"

Collins smiled. "I'm afraid we used all our C-4 at Turner's house."

Kitch sat up a little, painfully. Collins leaned forward to help him adjust his pillows, but the lieutenant waved him off.

"You realize of course that you're going to spend the rest of your life in prison."

"Yes," said Collins, expressionless.

"I admire your passion, Kevin, however misdirected it may be. The fact remains, however, that you broke the law. You murdered people in cold blood, with definitive planning beforehand. The courts will fall upon you like an avalanche on a cabin."

"I understand."

"You don't seem very concerned."

Collins stood and began pacing in the small hospital room. "I have no desire to go to prison, but I accept it as the outcome of my life. I knew long ago that someday I'd be caught. I wrestled with it, the idea of going forward or stopping my activities altogether.

"Believe it or not, the idea of living in a cage for the rest of my life seemed a distant second to forsaking the animals of the world. Someone had to try and protect them."

"And you felt it was your responsibility, your mission to save them?"

"I knew if I didn't do everything I could my life would've have been a waste, worse than that, a travesty. To do nothing seemed a worse sentence than life behind bars."

"You may be looking at the death penalty."

"That'd be even better," said Collins. "I could sit on death row for forty years and write a book."

Collins finally sat down again. He looked at his shoes briefly before asking the next question. "What about Capuana?"

Kitch smiled. "Cosimo Capuana could very well end up as your cellmate."

Collins jerked his head up and stared at Kitch.

"My counterpart in New Jersey paid a visit to the dock-yards yesterday. After a brief confrontation between his forces and Capuana's men, Mr. Capuana, along with one of his brothers and a handful of advisors, was taken into custody. They will be tried on several counts of murder, conspiracy to commit murder, and terrorist acts in our city."

"I killed his son," said Collins. "His *only* son."

"You killed a great many people, Kevin. Tell me, how do you feel about the others?"

Collins sat immobile, his features a sculpture of non-expression.

Two uniformed officers appeared at the door of Kitch's hospital room. The lieutenant gave a brief signal, motioning for them to hold their ground.

"I understand and sympathize with you, Kevin. Holding dominion over animals doesn't mean having free license to abuse them. Animals should be cherished, not tormented. Unfortunately, what you lost along the way is the principle that human life is also sacred, and as such it is protected by the laws of man and God."

Kitch gave the officers leave to enter his room and arrest Collins. "I assume you know your rights?"

"Lieutenant," said Collins, standing and placing his wrists together behind his back. "I mean, Sam, will you do me one favor?"

"If I can, yes."

A **Pound** of **Fur**

"Take care of Chambers and Galten. I wouldn't feel comfortable if they were anywhere but in your home. I promise you a hefty allowance; neither you nor they will go hungry."

"Of course," said Kitch. "You needn't worry about their safety or happiness."

The officers turned toward the door.

"Kevin?"

Collins stopped.

"Are you sorry for what you've done?" asked Kitch. "Do you feel any remorse at all?"

He turned slightly, not wanting to look directly at his friend. Instead, he spoke into a vacuum, staring at the restroom door. "Someone had to take a stand. Someone had to try. I have no regrets."

Turning toward the door, he slowly dragged the officers out of the room.

www.ingramcontent.com/pod-product-compliance
Lightning Source LLC
Chambersburg PA
CBHW031602240626
47153CB00002B/603